Witch Armageddon?

Book 2 of The Witch, the Dragon and the Angel Trilogy

Witch Armageddon?

Book 2 of The Witch, the Dragon and the Angel Trilogy

Paul R. Goddard

First published in the UK 2014

2nd edition 2015

ISBN   978 -1- 85457- 055- 0

Published by: Clinical Press Ltd., Redland Green Farm, Redland, Bristol, BS6 7HF, UK.

Innumerable thanks are again due to Jem, Allan and Lois.
Thank you!

Prologue

'So that was the case for the defence?' the elderly judge spoke with incredulity in his voice.

I, myself, thought the defence sounded absurd and I was the one in the dock. Who could possibly believe that I had stumbled across a seated ring of naked cannabilistic teenagers eating a harmless old man and about to start on a screaming young girl? Who indeed, especially when the teenagers were from a new church denomination and the girl was here in court as a witness against me and I could hardly string two words together comprehensibly?

I was confused. Where had the forty eight hours gone and why was my mind so foggy? My last really clear memory was of a period two days before the police arrived and after that I had scattered images but the continuity is a blur. That's the New York Finest I'm referring to who found me with the Morning Star, an elfin sword, gripped tightly in my hand and dead teenagers around me, the girl tied to a stake in the middle of the floor and no sign of the old man or his remains.

I found it hard to concentrate on the rapid court case. Things were rushing past me and my mind was not working properly. I was not entirely surprised by the verdict. Guilty of murder of the second degree..... unpremeditated homicide. However the addition of "by reason of insanity" was strange and did not fit any definition of murder that I understood. In view of the verdict I expected incarceration in a hospital for the insane so I was severely shocked by the sentence. "Death by the electric chair after the devil has been exorcised from his soul."

I am Jimmy Scott, or to be more accurate James Michael Scott, often known as Jimmy. I have found myself in awkward situations before but this did take the biscuit. I have fought devils and ogres in the land of Faerie, pitted my wits against a sphinx and conversed with elementals, dwarves and werewolves. I had even crossed through Hades or the Slough of Despond with the elf queen on my shoulders. However, I always had the belief that once I was back in the real world all would be sorted out. But this *was* the real world and I had travelled to New York by jet plane rather than on the back of an airborne golden dragon. I was pretty sure that I had walked out from the downtown Hilton to attend a small party in the Bowery........ and this massacre had happened. I could just about remember stumbling into the orgy of bestial gratification and being attacked by the cannibals. Or was it all a dream? I believed that, in self-defence, I had prepared myself for a fight by drawing my sword from its slightly curved scabbard which was disguised as a walking stick. I remembered no more so perhaps I did kill them? There were too many questions and too few facts in my own mind.

The sentence was to be carried out tomorrow, within twenty-four hours of the judge's pronouncement. This was an amazing change in a city and state which until a few months previously did not even permit the death sentence.

I was taken to a cold cell and I lay on a hard bench. I had just a few hours to contemplate my fate but my mind went backwards and forwards over the events of the previous two years. Perhaps there was something in my recent history which explained my present predicament? Maybe the trauma had affected my mind?

Think every incident through, I told myself as I lay back on the rough surface. *And look for clues.*

I remembered, firstly, all the details I could about the funeral of my mother-in-law, Mary.

Chapter 1

The crematorium was packed. Mary's funeral was much better attended than I had expected. She was, as everybody now knows, a witch so it seemed strange to have a standard religious service but Mary had insisted.

'I've no intention of going where Lucifer is in charge so I'll hedge my bets with a Christian funeral, if you don't mind.'

Her terminal illness had been a big surprise to all except her. Apparently she had suffered from cancer for some time and it had spread all round her body before it had been diagnosed.

Nothing could be done about it and she died within weeks of first presentation on the exact day that she predicted in the big diary she kept for engagements. She had made absolutely no commitments beyond the presaged date.

She bore the illness stoically, unlike her normal complaining attitude. She even managed to make a few jokes.

'I thought I would be like Mrs Thomlinson,' she once said to me.

'In what way?' I asked.

'She got cancer of the uterus but she was such a malignant personality that the cancer did not stand a chance,' she had chuckled at this memory of another member of her cabal, which is what I called her coffee morning group.

The whole cabal did turn up for the funeral but the press and quite a few politicians were there also. Mary had become famous at the "Stonehenge Incident" as it is sometimes called. Realities had been colliding and alien deities from parallel worlds had been forced, by Mary, to stabilise our reality. It had taken more out of her than we realised at the time and her funeral was only eighteen months later.

It was a cold December day when we walked into that church following her coffin. Her only living relatives were her daughter Sienna, myself (her son-in-law) and our two sons, Joshua and Samuel. We, the family, sat at the front of the church on the hard wooden pews listening rather numbly to the vicar welcoming everybody. Then we stood for the first hymn.

Abide with me fast fall the eventide
The darkness deepens,
Lord with me abide
When other helpers fail and comforts flee
Help of the helpless,
O abide with me

The organ wheezed and spluttered and we sang the words in a desultory manner. Mary had chosen the first hymn. I have heard it at so many funerals that it always makes me feel desperately sad and today was no exception. Mary and I had not always been the best of friends but in the months running up to her demise we had developed a mutual respect. Partly this was because of our shared experiences at Stonehenge but also because we knew that life could be fleeting and we both loved Sienna and the lads. I was fighting hard to hold back the tears and I could see that Joshua was doing the same. Sienna and Sam were both sobbing. I resolved, there and then, not to have the hymn at my funeral ...I would expressly forbid it!

Mary had insisted that she should be cremated.

'I don't want to wake up in a coffin when they've misdiagnosed me as dead and find that I'm six feet underground in the dark, scratching away at the wood, screaming my head off and dying of suffocation. I'm just not going to do it and that is all there is to it.'

'But Mum,' Sienna had said. 'That doesn't happen these days.'

'That's because people are cremated instead of buried,' was her reply.

The vicar gave a sermon which incongruously was mostly about giving money to the church. Sienna and the boys gave short eulogies and I read a favourite poem by Henry Scott Holland

Death is nothing at all.
I have only slipped away into the next room

If my experience in the previous year was anything to go by it may be that Holland was right. Just like Alice, I had slipped through a rift in realities and landed in a parallel world. I had spent two and half months trying to get back home and when I had done so I was only just in time to prevent mass slaughter and worldwide catastrophe ... with the help of Mary and the Faerie host. In my quest I had travelled through Hades and ridden on the back of a golden dragon.

I had met a few people in Hades and Valhalla but nowhere near the number who must die every day. Where did the others go?

The answer, I understand, is that there is another parallel world on the other side of us which some call the Eternal Realm. Part of that is where Mary wanted to avoid going.

Ruled by her former boyfriend, Lucifer, it is reputed to be an evil place so I am sure that she is right to stay away though I am not certain you get the choice.

The alternative place in the eternal realm, heaven, has an altogether better reputation and I had thought the vicar might say something about it. A few words that would focus our minds on something higher than money. Something more divine.

We came to the bit which I think they call the committal. The vicar pressed the button and the coffin slowly disappeared.

As the curtains drew across the last mortal remains of

the remarkable woman a ghastly, unearthly laugh was heard throughout the room. It frightened the wits out of me until I realised that it must have come from the sick organ expelling air from its punctured bellows. At least, that is what I think it was due to, anything else was too horrible to contemplate.

Behind me I heard a groan. Sienna and I turned round to see an overweight man being propped up by his neighbours in the pew. His face was ashen grey and his eyes had rolled up so that just his whites were showing. He was twitching with convulsions.

'Quick,' said my wife, Sienna, who was a nursing sister at a major hospital when I first met her. 'He's fainted and about to have a cardiac arrest.'

We both ran round to the pew, scattering people as we went. We grabbed the man and laid him out flat on his back. Sienna discovered that he had a very slow pulse. We raised his feet in the air and his colour improved.

Meanwhile the priest stood in the pulpit, mouth open, speechless. Another sound came from the organ much like a groan of annoyance, as if we had spoilt somebody's fun.

The man gradually came round and was eventually able to sit up. The last hymn was sung, the organ working impeccably. The blessing was given and nearly everybody filed out.

'Something came for me!' exclaimed the man as we helped escort him from the chapel of rest. 'I'd swear something came for me when there was that awful laugh.'

'You mean the organ?' asked Sienna.

'Was that what it was?' asked the man, who turned out to be one of Mary's many bridge partners. 'Sounded more like someone laughing to me. The sort of laugh that the devil might make. Knowing Mary that wouldn't have surprised me.'

Shouldn't have surprised me either, I thought. *And maybe it wasn't the organ?*

*

'CAP, the Church of Armageddon Prophets? What's that Dad?' asked Joshua, our fourteen year old son.

My memory was replaying another significant conversation so clearly that I was reliving the event.

'No idea. Why?' I had replied.

'It says in this article that the latest President of the USA, Theodore K. Z. Armstrong, is a founder member of the church,' he answered.

'I thought he was a methodist,' I countered, 'Either that or UCC, United Church of Christ.'

'Says here that he has become the leading light in a movement of religious renewal leading to the rapture,' answered Josh. 'Their motto is "Let it be soon, Lord".'

'Do they have a website?'

'I'm just googling it, Dad,' replied Josh. 'Got it. The church is the fastest growing Christian denomination according to this site. Their main call to fame is a rapture index....supposedly how close we are to rapture based on Biblical Prophecy.'

'I thought that the *Ship of Fools* website ran that one?'

'They did before the cataclysm but they've stopped doing it now. Their page was always a bit of a spoof but CAP say it is for real.'

'OK, Joshua, so what is their index saying?'

'That's the really worrying thing, Dad,' replied Josh. 'Both the article and the website say the same thing. They reckon that Armageddon is going to occur within the next month.'

'And the USA President is backing that?'

'Yep, he's 100% agreeing with the prediction.'

*

The world had got back on its feet surprisingly quickly. Once the realities had been stabilised and a few adjustments made the power stations had come back on line and in most places sanitation had been restored.

Billions had died, mostly in the developing world. This was hugely upsetting however most places had buried their dead and then ridden out the calamities better than I, or anyone else, might have predicted. There were a lot of grieving and ailing people all over the Earth but in a short space of time the developed world had responded by sorting their own problems and had sent aid to the parts that were not doing so well. Some help had also come from the better organised developing countries to the previously rich areas.

The large drop in population meant that food production should have been sufficient to feed all for the first time in decades but distribution remained a problem . Some cities were still starving and had become no-go areas whilst relatively short   distances away there was a bountiful supply of provisions. The main worry was that of disease ... and, of course, that the supernatural might return.

The knowledge of the intervention in our reality on one hand by Lucifer, or at least a creature claiming to be Lucifer, and the Faerie Realm on the other had, unsurprisingly, led to a massive increase in support of fundamental religions. Some claimed that Lucifer was in fact Loki, or maybe Ravana or Shiva. Others claimed that the faerie hordes were angels. At an election in the USA a new President, an unknown, had swept to power on a tide of religious feeling. The Congress and Senate had   rapidly endorsed his programme and to all intents and purposes the States were now a theocracy.

It now appeared that the President himself was the founder of a new religious sect. His Vice-President was Archbishop of the Church of Armageddon Prophets. The Secretary of State was a bishop. The Chief Justice of the US Supreme Court was Dean of the Cathedral Church of Armageddon Prophets. The entire thrust of the greatest economic force in the world, the only real superpower, was towards Armageddon.

Some critical pundits believed that the fulfillment of prophecies and movement to a final cataclysmic war had been at the back of some political decisions for many years. So the prophets stated that the rapture would not come until the Jews were back in Israel.....the Balfour declaration of 1917 had started that home-coming process. However, the Rapture Index included many more factors than that.

Following the well documented supernatural events at Stonehenge many "false Christs" and other false prophets had appeared. Satanism was on the rise, unemployment was high because industry had not yet got back up to speed. There had been widespread floods, plagues and famine and more than one sighting of an anti-Christ. There was even an Iraqi comedienne who claimed to be the Red Whore of Babylon.

Times were undoubtedly strange.

Chapter 2

None of this reminiscing was helping me to relax. I needed to be rested tomorrow and my thought processes needed to be in order as I intended trying to escape at any opportunity that presented itself. There was no way that I could get out right now. I was locked in a cell, chained and manacled to the bed, so there was no point in even trying. However, tomorrow was another day... a day that would probably be my last if I did not manage to break free. I certainly did not think that any rescue mission could help me. The trial had been in secret and I was not sure that the British Government even knew where I was right now.

So why was I in New York? My thoughts were clouded and my memory confused. I found it hard to recall why I was there but it gradually came back to me. Some of the States of America were fighting the religious legislation but New York, strangely enough given the East Coast's depth of liberal feeling, was one that had immediately implemented the new theocratic laws. I had been sent as a representative of the new British Government ostensibly on a trade mission. In reality they intended me to be a spy acting on behalf of the Queen. A latter day James Bond observing what was happening in the great U.S. of A.

The trade mission was to start in the Big Apple and move on to Washington where we were due to meet the President. In particular the British government wanted me to find out about the new religion.... the Church of Armageddon Prophets, CAP for short.

I had responded to an invitation which our agents stated had a connection with the new Church and here I was in jail awaiting a death sentence. What had happened to the two days after I blundered in on the killing orgy? Someone must have knocked me unconscious and then set me up as the killer. Presumably they had drugged me and that was the explanation for my confusion. But who and why? And what could I do about it?

*

At midnight my lawyer arrived to tell me that the judge had turned down the application for an appeal. The legal team were not even going to be allowed to present their arguments on my behalf.

I was not surprised. I was convinced by now that the whole thing was a set up. Even our agents and my lawyer had to be party to it. In retrospect I was a foolish choice as a secret agent given that my role in the Stonehenge incident had become international news so there would be a good number of people who suspected I was up to something. I had been chosen because of my contacts in the Faerie reality and the belief of the British Secret Service that there had to be some supernatural input to the new Church. From initially being total sceptics the spy masters now imagined Faerie interaction in all strange events and they considered me to be an instant expert.

I was extremely polite to the lawyer when he came into the cell, simply telling him in a jumbled way that I was confused, innocent and heartbroken about the whole thing and asking him to pass on my final words to the British consul in New York and thence to my family. He agreed to do this and I wrote a short, badly written note sending my love. I had no intention of giving any impression that my mind was clearing or that I would be attempting escapology.

After he had left I slept very fitfully, waking every few minutes. I still had my watch on and I could not help but constantly work out the number of minutes I had left to live if the execution went ahead. Although I was mentally convinced that an opportunity to escape would arise my body told me otherwise. If an opportunity for a break-out occurred I wanted to be ready to take it but a constant feeling of anxiety brought on by adrenalin was not helping me. I had never been a particularly fearless person and I could not help but be in a funk over this predicament. If this went on all the way to noon I would be too exhausted to respond even if there was a chance to flee. Part of me could not believe that they would really execute me..... Surely the whole charade was there to frighten me and they were softening me up in order to break me and find out what the Brits were up to and why I was there? The problem was that they were succeeding and I was becoming more and more scared.

★

'Don't worry Mum, It's just a youth club,' Joshua tried to reassure his mother.

They were talking in the kitchen as Sienna prepared the evening meal.

'But what do you do there? You've stopped going to judo because it's not "cool". What's so special about the church youth club?'

'Loads of things. There's pool, table tennis, darts and there's a disco. It's great.'

'But why do you have to dress in black? You used to enjoy such bright clothes and now it all has to be black.'

'You don't have to wear black, Mum. It's not a uniform. You can wear what you like.'

'But you all wear black.'

'We wear black because it's cool.'

It does not help that Jimmy has been sent over to New York, Sienna thought to herself as she over-enthusiastically chopped the vegetables with a large knife.

In fact she felt she knew more about Jimmy's whereabouts and what he was doing than she did Joshua's. If he was in trouble Jimmy would undoubtedly have flitted over into the Faerie reality where he had useful contacts. She was sure that he would be fine if things got hot for him in the new theocracy of the USA. Jimmy would be fine but Josh was a worry.

*

The seconds ticked by slowly throughout the night which was planned by others to be my last. Time dragged on with barely more than five consecutive minutes during which I did not look at my timepiece. One positive aspect was that the fogginess in my mind was definitely receding. My usual sharp wits were returning and perhaps the adrenaline was helping this by counteracting whatever drugs they had pumped into me.

At six in the morning when I was at my wit's end but my mind had cleared remarkably, the guards came for me with a CAP priest clad all in black and wearing a wide-brimmed, floppy black hat. They woke me from fitful sleep and dragged me into a nearby cell. I had been assured that the sentence of death would not be carried out until midday so I was not alarmed that I was immediately going to die. This was likely to be the interrogation and if so it represented a chance, however small, for me to turn the tables on the interrogators. The room I was taken to would in itself have scared most people to death and the entire ambience was chosen to create a frightening effect. The light was a flickering red glow, the walls were coated with demonic symbols and there was a large metal chair in the centre. I was roughly strapped into this by my legs and around my waist and one of the guards approached me with a hypodermic syringe in his hands.

The priest, who I noted was about my size but overweight, marched up to me from the other side, stared me in the eyes and whispered harshly. 'Sodium pentothal truth serum is my form of exorcism. It may not extract the devils but it does extract the truth.'

I stared back at the man in an uncomprehending manner trying to give the impression that I was still under the influence of whatever they had been giving me previously. Simultaneously and very carefully I studied his posture, his movement and his voice.

He had made his first big mistake.... he had told me what was in the syringe. I knew about sodium pentothal, otherwise known as thiopentone, and was fully aware that its use was over-hyped. Certainly it was easier to get people to talk when they were under its influence but did they tell the truth? Sorting the chaff from the wheat was the perennial problem. They were certainly going to have that problem with me. I would talk at great length and most of it would be true but I would be damned careful to make sure that I avoided saying anything that was of value.

The guard with the needle inserted the object into a vein in my arm and I felt the drug enter my venous system. The priest immediately fired questions at me.

'How did you get here? Who sent you? Why did you come? Who do you answer to? Who are the other British agents in the USA?'

Second mistake. Too many questions before I could answer any of them. This man was not an experienced interrogator.

'I took a taxi to Heathrow airport then flew in a Boeing 737 over the Atlantic. When I say flew I would not like to imply that I myself was capable of flying an aeroplane. No, I was a passenger in business class whilst a pilot or maybe two pilots flew the aeroplane. We had a very good meal half way across the Atlantic, or possibly over Greenland's icy mountains,' I replied with hardly an intake of breath, on and on I went.

Then, while the mood was with me, I burst into wild song, gabbling the words as I did so.

'From Greenland's icy mountains to India's coral shores, La, la,la,la,la,la la. Sorry, can't remember the words.'

The priest was becoming annoyed.'Just answer the questions. Don't sing,' he shouted in my ear.

The guards looked amused.

'Forgot what you asked, too many questions' I replied and felt a tear dribble down my face. 'Don't shout at dear old Jimmy. I haven't got long to live. Still, I don't have to worry about getting cancer or being run over by a bus do I?'

I turned my head to look at the priest and could not stop myself from starting to sing again.

'Swing low, sweet chariot, coming for to carry me home. Swing low, sweet chariot.....'

'SHUT UP!,' shouted the priest in my ear. 'Stop talking and stop singing!'

I obliged by stopping completely. Not a a word would cross my lips.

'Why did you come here?' the priest spoke insistently but was no longer shouting.

I looked at him and shook my head. I exaggeratedly held my finger up to my lips in the universal sign for silence. At the priest's signal the guard who had wielded the syringe came over and gave me a further shot into the vein.

The interrogating clergyman roughly urged me to reply to his questions, shaking me by the shoulders.

'You can talk now, fool. Why did you come here and who sent you?'

I pretended that the injection had knocked me out completely and the priest slapped my face hard and repeated his question.

'Why did you come here? Who sent you?'

'Came because I was told to. On behalf of the Government,' I answered, acting drunk and lightheaded.

'Go on,' urged the priest. 'Who exactly sent you?'

'On behalf of the Queen. S'posed to tell them exactly what I see? Mustn't give away secrets though,' I spoke in a slurred voice and tapped my nose in a knowing way as I did so.

'You can tell us,' replied the priest. 'We are your friends.'

'Funny friends,' I answered. 'Funny friends who tie someone up and arrange for him to be executed. Very funny friends.' I started to laugh again and to sing the spiritual hymn once more.

'Swing low, sweet chariot, coming.....'

'Stop that!' shouted the priest. 'What are you supposed to be looking for?'

'I'm supposed to be looking for trade agreements,' I answered truthfully. 'That's what I am supposed to be doing.'

'And what are you really doing?'

'I'm in a cell waiting to be executed and at the moment I am being questioned ,' I replied. 'I think you would call it in-terr-o-gat-ed.'

I pronounced each syllable as if I was finding it difficult to form the word and then continued quietly.

'But I have a secret plan that I won't tell you.'

'Which is?'

'Wouldn't be a shee-cret if I told you.'

'You can tell me. I can keep a secret. I'm a priest.'

I looked round, lowered my voice even more and did my best drunk impression.

'I'm going to escape.'

The priest laughed. *Third mistake*, I thought to myself.

'You can't escape,' said the priest. 'Nobody escapes from here.'

I beckoned for the priest to come closer and, slurring my words, whispered conspiratorially in his ear.

'If you shend the guards out I'll tell you how I'm goin' to do it. And why they shent me over here. Really why they shent me.'

The inexperienced interrogating priest swallowed the bait and waved the guards out with a command.

'Wait right outside. There is no problem. He cannot escape. I'll tell you when to come in.'

When they had gone he leant over to me and asked again.

'How do you think you are going to escape and why did they send you?'

I instantly grabbed the man in a powerful stranglehold and, before he could let out a word, told him truthfully.

'I'm going to take your place and I was sent to find out about people like yourself. Whether or not you and your church are a threat.'

I continued to squeeze until he was unconscious and then rapidly removed the ropes that had been wrapped around my body and legs. The biggest mistake, I reflected, had been to allow my arms to be free. A really stupid mistake compounded by not realising that the effects of thiopentone were so fleeting and that before they started on me I had already recovered from the drugs they had given me previously.

I took the unconscious priest's clothes off and swapped them with mine. There was no time to lose as the guards could decide to return at any moment despite the instructions from the priest. The clergyman started to stir so I jabbed the hypodermic syringe into his arm and gave him a much more generous shot of the truth drug than I had been given. He immediately fell back and started snoring.

I lifted the man onto the hard metal chair and strapped him in place. Moving his deadweight was the hardest bit so far but I managed it as quickly as possible. The priest did not facially look like me but I put a towel over his head to hide his features. Clad in my clothes he would pass as the prisoner for a short time.

I placed the large floppy hat on my head and walked boldly over to the door and rapped on it. The guards undid the lock. I tapped my ability to create illusion which was something I had been introduced to when I was in the Faerie realm nineteen months previously. It was a talent which worked best in that alternative reality but could be effective in the real world if the illusion was not a completely unexpected development of events. I thought of it as being a form of very effective impressionist act and it was considerably assisted by props such as the correct clothes. Over the past eighteen months I had sometimes reckoned that I could earn a fortune using my newly found ability with a satirical act on television.

The guards came into the cell and I ordered them to sit down.

'Call me on my cellphone when he wakes up,' I concluded, feigning the priest's American accent, moving like him and imagining that I looked exactly like the man.

I then marched out leaving them sitting, suspecting nothing and guarding the unconscious snoring clergyman. I reckoned I had about five to ten minutes before the sodium pentothal wore off and the priest regained consciousness so I did not have very long to make good my escape.

As I walked rapidly down the corridor I searched the pockets of the man's clothes. Wallet with money and credit cards, pen, diary, cellphone, car keys with remote fob, house keys separately, security access visitor's card. Bingo!

The latter let me straight out of the building and I walked past the police and security staff detailed outside with just a faint nod of my head. There was a car park right by the complex and I pressed the remote control of the car keys. A large black saloon immediately responded by flashing its lights. I jumped into the car and drove away.

Chapter 3

I had no intention of going far in the priest's car. As soon as he awoke all hell would be let loose and they would trace the car and the phone. I drove round the corner, passed a few blocks then steered straight into a car park. The valet parking attendant took the keys from me and gave me a ticket. I walked off and went down into a subway station. A few dollars on a Metrocard and I was in. I walked onto a Brooklyn train, sat down and took the phone from my pocket, turned it on and rapidly wrote down as many numbers as I could bring up. This took several minutes and two stops. Then, carefully unobserved, I pushed the phone down between the side of the seat and the metal upright at the end of the row. At the next stop I got off the train and rode in the opposite direction.

I had a "safe house" to go to in the Bronx so I stopped at the Grand Central Station and prepared to transfer to the overland railway. It might be a bit faster than continuing on the subway and it was less likely that they would look for me on the overland. The station, the largest in the world by number of platforms, was celebrating a landmark birthday and was a bustling lively place despite the early hour. I bought a few new clothes in one of the station's forty retail outlets and changed out of the priest's garb in the men's bathroom facilities.

I took the priest's clothes with me in the carrier bag supplied by the shop and then bought my train ticket to the Bronx.

The train journey was uneventful. The address of the safe house was close to the Bronx Zoo and I hurried to the place. The building turned out to be part of a large, peculiarly orange-coloured post war tenement on a road between the station and the zoo. I banged on the door rapping my knuckles on the wood with a Spanish

Tango beat... One, two And Three, Four. It was opened at my first knock and I was bustled inside. I gave the correct code for the day and the man who had opened the door replied with the appropriate response.

'We were just about to mount a rescue attempt,' said the agent after ushering me in to a side room. He was an Englishman from Lancashire, judging by his short vowels. I had never met him before but he knew me. 'We assumed something had gone wrong when you didn't turn up at the trade meeting.'

'You would have been too late,' I replied, in an aggrieved tone. 'They were going to execute me at noon.'

Bloody hell!' exclaimed the Lancastrian who told me his name was Bill from Chorley. 'That's a bit quick. I thought we had at least a few days to work something out.'

'Things have changed over here,' I replied. 'And not for the better. I was set up.'

'Are you sure?'

'Certainly. I had a good few hours to think about it last night. Your agents over here sold us a bum deal or they were being purposely misled. The second I arrived at the place I was in trouble.'

'Did you get anything out of the foray?'

'Not that much except that they are a bunch of homicidal religious maniacs.'

'We'd assumed that already judging by the political opponents who have gone missing or have turned up insane. Still, it is further proof.'

I then explained how I had been interrogated and escaped. Bill indicated that I should continue to tell my story.

'That's about it,' I replied. 'My cover is completely blown. I need to get out of here.'

'Sure. But did you get the priest's phone or anything else that might give us a lead?'

'I ditched the phone.'

Bill winced.

'We could have learnt a lot from the phone, Jimmy.'

I gave him the list of telephone numbers followed by the wallet, pen, diary, cellphone, house keys, security access visitor's card and the ticket for the parking lot.

'Well done lad. That's a treasure trove!' Bill congratulated me.

'The priest's a monster,' I told the Lancastrian. 'But I bet this new church and theocracy has spawned a whole load of them.'

'The Church of Armageddon Prophets security force is bound to go to the priest's home and to his car but before they do we'll undertake a thorough search then leave it as if it had never been touched,' said Bill, picking up his mobile phone. 'I'm getting on to it right now. Our team are working closely with a group in the FBI who are not in agreement with the Theocracy. They will pick all this up in a few minutes and then you can tell them...'

'I can't stay here,' I said interrupting his flow. 'I don't know which of your agents to trust and which are traitors.'

'It would be better if you can stay to debrief the team.'

'I'm not doing it Bill,' I countered. 'This place is not safe and I've escaped once. I'm not putting my head back into the hornet's nest.'

'OK. I thought they could get you on the next plane,' said Bill, thumbing his phone and looking for flight details.

'I'm not going by conventional means,' I replied. 'I'm going out of here via Faerie.'

'How can you get out that way?'

'I researched this with my contacts in Faerie before I came on this jaunt. There is a gateway to Faerie at the New York Shamanic Group meeting house....'

'Which I happen to know is right here in the Bronx,' added Bill. 'Just up the block in an old house that is also used as a dance studio..'

'...And my contacts have made a few introductions for me. The only problem is that the gateway sets you down somewhere in the middle of the Slough of Despond....'

'Which is otherwise called Hades according to the reports you wrote on your last jaunt there,' said Bill.

'....And I won't find my way out too easily as nobody quite knows where it will set me down, I will have no map and no idea which direction to go in,' I continued. 'But it would be a perfect place to hide away from the Armageddon Prophets.'

'Is there anything you need if you are going to Hades?' asked Bill. 'A lute perhaps?'

'A couple of silver dimes, a compass, a bottle of water and some food,' I answered. 'Then I shall pop round to the Shamanic meeting house, dive into Faerie and blunder my way through hell.'

'Is it really Hell?' asked Bill, a little worriedly. 'I'm not happy about this solution to your problem.'

'It's only hell for some people,' I replied with a grin. 'Looking back on the experience it doesn't seem so bad. Just animated skeletons grabbing at my legs and a general miasmic smell of death....Oh yes, and a sucking bog if you put a foot wrong.'

Poor Bill shuddered at the description. 'Rather you than me lad. I want to go to t'other place.'

'The real Hell?' I answered, purposely misunderstanding the Lancastrian.

'No, no, lad. Heaven forbid. I'm a good church-going Baptist. I want to go to heaven.'

'Who knows. I might meet you there,' I grinned at the agent but secretly wondered if the leak had come from him. Was our top man in the USA the double agent?

If you are the double agent, I thought studying his bland, honest-looking face, *you will definitely go to Hell.*

Chapter 4

'So how and why did you let James Scott go?' asked the CAP bishop. The priest was now receiving some of his own treatment. He was tied up to the metal chair being interrogated by the bishop, a grey-faced individual with eyes like marbles.

'He managed to trick me, your Grace,' gasped the priest.

'It took some considerable effort to lure him into our grasp and you let him go, you idiot.'

'I did interrogate him as instructed, your Grace.'

'And what did you learn from your so-clever interrogation of him?'

'He worked for the Queen of England, your Grace.'

'Of course he did, fool,' shouted the bishop slapping the priest hard on his face. 'They all work for the Queen. Anyone employed by the British Government is working for the Queen. It goes with the territory. Did you learn anything else? Anything of value?'

'Just that he was planning to escape,' admitted the priest.

'And then you helped him?'

'Not purposely, your Grace. He must have had inside help. I don't see how he could have tricked me so easily.'

'Because you are an idiot, a complete imbecile' screamed the bishop. 'That is why he could trick you. I shall hand you over to our God. He will find out whether or not you purposely helped the man escape and whether you are a traitor.'

'No, no, please no!' pleaded the priest. 'Don't sacrifice me to our God. I am more use alive than as half-dead zombie or a burnt out corpse. I would not make good eating. I'm too fatty. No, not our God. Anything else but that.'

The bishop smiled with a cruel half-grin. 'Then you had better be more successful on your next assignment. You must be much more successful.'

'Anything, your Grace. Anything.'

'Of course anything,' grimaced the dead-eyed bishop. 'I shall send you to Hades. I have reason to believe that James Scott will go that way.'

The priest shuddered at the news.

Hades, he thought. *The abode of the dead. An awful place but it is surely not as bad as meeting God after being eaten.*

*

The NY Shamanic Group meeting house was an old detached brick-built property less than a stone's throw from the safe house. It was on the same block and normally it was a matter of walking out of the front door, past two buildings and into another. I picked up the various items I had requested from Bill, bade him farewell but left via a back exit and hopped over a few low walls. It was always possible that the house was under surveillance and this could just forestall the pursuit.

I entered via a back door in the basement and was stopped immediately by a very large black man .

'Hey Dude,' he said as he grabbed me. 'Where do you think you are heading to?'

'The New York shamanic group?' I queried. 'Is this their headquarters?'

'Whose asking?' asked the man.

'Jimmy Scott's the name,' I replied.

'And creeping in round the back's the game,' came the rejoinder.

'I think you'll find that they are expecting me to turn up some time now,' I countered.

'I'll find out whether that is true or not,' replied the security man and he started gabbling into a walkie talkie. I could not hear the reply but his mood lightened considerably. He turned to me and remarked. 'It seems like you are some sort of star, man. Go right on up to the main floor. It's on the first level immediately above us.'

I climbed the stairs rather than take the elevator and was astonished when I entered the lobby area. The building looked old from the outside but had been completely gutted inside and the vestibule rose to three stories in height with balconies looking inwards to it on each of the levels. There was jungle growth centrally maintained by ultraviolet arc lights and a sprinkler watering system. Right in the middle of this I could see a totem pole and a very large wigwam. I walked over to this and a young woman, maybe twenty-five years old, came out of the tent to greet me. She was clad entirely in black leather with metal studs on the shoulders. I had expected that the leader would be an elderly native American so this leather lover was a shock. One that I quickly overcame but a shock nevertheless.

'I am the Shaman. I'm a witch doctor,' she informed me as she shook my hand and looked me straight in the eyes. 'And you are Jimmy Scott. I'll be going through the gateway with you.'

I had major misgivings about this but the girl, who told me her Shamanic name was Vole, wasted no time. She took me towards and into the wigwam. The back of the native tent was very dark and, with Vole holding my hand, we stepped into the blackness.

*

'You will travel to Hades the normal way,' intoned the bishop in the slightly melodic voice often assumed by the clergy.

'Which is what?' asked the priest.

'You will have to die, of course,' replied the bishop. 'But I will provide you with all the correct and best known ways of returning to the living world.'

'But I'm not ready to die!' protested the priest. 'I'm far too young. I've still got a lot of living to do.'

The grey-faced bishop laughed a sepulchral laugh. 'Ha, very

good. Too young to die. They all say that.'

'But how do you know where my soul will end up and how do you know that I can come back? Who has told you that Scott has gone to Hades?'

'Our God has told me where Scott is going and He will send you there. You are not going to disagree with our God, are you?'

'No, no. Not that. I will obey,' the priest shrank back despite his bindings. 'But has anybody ever returned from Hades who went there by dying?'

'I have,' said the bishop with a sigh. 'Our God killed me, sent me to Hades and brought me back. A little death now and then is good for obedience, don't you think?'

The priest felt too weak to nod his head in agreement or even to shake it in disagreement, which was how he really felt. He did not have long to think about it before the reanimated bishop plunged a long serrated knife into his body and up into his heart. The pain was unbearable for a few minutes before he expired and the normal world went black.

*

There was a momentary sensation of intense chill, a second or two of weightlessness and then Vole and I were through into the Faerie reality.

We landed with a slight bump on a soggy island in the middle of a great bog that stretched to a foggy horizon in every direction. Around my feet I could see a pile of wet bones and in the adjacent swamp I could hear moaning. A skeletal hand came up out of the mud and tried to grab at my ankle and an insistent murmuring assaulted my ears.... "Join us, join us, join us."

A sickening miasmic smell pervaded the atmosphere and I felt a great weariness wash over my soul.

Despite the appalling habitat I smiled at myself. I was back in Hades without a doubt. Yes, this was the Slough of Despond.

Chapter 5

The dead priest opened his eyes and looked around him. He was lying on a sandy shore beside a foul-smelling river. The water was to his left but if he looked to the right there was just blackness and nothing else. He tenderly examined his chest. The wound was still there but was healing. Whilst he looked at the damage the priest pulled himself painfully to his feet. As he did so a handwritten note fluttered down from his body to the ground.

The bishop placed the note on my body while I was dying, thought the priest very grumpily. *There must be other ways to get to this place but the bishop has to kill me. Typical.*

He knelt to pick up the note, sat back down on the shore and in the dim half-light of dusk read what his boss had scribbled.

I have placed two silver coins in your pocket. Each is good for a trip with Charon across the River Styx. In order to return to the living world you must cross over into Hades and find Scott, who will be there.

Follow the man until he returns to Earth and cross over with him. Report back to me exactly who he is with, who he meets, what he does and when he arrives in the land of the living simply kill him and your job will be done. Bon voyage dead man and may the blessings of Hadad go with you.

*

'Have you been here before?' I asked the leather-clad shaman who called herself Vole.

'Am I dead? Have I died?' replied Vole in a small, beaten voice, failing to answer my question.

'We haven't but they have,' I indicated the various scrabbling skeletons and half-decayed creatures mired in the filth. They were still trying very hard to attack us but I just ignored their attempts. Clearly Vole was not finding it as easy as myself.

'We'll never leave here,' moaned Vole. 'This place is evil. Why did we come here? Why did you make me come to this awful place?'

I looked at her with feelings of sympathy tinged with surprise and minor irritation. I knew exactly how the place made you feel if you were not prepared for it so I felt empathically bonded with the girl. The surprise was there, however, since I had assumed she had been here previously. After all, she claimed to be a shaman and shamans, in turn, claimed to walk the path of the spirits. Irritation because she had insisted on coming with me, not the other way round.

'I needed to escape pursuit, Vole,' I replied. 'And there are various people I need to meet.'

'In this place?' she looked perplexed. 'How can anybody in this place be worth meeting?'

'This plane of existence is not all like the Slough of Despond,' I answered. 'It is not all Hades. It is also intimately connected with kingdoms of the elves, dwarves and fairies, lairs of the dragons and Halls of Valhalla. That's just a few of the many delights.'

My mind wandered through memories of the time I had spent with Lady Aradel snuggled safely in my arms but then my recollection jumped to the horrendous period when I had carried her through Hades, half dead and lying motionless on my shoulders.

'Well, this place is the pits!' exclaimed Vole.

I agreed with the poor girl. It certainly was a dire place but I needed to know a bit more about Vole in order to help her.

'I don't want you to think I am being brutal but I must ask you whether or not you are a genuine shaman?'

She looked at me reproachfully.

'Of course. Do you think that they would let me guard the

gateway if I wasn't?'

'In what way are you gifted?' I asked.

'I have healing powers and just a little ability with telekinesis,' she replied distantly. 'And I predicted the collision of the realities. It was all published but nobody believed me until it happened. In fact most of my circle of friends thought that I had finally lost my mind.'

'But it was the opposite,' I surmised, quietly. 'You had found it.'

She looked at me with greater appreciation than before.

'You are so right. I had finally discovered what I was good at.'

I nodded.

She returned the question. 'Jimmy Scott, do you have any supernatural abilities?'

'That's not what I would call them but the answer is yes. Just a little.'

'Such as?'

'A moderate ability with illusion,' I answered and imagined myself to be a rat.... a large fat gobbling rat.

I fell down onto all fours and felt my face extend to a whiskery nose and my ears perk up. I had a long scaly rat tail which I curled round Vole's leg.

The shaman screamed and jumped backwards off the little island. I had to change straight back into my normal human form and grab her before she sank too far into the mire.

'God,' she cried. 'You gave me such a fright. I hate rats. I'm just a timid creature out of love.'

I smiled at the implied anagram with its clue of timidity.

'The sphinx would enjoy that, Vole.'

'Sphinx?'

'We'll probably meet it when we get out of here.'

'Do you think I could create illusions like you? '

'Very likely. We'll have a try when we are out of the Slough,' I replied then asked again. 'I don't suppose you have been here before?'

This time she answered the question.

'No way,' she said sounding a little happier than when we first arrived. 'The gateway has only been open since the clash of realities. But I have received some visitors from this place. I wondered why they all looked so muddy and now I know.'

*

The dead clergyman weighed up the options. On the riverside bank nearby he could see a party of revelers around a table groaning with food. Totally ignored by the partygoers was a sick looking man trying to catch their attention. The man suddenly spotted the clergyman and walked over to him.

'Can't seem to get them to notice me,' said the man with the malaise. 'I've no idea what is wrong.'

'You're dead,' said the clergyman bluntly.

'Dead?' queried the man. 'No, I can't be dead. The doctors said that my disease had a very good prognosis.'

'Your disease might have a good prognosis but you certainly don't,' replied the priest. 'You have expired. You have died and they are enjoying your funeral wake.'

'But I don't know half of them and I hate the rest of them,' answered the man. 'Sick of the sight of them, sycophantic fawners. They're just after my money.'

'Well, they've got it now,' said the priest.

'No they haven't,' countered the dead man. 'They won't be so happy when the will is read. I've left all my money to a donkey sanctuary. I chose one that had plenty of money already just to be spiteful. Just so that I could get the last laugh. Ha, ha, ha.'

Evil old miser, thought the priest. *He could have left it to my church. We always need money.*

The man at his own funeral wake stood watching the partygoers with amusement on his face. The priest left him and walked over to the riverside wondering how he would catch the attention of the ferryman. As he did so he could see other funeral parties up and down the riverbank, some with many guests, others with just one or two. The common factor at each party was a desolate looking man or woman being ignored by the partygoers.

The priest did not have to work hard in order to attract the ferryman and his concern was misplaced. Charon was already waiting for him with his hand outstretched to accept the standard payment of a small silver coin. Incongruously the ferryman was playing a game on an old mobile phone whilst waiting for the clergyman. The priest thought that it looked suspiciously like Tetris and Charon's points score was high in the millions.

*

One of the items I had brought with me was a short rope. I attached this to my belt and asked Vole to hold on to it. She did this rather reluctantly.

'How will this help, Jimmy?' she said with a pout. 'I feel like a child on reins.'

'Better to feel like that than to sink into the swamp without a trace,' I replied. 'Unless, of course, you have a better idea?'

'Put that way I suppose I should actually be attached rather than just hang on,' suggested Vole, reluctantly. 'I'll tie this end to my own belt.'

We struggled onwards taking as straight a course as possible, rising upwards to a small hillock. I thought that I knew this part of the route but I could not be sure.

At every step I held a compass in front of me tipped on its side and only stepped forwards if the arrow was not being deflected. When I had forayed into Hades previously I had discovered that it was awash with monopole magnets, something that could not be found in the normal world.

In this reality the monopoles interfered with one of the five fundamental forces ..... the extra one which hardly existed in our own world and was loosely called magic. Since every living creature in this world had some magic within them the monopoles interfered with the living essence, created despondency and despair. What is more it made people insubstantial and land that should have been solid became a sucking bog, a quicksand of miasmic filth that drew the unwary into its quagmire.

The monopoles deflected other monopoles and also sent my compass spinning. Avoiding such areas meant that I could, in theory, stop us from falling into the sucking Slough of Despond.

The theory was easy but in reality we stumbled our way across Hades through a fog of horror and wretchedness. The very elements were arraigned against us and the going was slow. As we went skeletal hands came up out of the bog to grab at our ankles and I became aware of something much larger on our trail.

Something monstrously large was following us but was keeping out of direct sight. Just occasionally I could see it in the corner of my eye... a huge black shape, slobbering with gore. I stopped abruptly at one point and Vole stumbled into me, nigh on pushing us both into the mire.

'Have you seen or sensed a monster following us?' I asked, looking back over my shoulder as I said it and seeing nothing but the mists and fog of despondency that bathed the noxious atmosphere of that godforsaken place.

'Yes,' replied the young shaman. 'And I know what it is.'

'What?' I queried. 'What is it that is following us? What foul creature is dogging our path.'

'It's my familiar. The spirit I usually converse with on the shadow plane,' she answered a little reluctantly.

'But it is a huge slobbering monster,' I interjected. 'There is nothing pleasant about it at all.'

'I know,' she timidly replied. 'I've never liked it and hoped that I would never meet it in the flesh.'

'What is it?'

'I call it the Devourer of Souls.'

Chapter 6

'Armageddon is nigh, Armageddon is nigh,' the sandwich board wearer marched up and down Whiteladies Road in Bristol. The man stopped every second passerby and handed them a leaflet entitled *Repent of Your Sins Now*. Beneath this heading in smaller writing were the additional words *Before it is too late*. On the back the leaflet described the way that the board wearer reckoned you could be saved.

The man handed a leaflet to Sienna and she passed it on to their younger son, Sam, who was now eight years old. Sam had been making a collection of Apocalyptic leaflets ever since the Stonehenge incident. At first Jimmy had tried to stop this but Sienna and Mary had persuaded him that it was a harmless enough pastime.

'If that's the worst thing he does when the devil has tried to sacrifice him I don't think he's doing too badly,' Sienna had argued.

Mary had added her own thoughts only weeks before she died.

'They're probably quite right. The end of the world was practically on us at Stonehenge so it is probably getting close. Anyway, stop being a wimp and be pleased that he has a hobby.'

Joshua, now aged fourteen, had also been on the sacrificial altar stone and had not fared so well as Sam afterwards. He had become a troubled teenager and would have died with embarrassment if he had been seen out with his mother. Sienna was worried that he might be on drugs and he had definitely taken up with a group of rough kids from the Southmead area whose only hobbies seemed to be getting into trouble with the local community policemen and truancy from school. Where he was right now she could not tell... he had disappeared on Thursday saying that he had a job to do after youth club and not to worry, he had his mobile phone with him. It was Saturday and not a word had come back to her. When she tried ringing he had not replied so she was considering calling the police.

Sam was examining the leaflet.

'It's great Mum,' he cried with delight. 'I haven't got this one. It's amazingly weird too. He reckons you can save the world by not eating eggs and by standing up to work and never sitting down.'

'Good idea, Sam,' replied Sienna without listening to a word Sam had said.

Good idea? thought Sam. *She's not listening again. This is almost as silly as the leaflet I've got that says you can save your soul by eating goldfish. None of these things could save you from the devil. You need a flaming sword like my Dad has got and a bad temper like my Granny had. She was great. I wish she was still here.*

*

I wish I still had my sword, the Morning Star, I thought as I trudged onwards, never quite sure whether or not we were going in the correct direction. The last I saw of the weapon was as an exhibit in court. I'm pretty certain it could make short work of the Devourer of Souls .... it certainly gave Lucifer something to think about.

We reached another dry mound which rose above the general level of the swamp and I decided that it was time to stop for refreshment. Vole was very relieved and immediately sat down on a large rock. Her weight displaced the boulder and she had to scrabble back onto her feet. The stone rolled down the small slope and over the edge into the swamp. To her amazement the heavy boulder, instead of sinking into the bog, bounced on the watery surface and then floated a foot or more above the marsh.

'Is that an example of a monopole?' she asked me as I passed her some food.

'Absolutely,' I replied. 'That is for all intents and purposes a pure monopole ore of iron. Very heavy normally but over deposits of the same stuff it floats because it has the same polarity.'

'Why don't the ores just break up and explode?' asked Vole.

'They do and there is a lot of volcanic activity here. But they are also held together by the four usual forces ... gravity, electromagnetism, the strong interaction and the weak interaction.'

'And they are the forces in our Universe?' queried Vole.

'They are, although some people postulate an additional force or energy field called Dark Energy.'

'Could that be magic in our Universe?' asked Vole.

'Possibly,' I replied shrugging my shoulders. 'Nobody knows. It only appears to manifest itself in a big way when we look at the expansion of the Universe. It can be considered as a constant in Einstein's equations.'

'The one he said was his biggest mistake?'

I was surprised that Vole knew this.

'That's right.... and now the cosmologists think he was correct all along.'

'Do you think he was right?' asked the young shaman.

'No I don't. Not exactly. But I'm a heretic with regards to this,' I answered candidly. 'But his ideas are a very good model and help explain quite a lot on the cosmic scale. Quantum theory helps explain things on the smallest scale. It's making the two tie up that is difficult.'

'Has the clashing of realities affected physics and cosmology as much as it has religion?'

I looked at her and replied to this young girl who had a knowing look and faraway eyes.

'It will eventually but at that moment the physicists don't know what questions to ask anymore.'

'And who should they ask the questions of?' she queried.

'They need to ask the dragons,' I answered. 'The golden

dragons of the Southern Mountains could explain much about the multiverse. If they cared to.'

*

The ferryboat glided over the River Styx. The priest looked down into the murky depths and saw writhing eels biting at each other. They did so in an aggressive cannibalistic way and the clergyman thought about the flesh-eating rites of his new religion.

The Church of Armageddon Prophets had not always been his religion. He had been a good Roman Catholic until he had been converted to the new sect.

Perverted, he thought to himself. *Perverted not converted. I've been perverted away from the paths of righteousness.*

There was no doubting the new religion's potency. He had seen it in action and witnessed its force. He had even caught a glimpse of his new God. He had only seen the tail end of a manifestation, the initiates were not allowed to see more. What he had observed had been extraordinary..... white light illuminating a vast section of the city and a huge but beautiful face framed against the sky by a window of stars. It had been no projection or trick of lasers. It was the real thing and had turned and spoken to him in person right inside his mind, opening vistas to space and time and demonstrating the vastness of creation.

The things his new God had told him were predictions and so far they had all come true. The presidency of the United States had, against all the odds, been captured by their founder, Obadiah Brabec. Before going into politics the founder had changed his name to Theodore K. Z. Armstrong, arguing that it was more American sounding than Brabec. That alone would have prevented most people from winning the presidency but the new God's prediction had proved correct. Armstrong had a landslide victory and once he had been sworn into office the man had immediately drafted laws that would create a theocracy out of the USA, overturning the constitution in myriads of ways. The priest had thought that they would never pass through Congress and Senate but they had.

The student priest had been formerly admitted to the priesthood and it was only then that he witnessed the more horrifying side of the church. It was not just that they had to kill opponents. He had expected that. All religions killed their   enemies, except perhaps Buddhism and Jainism who were simply too feeble in his opinion. It was necessary for the correct view to prevail and if you knew what was right you had a duty to explain that to people and convert them to your cause .... even if doing so meant stoning, burning, shooting or ripping them limb from limb.

No, it was the literal sense of the communion in the Church of Armageddon Prophets that shocked him. True, in the RC church he was supposed to believe that the wafer actually turned into the body of Jesus and the wine into his blood. This was an act of faith that he had struggled with many times. But in the CAP you killed people and ate them. You actually killed church members and ate them. You killed your *friends* and ate them!

The theory was that you absorbed the ideas, intelligence and strength of the people you ate. Moreover, they did not stay dead. If killed and eaten in the correct way they returned on the third day. They rose from the dead and rejoined the congregation just as if they had never died. Well, perhaps not exactly as if they had never died. You could tell the undead ones in the church as they were the most fervent followers willing to risk anything. That and the fact that they did not smile or laugh. They moved like normal people and went back to work as if they had just had a few days off with a cold or "man flu". In fact they worked harder than previously at whatever occupation they were employed in, taking no extra breaks and sometimes working all through the night to further their ends. If their job did not serve to strengthen the church they either changed the nature of their employment in the post they were in or they changed their job so that they were all working for the common good of the Church.

The priest had been given a new name once initiated. He was now Brother Habakuk and his bishop had killed him just to send him to Hades. It would probably have been better if he had been despatched in a communion service and eaten by his fellow priests. Here he was on a smelly river watching cannibal eels, or maybe snakes, taking great chunks out of each other.

'Does everyone who dies come this way and do only the dead pass over the river?' Brother Habakuk asked Charon.

'Quiet for ages staring into the water and suddenly two questions at once,' replied the ferryman, looking up from his game of Tetris.

'Well, I've not been dead before,' said the priest. 'So what's the answer?'

'No and no,' the ferryman retorted the ferryman.

'So not all the dead cross the Styx and live people do cross the river.'

'You've got it,' answered Charon.

'Has James Scott passed this way?' asked Habakuk.

'A common name so the answer is inevitably yes,' responded the ferryman, getting just a little irritated by the priest's interrogation.

'Perhaps you knew him as Lord James Scott?' asked Habakuk.

'Perhaps I did and perhaps I didn't,' replied Charon, looking up from the smart phone and losing a game at a low score because of the interruptions. 'Look, I do not have to answer your questions. It's not part of the package. I just have to take you across the river and the journey is almost over.'

'So what are you?' asked the priest, unable to stop himself from asking questions.

'That I will answer,' replied Charon. 'I am an old, bearded Athenian seaman who was granted immortality by the gods, provided that I stayed at my post ferrying newly dead souls across the river to Hades. I do it and they're satisfied. Is that OK?'

'Then why are you playing Tetris on a smart phone?' asked the priest. 'It's anachronistic. There were no smart phones in Ancient Greece.'

'You think that things stay the same with immortals?' asked Charon. 'Never changing, immutable? Is that it?'

'No, but a smart phone is a strange thing for the ferryman of the dead to possess and why play Tetris?'

'You don't think that this job gets boring?' queried Charon. 'Backwards and forwards over the same stretch of stinking water ferrying the newly deceased over to judgement? The dead don't make very good company as they are mostly too shocked to talk. Wouldn't you play a game or two if you could?'

'OK, perhaps I would,' agreed the priest. 'But how does it keep working? You can't have a ready supply of batteries.'

'I don't need them. I was given a dead phone. Full of precious metals but as a phone it was dead.'

'So how does it work?'

'Just like you, Brother Habakuk, Priest of the Church of Armageddon Prophets.'

'How is it like me?'

'It is the physical manifestation of the ghost of the phone. It's a ghost phone that I am playing Tetris on and I do it because I enjoy it. That and because I want to beat Thanatos the next time I meet him. He is far too good at the game and I want to give him a thrashing.'

'Will I meet him?'

'I hope so,' replied Charon. 'He is the daemon manifestation of death. He takes many forms but I hope that you meet him in his female form, as Ammit.'

'And what is Ammit?'

'Ammit?' Charon replied somewhat nonchalantly. 'Ammit is the Devourer of Souls.'

The boat glided into the shore on the Hades side of the river.

The foul smell of the swamp wafted over towards the boat. The priest looked back over the crystal flowing waters. The opposite bank looked more inviting from here than it had done from over the other side of the torrent.

'Yes,' remarked Charon. 'It's not so bad over there as you thought. But this is where you get off the ferryboat. Welcome to the land of the dead.'

Chapter 7

'Joshua,' said Sienna. 'You must not disappear like that. I get so worried.'

'Hey Mum,' Joshua was nonchalant. 'Don't hassle yourself so much. It's no big deal.'

'It is to me, Joshua,' his mother replied. 'I can't help but worry about you. What would your father think if something happened to you?'

'Dad? He's off chasing the fairies I imagine.'

'Don't talk about him that way. He's your father and he works very hard.'

'Yeah, but this Church deal can't be that important surely?'

'Your father thinks that it is a very big deal and is very dangerous.'

'I've met some guys from the Church and they are cool. Really cool.'

'Josh, stay away from the Church of Armageddon Prophets. Don't get involved. Stay away from strangers. If your father says they are dangerous he is right. They. Are. Dangerous!'

'OK Mum. No need to get heavy. I'll avoid strangers and stay away from the Armageddon Prophets. But you are being a bit unfair and I still think that they are cool.'

*

We set off again from the dry mound in the direction I thought was correct. I could just get an impression of mountains in the distance when the fog cleared momentarily due to the chill wind. I assumed that they were the Southern Mountain range where the dragons lived. If I could get to the end of the swamp I could then take the two of us over the river, past the sphinx and into Valhalla. There might be people in Valhalla who could help but if not I was sure that the dragons would have the answer to my queries. I wanted to know who and what was behind the Church of Armageddon Prophets. They had become powerful far too quickly for it to be due to simple faith. My experience with Lucifer and a fire elemental called Parsifal X made me think that some supernatural entity was behind the rise of the Church. Perhaps Lucifer himself had returned and was walking the Earth?

My mother-in-law was a witch and had saved the world by means of a promise she had extracted from Lucifer. Had that deal become unstuck? Was the devil controlling the Church of Armageddon Prophets?

My mind was mulling over these matters and not really on our route through the swamp which was not so bad until I stepped off the narrow path and into the maw of a gigantic monster. I fell deep into the slobbering jaws pulling Vole with me. We were swallowed whole much as a snake might swallow an egg.

This is the end, I thought, but then realised that the monster, which resembled a huge pike was being picked up and shaken. We were choking to death in the monster's gullet one moment but then the next second being regurgitated, coughing and splattering, onto dry land. Relatively dry, that is, until the rest of the contents of the monstrous fish spilled out all over us. Surrounded and submerged by half-digested bones and fetid gore ..... we were putrid, reeking, malodorous but alive.

Picking myself up I looked to see what had saved us. There was a battle going on between the gigantic fish, which must have been twenty foot long, and a creature that looked as if it had been put together by a committee. An Egyptian committee at that. It had the head of a crocodile, body and front legs of a lion and back end of a hippopotamus. I was sure that I had seen something like it carved into a pillar of a temple near the Nile when I had taken a cruise down that river many years before.

The giant fish struck back at the creature that had shaken it. The fish was much larger and had massive jaws and teeth which it crunched down on the committee beast's head. The struggling creatures rolled over and over on the drier part of the mound nearly squashing Vole and myself. Eventually the beast wriggled free of the fish jaws and using its two front legs picked the bigger monster up and flung it at least one hundred feet away into the swamp.

I found myself cheering for the beast. It had saved us from the maws of the ugly fish and deserved our praise.

'The enemy of my enemy is my friend' I said to Vole, half expecting her to tell me exactly who had said that first and where and when. In my mind I imagined an echo of Lady Aradel telling me "Vishnu Gupta. Three hundred BCE."

Vole, however, looked less than happy.

'That's the Devourer of Souls,' she said.

'What, the fish?' I asked.

'No, no. The other beast. The one that saved us,' she replied. 'And it wants us to follow it.'

'Where?' I asked.

'To Judgement.' Vole answered. 'We are to follow it to the Seat of Judgement here in Hades.'

*

Habakuk the priest stumbled off the boat and onto the shore. He looked askance at the stinking swamps stretching away from him into the distance in all directions.

Charon had been right. It was better on the other side. Perhaps I could ask for a lift back?

He turned back to the boat but it had vanished into the mists. When the fog cleared the ferry was nowhere to be seen. The dead clergyman of the Church of Armageddon Prophets stood and looked over the river. On this side the waters were clear and crystal flowing and looking over to the other side he could see fields of waving corn dancing with glee and distant mountains topped with snow. The sun was high in the sky but there was a slight misty rain and the priest could see a strong rainbow over the fields.

Glory Land and the promise of my former God, thought Habakuk. *I have turned my back on Paradise because I could not see it when I was there.*

The priest made the decision that he would not proceed into the swamps. If he could not go by ferry he would wade or swim to the distant shore. This was not the Styx, it was the Jordan and he wanted to go to the other side where the land flowed with milk and honey. He took a step into the water and it immediately chilled his body to such an extent that he could hardly move.

Chills the body but not the soul. I should have remembered that. Well, if I can't swim over there I shall just sit down and wait for the boat to return. If I'm dead already it can hardly do me any harm to wait.

He found a rock and sat down on it, closing his eyes as he did so. When he opened them to his immense shock he realised that the river had moved away from him. He was no longer sitting on the bank but was half way up the shore towards the swamps. Standing up in annoyance he took two steps towards the bank and found that in doing so he had moved even further into the edges of the mire. He took an enormous jump in the direction of the river and landed in the middle of a bog which started to suck him down. The dead man struggled against the sucking mud but slipped and sank further and further into the filth. The smell of the swamp made him gag and retch and he was up to his neck when a hand reached out to him. He gratefully pulled on the hand and then recoiled further into the swamp with horror. He was holding not a hand but a rotting skeleton.

He sank completely under the surface of the filth.

*

'Come to our communion service,' suggested the young CAP

acolyte to Joshua as they walked past an area ripe for redevelopment. 'You can't totally understand where we're at until you've undergone communion.'

Joshua looked at the his friend admiringly. The follower of the Church of Armageddon Prophets was dressed in high Goth style ..... all black and silver. His hair was dyed black and his face was made up with white foundation and there was blue-black mascara round the eyes. At least Josh assumed it was make-up. You could not get to look quite so pale and have such deep sunken eyes without the help of cosmetics. All of this Joshua found deeply fascinating and what is more this guy was not a stranger. This guy was Rupert, Josh had known him for at least eight years. Rupert had been round to their house for parties and Josh had been in the same class as him for a couple of years at his junior school, St John's in Clifton. So if he went to the Church with Rupert he would not be disobeying his mother so much since Rupert was not a stranger.

It's true I've not seen him for a while, thought Joshua. *But the guy is not even a stranger to my parents. Surely he can't really be dangerous?*

Josh had just about decided that he would go to the communion service when Rupert smiled at him. This was the first thing that made Jimmy's elder son really uneasy. It was truly disturbing. The smile was more of a grimace than a genuine smile and all of the Armageddon Prophet's teeth were filed to points. When Josh had last seen Rupert he did not have peculiar teeth, Joshua was certain of that.

Rupert came closer to Josh and Joshua could see that the guy's eyes looked like two cloudy marbles. Josh decided to run ... this guy had become just a bit too weird even for him and he, Joshua, had almost been sacrificed to the devil, so he knew what weird was like. No he did not like the look of Rupert's teeth at all and he was sure that just a little blood had dripped out onto the acolyte's chin.... and those scary dead eyes!

Joshua turned and began to sprint but more of the CAP

acolytes appeared from behind the derelict buildings. Joshua turned nervously in all directions.

The Armageddon Prophets were closing in on him and he could see nowhere to flee to.

Chapter 8

'You may know me as Ammit, the Devourer of Souls,' intoned the committee creature. 'Or perhaps as Thanatos, the daemon personification of death.'

'Do you rule Hades?' I asked.

'Rule Hades?' the monster laughed. 'Hades rules Hades.'

'What does that mean?' I queried.

'Hades is the lord of the dead and ruler of the nether world,' Ammit waved an arm in an expansive gesture. 'This is the domain of Hades.'

'We have conversed before, Devourer,' whispered Vole. 'Do you not recognise me?'

The monster turned its crocodilian head and peered closely at her. Then it jumped right up next to the shaman who tried not to flinch away. It stared into her eyes.

'Yes, it's little Vole. I did not expect you to me so big,' it chimed. 'You will both come with me to judgement.

Damn, I thought to myself. *One judgement after another. But perhaps we can still escape.*

There was no escape. One second the monster was talking to us and the next we were standing in front of a huge throne made of dark, dark ebony. A large figure sat on the throne, unmoving. The figure held a scepter in his right arm, a helmet on his head and wore a Greek tunic and sandals. In his left hand he was holding scales. On one scale, just about tipping the balance, was a large ostrich feather. The other scale was empty.

The figure on the throne slowly turned and looked at us.

'I am Hades, Pluto, Orcus and Anubis. This is your Day of Judgement.'

Here we go again I thought. *Out of the frying pan into the fire.*

'I shall judge all three of you using the scales of justice and the feather of Ma'at. If you are judged impure your soul will be devoured by Ammit.'

All three of us? I wondered. *Surely he can't be including Ammit if Ammit is to be the devourer?*

I looked round. Standing away from me on the other side of Vole was another figure, a person dripping with the stinking mire. It took me a while but I eventually recognised the stance if not the face. It was the priest who had been interrogating me in the New York cell. He was here, in the Slough of Despond, the Domain of Hades.

He had followed me to the very Seat of Judgement and we were to be judged together.

★

Rupert pulled a closed knife from his belt and flicked it open.

'Don't worry new boy,' whispered the pale friend with the pointed teeth. 'Just a little snip or two and you can be like us.'

'I'm pretty sure that I don't want to be like you,' Joshua replied and disarmed Rupert with a quick judo move.

He ducked under the nearest of the other acolytes and ran as fast as he could towards the lit road and away from the ten or more black clad youths. He had almost made it to the light when a large figure stepped out from the shadows and tripped him up so that he went flying onto a sharply graveled drive.

The Armageddon Prophets closed in for the kill, knives and teeth flashing as they did so.

★

I felt a searing pain in my chest and in horror looked at my body where the anterior thorax had split open like an over-ripe seed pod.

'I shall weigh your heart against the feather. If you are found wanting your soul will be destroyed. You will not continue your voyage to immortality,' Hades voice battered my ears.

'But I came here alive of my own free will,' I protested. 'Without my heart I will inevitably die. I don't even understand how I am able to stand here and talk.'

'Petty mortal concerned with petty matters,' growled the Devourer who was standing next to me. 'Time stands still at the Seat of Judgement and your body is only a representation.'

'Don't I get to say something in my defence?' I asked.

'No!' replied the Devourer.

'Arrgh!' I turned to see that Vole had been inflicted like myself.

Then again.

'Aaaarrgh.'

The last sound had come from the priest who collapsed in a moaning heap on the ground.

'Lord James Scott stand forward,' the voice of the god of the underworld battered my ears yet again. 'You will be the first to be weighed in the balances.'

And hopefully not found wanting, I mused

Hopefully not, replied Hades in my thoughts. *And yes, I can hear everything you think.*

Then I had better be careful not to think anything bad about the big guy, I thought.

'Ha, ha!' Hades laughed out loud and the sound shook the earth we were standing on. 'Droll humour at the seat of judgement. I admire the courage.'

The others looked on bemused.

'Your heart must balance the feather if it is found to be true,' said Thanatos, otherwise known as Ammit the Devourer.

He was now standing next to me in the form of a gigantic man in Greek attire. When he saw me peering at him he added.

'I like to look my best when we come to the formal part of the proceedings.'

The devourer reached into my body and pulled out a mass of quivering flesh with blood dripping from the tubes. He placed the heart on the empty scale. It immediately swung wildly down, pushing the scale with the feather upwards.

Doesn't look too good, I thought.

'I allow a few moments for the scales to settle before the judgement is made,' the voice of Hades spoke, again shaking the local reality. 'We shall wait while the balance is formed.'

*

'You are all under arrest. Do not move. Lie down on the ground and stay still.'

The echoing voice came over a loud hailer system and Joshua realised that the person who had tripped him up was not an acolyte of the Church of Armageddon Prophets.

He looked around as best he could without shifting his position and could see that he had been floored by a policeman who was part of a team subduing the Prophets. There were as many as thirty policemen in protective gear, armed with guns and tasers. They were rapidly disarming the CAP acolytes and the haul from the Prophets included numerous knives and several guns.

Joshua could see all of this from his position on the ground. In total he counted thirteen CAP acolytes. The police would presumably think that he was the fourteenth. It was vitally important that he was kept away from the new church followers as he did not trust them at all with their pointed teeth and their marble eyes. Not at all.

*

The balances slowly equilibrated and eventually held with my heart and the feather level at the same height.

'You have truth in your heart but the balance was only just in time,' the voice of Hades thundered.

I had passed the test and been proved worthy of life. The heart vanished and I looked down at my chest. It was completely whole again with no trace of trauma.

'And now for my little Vole,' said Thanatos, alias the Devourer and Vole's familiar in the spirit world. Vole's heart appeared on the scales with no visible signs of trauma on her body. She looked on impassively as if she had always known this moment would come and was resigned to whatever fate would send.

The beating heart of the young shaman balanced the feather immediately and the heart disappeared off the scales.

'A truly noble heart,' Hades declared, shaking the ground with his intonement.

'Now the heart of the priest who followed you into Hades by the more conventional route,' remarked Thanatos.

'You mean he died to follow us?' I asked amazed.

'He was killed by his bishop,' replied the Devourer of Souls. 'In order that he could follow the pair of you to the Domain of Hades.'

Habakuk the priest scowled as they talked about him. He had been pulled out of the mire, where he had been completely submerged and could see nothing, and dragged to this judgement throne by a baboon that incongruously called itself Babi or perhaps Baba. The creature had been nothing like a baby and had been immensely strong.

'I protest,' shouted Habakuk. 'I serve a different god and do not recognise your authority over me.'

'And yet you have come to my domain and you are therefore subject to my judgement if I so desire,' the voice of Hades bellowed, the whole firmament shaking as he did so.

Vole and I fell to our knees due to the disturbance and the priest fell face forward, prostrate in front of the ebony throne.

The clergyman's heart appeared on the scales and the feather immediately dropped, the heart being lifted right up. It stayed that way for several minutes whilst we all stared at the ethereal weighing machine.

Eventually Hades spoke.

'Sins of omission make your heart untrue. You have not done the things you should have done or promised to do, so your soul will be devoured.'

I looked round at Thanatos and saw him change his form into the peculiar committee animal, with the head of a crocodile, body and front legs of a lion and back end of a hippopotamus.

'This is my form when I am the Devourer,' the creature said to me almost apologetically.

'STOP,' came a loud voice, equal to that of Hades thunderous tones. 'The clergyman is my acolyte and my priest. He is not subject to your judgment but to mine. His soul belongs to me.'

'Who dares to countermand my orders?' the voice of Hades roared in my ears.

'I am the Lord of the Covenant and he is mine.'

'No, he is in my domain,' countermanded Hades.

'I broach no argument,' came the reply and a huge thunderbolt smacked down at the base of the throne. In the same instant the clergyman and his heart disappeared leaving the scales swinging wildly. Hades stood and the ground shook.

'This is sacrilege,' said the Devourer quietly. 'This is tantamount to war between the realms.'

Hades sat down again with a weary look on his huge face.

'I detect the priest not. I believe he is no longer in this reality,' thundered the god of the dead. 'Can you detect him, Thanatos?'

The Devourer lifted its head and sniffed the air through its crocodile nostrils.

'He is no longer in our realm, your deity. The clergyman has gone,' the Devourer replied to his overlord. 'I do not believe that he is in the Earthly land of reality. If he is anywhere he is in the Eternal Realm.' The Devourer paused, sniffed the air again. 'Yes, the trail definitely leads to the Eternal Realm.'

'We will have to consider this very carefully,' replied the lord of the underworld. 'The entity that took the priest is clearly very powerful and we must plan our moves well.'

'Perhaps I can be of help?' I suggested.

'You? A mere mortal?' queried Hades. 'In what way can you help a god?'

'It has been known before,' I replied. 'And I think that this so-called Lord of the Covenant has a lot to answer for in my own realm. I would like to pursue him into his reality.'

'And does your companion Vole wish to pursue the Lord of the Covenant also?' crashed the voice of Hades as he talked to us from his throne.

'I think I do,' replied Vole. 'Although I am rather worried about the prospect.'

'You now both have the protection of the Underworld,' Hades answered. 'But if things go wrong for you all I can offer is an eternity within my Domain.'

'Does that also include Valhalla and the Elysian Fields?' I asked.

'Of course,' replied the god from the ebony throne. 'But if you die whilst fighting the Lord of the Covenant you cannot return to the reality of the living.... you can only come here.'

'And the Heaven of the Christians, is that forbidden?' asked Vole, quietly. 'You see that as well as being a shaman I am also a fully baptised Christian.'

'There is a Heaven of the Christians,' replied Hades. 'It is part of the far realm. But I have no direct knowledge of it. Perhaps the Lord of the Covenant is also the Lord of the Christians?'

'Perhaps,' I replied. 'That is certainly something I would like to find out. If so there is a lot awry with our present-day Earthly religions.'

The Lord of the Underworld simply laughed in reply. But the laugh was so powerful that the whole of his domain shook with his mirth.

Chapter 9

'Inspector Blake here,' said the policeman over the telephone. 'I'm at the central police station in Bristol. We have a collection of Church followers in the holding cells and I need to talk to the chief constable about one of them.'

'I'll get him for you straight away,' replied a female voice, probably that of the chief constable's wife. The call was immediately picked up by a gruff sounding, military voice.

'Maxwell Devonport here, how can I help you?'

'Hello sir, Inspector Donald Blake here. I have a problem,'

'Which is?'

'We arrested a group of fourteen CAP acolytes,'

'Yes, from the new Church '

'They were breaking the curfew and had started a kerfuffle in waste ground. We took a total of twenty knives off them and four guns.'

'So a successful purge, I would say.'

'Yes sir, but there is a slight problem.'

'Go on.'

'One of the acolytes, the one they were chasing, went completely mad when we tried to put him in with some of the others from the Church of Armageddon Prophets.'

'You are sure that he is one of them?'

'He's dressed in their type of clothes and was hanging out with them. He was chatting to them, there was some sort of argument and he ran away. I personally tripped him up and arrested him.'

'So where is he now?'

'He's in the holding cells next to the others but on his own.'

'I don't see the problem, Blake. You can arrest him for resisting arrest. Was he armed?'

'No, I don't believe that he was. The troubling feature, and why I have telephoned you, is that his family are very high profile.'

'Tell me more?'

'He is Joshua Scott. His father works for the government as a roving trouble-shooter. Has some sort of ministerial appointment.'

'Not Jimmy Scott? The one whose sons were almost sacrificed to Lucifer?'

'If you believe that sir.'

'Believe it? I was damn well there and almost got killed myself by a ruddy cyclops. Of course I believe it.'

'So what do we do with him?'

'Be very careful and don't let the acolytes near him. Contact his parents and I'll be over right away.'

'Sorry to have disturbed your sleep sir.'

'Sleep? I wasn't asleep. I was catching up on paperwork. That's all that this job entails most of the time. I'll be over right away. It will be a relief to get away from the ruddy form filling.'

*

'Do you or the Devourer of Souls have any practical suggestions?' I asked the Lord of the Underworld. 'Are there any allies who could help us?'

'You will find allies along the way,' replied Hades.

'Is Lady Aradel likely to be of assistance?' I asked, hoping that my close friend would be able to help us.

'The Queen of the elves and dragons is not on this world at present and my Domain is that of the dead,' replied the huge figure on the ebony throne. 'You are still alive and must pass from my realm to the far realm. I cannot aid you in that endeavour except to say that there is a bridge through the multiverse and one part of that bridge touches my Domain.

My power does not extend to that bridge and whether you can pass over it will depend on yourselves.'

'Where does that bridge meet your realm, your deity?' I asked Hades.

'In Valhalla,' the god replied. 'You must go to Valhalla and attempt to cross the Bifrost Bridge via Midgard to Asgard. The bridge ends in the Eternal heaven at Himinbjorg.'

'And how will we pass over the bridge?' Vole asked.

'Dear mortals, you have passed the test of truth via the scales of justice. Noble souls can cross the bridge so you are likely to succeed if you persevere,' replied the Lord of the Underworld. 'I repeat....go to Valhalla and the blessings of the dead go with you.'

Blessings of the dead? I thought. *Is that what we need?*

It's what you have got, replied Hades in my mind. *Go now. The Devourer of Souls will escort you to the River Styx.*

*

Maxwell Devonport drove swiftly into Bristol and parked his car in the space reserved for the chief constable. He glanced at his watch as he walked into the building. Five minutes to two in the morning and most sensible people were asleep in their beds but here he was marching into the refurbished "new" central police station. The place had been completely gutted by the hurricanes and the hastily mended building was almost unrecognisable compared with the modern, sleek, glass and concrete structure that had been opened in 2012.

The sergeant at the desk greeted him and told him that they had telephoned the Scott home. Mrs. Scott would be coming in to the police station as soon as she had arranged for someone to look after her younger son.

'I told her that he was perfectly safe but we would appreciate it if she could come in at least by midday,' the sergeant explained to the chief constable. 'I added that she could bring her younger son with her if she had to.'

Maxwell Devonport huffed.

'I hope she comes in considerably sooner than that. You've

brought me in when it should be my beauty sleep. Lord knows I need it, I'm feeling ugly enough.'

The sergeant smiled. The chief constable was noted for his gruff wit and was one of the most approachable chiefs he had known in the twenty years he had served in the Avon and Somerset Police.

'Where's Blake?' asked Devonport. 'I thought he'd be here?'

'He is, sir,' replied the sergeant straightening up. 'He's down in the holding cells talking to the acolytes.'

'And is there anybody else here?'

'No sir, the remainder of the arresting team have been disbanded for the night and have gone off home to bed. Judging by their looks they needed their beauty sleep even more than you, sir.'

The chief constable huffed again in reply.

'I doubt that. You're looking at me with rose-tinted spectacles, sergeant. I'm even uglier than I look.'

The sergeant laughed again and the chief constable smiled and walked on down the passage and descended to the cells.

As he did so a strange smell afflicted his nostrils. The smell had a metallic tang to it. Blood! He'd recognise that anywhere. The smell of blood.

*

Ammit, the Devourer of Souls, led us through the swamps. I was becoming tired and hungry despite the Devourer's previous pronouncement that time had stood still. It certainly was not doing so now and I could feel every step we took wearing me down. Vole was a changed person. Where before she had been morose and withdrawn she now was ebullient. The Slough of Despond was no longer making her despondent and eventually I asked her why.

'I'm no longer worrying about judgement day, Jimmy,' she replied instantly. 'Ever since I became a shaman I have known that judgement day with the Devourer of Souls was on its way. Any thing after that was blank so I feared the worst.'

'But we've got a lot of work to do yet,' I answered. 'And I don't think that there is much our new found friends can do to help us.'

'Hades has guaranteed us a place in the Elysian Fields,' retorted Vole. 'I consider that to be a great gain for us and a superb offer on his part. You should be grateful.'

I looked at Vole. I admired her courage and her newly found optimism but I could not delight in our present predicament in the way that she could.

'I've a wife and two boys on Earth,' I answered. 'I want to see the boys grow up, get jobs, perhaps marry and have my grandchildren. I want to spend some time with my wife. I don't want to go straight to Valhalla or wherever.'

'Aren't you being a little selfish?' asked Vole with a toss of her head. Now that her manner had changed I could see that she was quite a fiery beauty. Her features were delicate but well-formed and she had high, oriental, cheek bones. Her black hair swung out in a lively manner and she gave me a provocative look. 'We could be happy together. Very happy.'

Gawd, I thought. *It's happening again. She's got her sights on me just like Lady Aradel.*

'I can't help worrying about my family,' I replied, trying to keep my roving spirits under control. The swamps of Hades were no place for an illicit affair.

'They'll be fine,' replied Vole. 'They're in the real world. They'll be OK.'

'Is that foresight or wishful thinking on you part?' I asked provocatively. 'Can you predict their future or are you just saying it to please me?'

'The future's blank,' answered Vole and her ebullience diminished a little. 'But I really do think that they will be fine. Stop worrying about them and concentrate on what we need to do and all will be well.'

*

'Oh my god!' exclaimed the chief constable and had to prevent himself from retching. As he entered the basement of the police station he could see directly into the cells. The holding bays were four large metal cage affairs in a row. They had also been hastily erected after the hurricane when dealing with hordes of invading forces from faerie land. It had taken months to sort through the troops and similar cages had been set up all over the country but particularly in the South and South West of England where the invasion had been greatest in number.

Now he was looking at a terrible sight. There was no movement anywhere and in every cell there were bodies lying in pools of blood, blood and more blood.

Inspector Blake lay dead in a pool of his own blood. He had clearly been grabbed by one of the prisoners, pulled up against the bars and stabbed to death.

The chief constable gathered his senses and looked carefully at each cell. There were five bodies lying in the far right cell. Four in each of the next two and just one isolated, immobile figure huddled in the far corner of the last cell, hood covering his head, a bloody knife near his feet.

That must be Joshua Scott, thought Maxwell Devonport. *God, this is a disaster. Better get the homicide crew in and let the new Chief Commissioner of Police know what is going on.*

Devonport swung round decisively. He must get the sergeant to call the homicide lads. How come Sergeant Andrews had heard nothing?

'Sergeant,' he started to shout to gain the man's attention and then stopped. The portly sergeant was standing halfway down the stairs with a grin on his face. Not a nice grin for in the dim half-light of the stairwell the sergeant's eyes looked sunken and dead and when the man opened his mouth wider the chief constable could see the sergeant's teeth. They were all filed to points.

'It has begun,' whispered Sergeant Andrews hoarsely.

'What has begun?' asked the chief constable.

'The assault on Heaven,' replied the sergeant. 'The assault on Heaven has begun and all acolytes are needed. You can join us.'

The grinning sergeant with the filed teeth walked down the remaining stairs and slowly approached the chief constable with a knife in his hand. Chief Constable Devonport stood stock still with shock as the man came closer and did nothing to defend himself as the sergeant raised his arm with the long, wicked knife grasped in his fist.

Chapter 10

We reached the River Jordan and I could see that the ferryboat was already waiting and Charon was standing in it playing a game on my old smart phone. The Devourer of Souls changed back into the Thanatos persona as we approached the shore and then turned to me with a frown on his face.

'I have a bone to pick with you, Lord James Scott,' he said, pointing to Charon. 'You gave the ferryman your phone in payment for a trip and now he is as good as I am at Tetris.'

'It was a fair payment,' responded Charon with a grin. 'Anyway, you were beating me too easily and now it's more equal. The challenge is more fun.'

'For you, yes,' said the Devourer of Souls. 'But not for me. I liked winning.'

'You still win most times,' answered Charon. 'So stop complaining and introduce me to your charge.'

'Lord James you know,' replied Thanatos.

'It's the beautiful girl I was asking about. She is the one that I don't know,' Charon stated. 'And I can detect that you have a special relationship with her. There is a golden rope joining you two.'

Golden rope? I thought. *I can't see anything of the sort.*

'It's another representation,' said Charon, clearly reading my thoughts. 'Thanatos and the girl are joined spiritually. They have a bond and I see it as a golden rope.'

Charon then looked more closely at myself, squinting as he did so and holding his head at a strange angle. 'You also have a spiritual bond. It is more difficult to discern but your golden rope connects you to Lady Aradel, Queen of the Elves and Golden Dragons of the

Southern Mountains.'

*

The sergeant stepped forward and swung his arm down towards the undefended chief constable. But as he did so he felt the sensation of a punch in his back which made him stumble and miss his target. The sergeant looked round in bewildered surprise. Who had hit him? There was nobody else in the room.

Then he realised that he was, himself, bleeding and that a knife was sticking out of his lower thorax. He stumbled again and locked eyes on his assailant. The person who had saved the chief constable was standing up against the bars, alone in his cell.

It's that cursed Joshua Scott, thought the sergeant. *When my God returns me to this world I will return that blow.* He then promptly expired.

'Well done my lad,' said Chief Constable Devonport, regaining his composure. 'That was an excellent throw. It certainly saved my life. Are you an expert at knife throwing?'

'Not at all, sir,' replied Joshua politely. 'I don't think that I have ever thrown a knife before in my entire life.'

'Probably beginner's luck,' muttered the police chief and then he looked more closely at Joshua. 'You wouldn't mind me looking at your teeth, would you?'

Josh opened his mouth and the chief constable peered in at him through the bars of the cell.

'Perfectly normal teeth,' remarked the policeman. 'Thank god for that.'

'I have a tendency to a cross bite, or so I was told,' replied Joshua. 'But at least they are not filed to points like all these homicidal maniacs.'

The chief constable fumbled around in the dead sergeant's pockets and eventually found a key to let Joshua out of the holding cell.

'Come upstairs away from this murderous mayhem,' ordered

the chief. 'I need to get all the details from you and a signed statement.'

The senior policeman strode up the stairs followed by Joshua. When they reached the top of the stairs the chief constable swung a heavy door closed and locked it with one of the sergeant's keys.

'Joshua, once we have got your statement down we must telephone for the homicide boys and then get your parents over here.'

'I have a very worrying feeling that we don't have long, sir,' remarked Joshua. 'I heard several of the Church followers say that the assault on heaven has begun.'

'Yes, Sergeant Andrews said the same. What do you think it means? Is it some kind of code?'

'I don't think so, sir,' replied Joshua. 'I think they meant exactly what they said and they all committed suicide to go and join the fight.'

'Very worrying,' said Chief Constable Devonport. 'Extremely worrying indeed.'

✳

Charon held out his hand. 'Do you have the fare?' he asked.

Vole looked at me slightly perplexed. 'What fare does he mean?'

'The ferryman requires a small silver coin as fare in order that he may take you across the river to the far side,' I answered.

'I don't have a silver coin,' retorted Vole. 'I was not told that there was such a requirement.'

'Look in the lefthand pocket of your jacket,' I said to her and she slipped her hand down into the black leather. After fumbling for a moment or two she pulled out a silver dime.

'How did that get in there?' she asked, surprised to find the coin.

'I slipped it in before we passed across the gateway into Faerie,' I answered. 'I knew that we might end up here and it was important that you carried the fare through Hades.'

'Thank you Jimmy,' she flung her arms round me and kissed me right on the lips.

A growl came from the large form of Thanatos...... the Devourer was jealous!

'Time that you both stepped onto the ferry,' said Charon looking warily at Thanatos. 'He can have a bad temper if he loses. At anything!'

'I am not a bad loser,' countered Thanatos. 'I just take life seriously.'

'And death even more so,' replied Charon. 'But these two have finished their business in this part of the domain and I needs must ferry them to the other side of the river.'

*

The priest Habakuk was straining on tip-toe to see who was speaking.

'The time has come for the assault to begin,' said a shining angel-like figure. 'I am the messenger of your God and He wishes you all to know that we shall succeed. The rewards will be great and a great wrong will be righted. The rightful Lord of the Covenant will retake his place in the firmament.... and Paradise will be yours.'

The messenger was addressing row upon row of black clad followers of the Church of Armageddon Prophets. They numbered in their millions like the sands of the seashore.

Habakuk sneaked a look around him. Every other eye in the place remained fixed on the shining angel but Habakuk still felt curious.

What is this place and how did I get here? he pondered. *It's been a very nasty experience ever since I interrogated that Scott man. Scott nearly strangled me, my bishop stabbed me, the Lord of the Underworld judged me. Twice I have had my heart assaulted and twice I've been revived. This had better all be worth it.*

He sneaked another look round. *No, nobody else is acting like me. Strange that I am doing it myself.*

Then Habakuk remembered. Nobody else had eaten his flesh or drank his blood. Perhaps that was why his soul still felt intact?

'We are Gog and Magog and we are the chosen of God.'

A loud chant had started and was sweeping through the crowds getting louder and louder as it was taken up by more and more of the soulless.

'We are Gog and Magog and we are the chosen of God.'

*

'So, if I have it right, you are saying that the Church acolytes all started stabbing each other and eating bits of their flesh?' queried the chief constable. 'I'd assumed that the sergeant had something to do with it.'

'No, not at all,' answered Joshua. 'I was worried about him because he had the pale sunken look of the others but he stayed upstairs.'

'So what happened to Blake?'

'The inspector?'

'Yes, Inspector Blake.'

'Well, he got too close to the cell and presumably several of the acolytes still had knives. Once one Church follower had stabbed the inspector all hell broke loose. Rupert, who used to be my friend but had become weird, grabbed a knife and stabbed himself saying that the assault on heaven had begun. Then they were all stabbing each other and eating each others flesh.'

'It must have been very noisy.'

'It was, they were all screaming and shouting.'

'Nobody came down?'

'No.'

'How did you end up with a knife in your cell?'

'I got as far away as I could on the other side of my cell and one of the Church followers threw a knife at me and missed. I then crouched down and pulled my hood over my head and stayed completely still, trying to block out the horrible sights and sounds.'

'Were you scared?'

'Scared? I was completely petrified.'

'What happened next?'

'When it was all quiet the sergeant came down and looked at the horrible, horrible sight of all the broken, bleeding bodies.'

'Did anybody else come down?'

'Not until you came down the stairs and looked in on the scene. I didn't know whether you were also one of them so I kept as still as I possibly could.'

'...And then?'

'And then the sergeant came down and tried to kill you so I had to do something. I threw the knife at the sergeant.'

'How did you get mixed up with these guys?'

'I met Rupert at the local Church youth club. Dad was investigating the Church of Armageddon Prophets so I thought I would do some investigation of my own. Quite a few Prophets came to our youth club from their church. I had no idea that they were a bunch of sick, murderous cannibals.'

'How much of this did you tell your mother?'

'I told her that I was going to the youth club, nothing else. This will be a horrible shock for her, sir. Am I still in trouble with the law?'

'Trouble? No, not at all. You saved my life and you deserve a medal. But I believe that we are all in trouble. If there is another supernatural battle just starting then we have to be prepared.'

'Well sir, we won't know who is a follower of the Church of Armageddon Prophets until they turn murderous.'

'Not entirely true, young Joshua. I instigated an investigation into their activities some time ago so we have a list. But what you said earlier is probably right. What we don't have is much time. Time is running out.'

Chapter 11

"......Israel and the United States of America have launched an attack on a Syrian army company that had invaded Megiddo, a small town in northern Israel. The President of the USA has stated that the attack was necessary to counter the aggression of the Syrian army. The Syrians deny any such aggression and have said that their small contingent of armed forces were only present as a peace-keeping force and that they had been invited there by the Megiddo elders. Their largest ally in the region, Iran, has put all their armed forces on a war footing. This is the voice of BBC World Service at exactly ten minutes past eight o'clock on the morning of Sunday the ...."

∗

The trip across the river was very peaceful apart from occasional gasps of surprise or exultation from Charon as he played Tetris on the phone. Eventually he let out a groan.

'Twenty-five million,' he muttered. 'Not a bad total but I won't beat Thanatos with scores like that.'

The boat drifted gently towards the far shore. Once again as we approached the bank I looked down into the water and I could see writhing snakes biting at each other. This side of the river was murky and gave off a nasty odour of decay.

'Why is the river so foul on this side but beautiful on the other?' asked Vole, staring with me into the impenetrable depths.

'There is some quirk of the flow,' I answered. 'You can see that the river is bending around a huge arc. That's one possibility.'

'And the other?' Vole queried.

'The other is that the whole thing is metaphysical. From the other side these are the crystal flowing waters of the River Jordan which lead to the Promised Land. From this side they are the murky sludge of the River Styx leading to the Domain of Hades.'

'Either way they are usually crossed by the dead.'

'That's right, Vole. But we are alive and hope to remain so.'

The ferryboat reached the shore and we bad farewell to Charon.

'You still have one free trip, Lord James,' Charon remarked as I stepped off the boat. 'This phone has revolutionised my experience of the river. After three thousand years I was getting a little bored with the journey.'

Vole's eyes opened wide with amazement.

'Three thousand years? You've been doing this trip for that long?'

Charon laughed.

'It's not always that bad. On a good day I meet a lot of interesting people. Oh, by the way, Lord James, there was a priest by the name of Habakuk who was asking after you. He depressed me.'

'About my height and overweight?' I asked.

'That's right. I told him nothing. That is not part of my remit..... I ferry them across and anything else is up to me.'

'We met up again at the Seat of Judgement.'

'The priest and yourself?'

I nodded in reply.

'Did he survive?' asked the ferryman.

'I don't know. He did not pass the test of the scales of justice but was not swallowed by the Devourer. A godlike voice told us that the clergyman was his acolyte and that his soul belonged to him. The priest just disappeared from this reality.'

'But that is interfering with the Judgement of Hades in his own domain! That is sacrilege,' Charon was shocked. 'This may be the beginning of the end for all things and all beings. Such sacrilege may signal the end of Time itself.'

'Let's hope not,' I replied, disturbed by Charon's response. 'Vole and myself are following the trail of the god and the priest over to the far realm.'

'I wish you luck, young man,' Charon answered. 'You will need it.'

'Thanks!' I replied.

*

'We are Gog and Magog and we are the chosen of God.'

'We are Gog and Magog and we are the chosen of God.'

The chant continued interminably. Habakuk the priest stood up and looked round. The shining figure of the messenger was orchestrating the chanting and the power increased to the point that Habakuk could not stand the agony of the sound waves battering against his ears.

'We are Gog and Magog and we are the chosen of God.'

'We are Gog and Magog and we are the chosen of God.'

So I'm twice dead and probably twice cursed, thought Habakuk. *And here I am amongst a sea of mindless, soulless, undead worshippers of our new God. Who, of course, claims to be an old God. I've met Hades, Charon, The Devourer of Souls. All of them are gods or demigods. In what way is this god any different? Are they all simply powerful aliens?*

As if in answer to his question a disembodied, multi-timbral and exceedingly loud voice started to speak.

'I am the Lord of the Covenant. The maker of the Promised Land. The Rightful owner of Heaven.'

In reply the chanting continued.

'We are Gog and Magog and we are the chosen of God.'

'We are Gog and Magog and we are the chosen of God.'

'The final battle has begun. Armageddon on Earth, Ragnarok in Asgard, Gotterdammerung in Heaven. Skoll will devour the sun, Hati will eat the moon. The stars will vanish from the sky. Let the assault continue.'

Habakuk could feel the presence of his God but could not see him and then, just for a moment he glimpsed the last fragment of his deity. He saw a blinding flash of perfection, a light so bright that it seered into his soul. Habakuk immediately went blind and could see nothing at all.

Bloody perfect, thought the priest. *Stabbed in the heart then the same organ is ripped from my chest, I'm about to be swallowed by the Devourer of Souls and I'm whipped up here to a war-party of chanting idiots and now I've gone blind. Gee, it's bloody typical.*

He sat down amongst the chanting throng and then, almost immediately, felt himself being bodily carried away by the movement of the crowd.

'We are Gog and Magog and we are the chosen of God.'

'We are Gog and Magog and we are the chosen of God.'

So they are all off to assault Heaven and I, blind Habakuk, am going along for the ride whether or not I want to. But if this is the God of the Covenant, therefore the God of the Old Testament, who is in control of Heaven?

✴

".....This is the voice of BBC World Service. Reports are coming in that Iran has launched a nuclear attack on Israel in retaliation for the assault by Israel and USA armed forces at Megiddo. Israel has immediately responded by firing several ballistic missiles at designated sites in Iran. Rachael Dayan, an Israeli spokesperson and former Mossad agent, would not be drawn as to whether or not the missiles were armed with nuclear warheads.'We will not tolerate any aggression against the State of Israel. We have targeted specific military sites only.'

China and Russia have issued stern warnings to the USA advising the US to remove their armed forces immediately or face involvement of the Chinese and Russian military. India has moved a major part of the Indian Army to the Indo-Pakistan border. The Prime Minister of Pakistan has appealed to the USA to calm the situation but it is understood that radical factions in Pakistan are advocating an immediate strike against India.

North Korea has invaded South Korea and also launched an Intercontinental Ballistic Missile targeted on the USA. The rocket failed and the ICBM is reported to have exploded in the Pacific several hundred miles north of Hawaii.

Tonight on HardTalk we will be asking experts whether the outbreak of hostilities in Megiddo, which has sparked off this latest round of violence, was a peculiar coincidence or whether they believe there is any significance that this is the prophesied site of Armageddon.

This is the voice of the official BBC World Service at nine o'clock on Sunday the...."

✶

It was a delight to set foot on the shores of the River Jordan. Just like the last time there were funeral feasts happening up and down the river bank and just like last time I was starving hungry.

'Fancy a snack, Vole?' I asked the shaman.

'I would,' she replied. 'In fact I'm starving and very thirsty.'

'Take your fill,' I waved my hands expansively. 'Nobody will mind. We've just been in Hades so it is likely that nobody will see you except the dead.'

I walked up to the nearest party and picked up a rather pleasant looking black plum.

'Oy,' came a cry. 'What d'you think you're doing?' A young lad with a cockney accent came running over. 'That's ours. You can't 'ave it.'

'Sorry,' I replied, putting the plum back. 'I didn't expect anyone to notice. Nobody did last time I was here except the person who had died and he didn't care.'

'Well I'm not dead, am I?' said the cockney.

I looked closely at him, noticing that his skin had a slightly blue tinge to it. 'You probably are but don't realise it,' I answered.

'Comes to the same fing don't it mate,' the young lad answered. 'Alf the world's dead but they don't realise it. If I'm really dead but can act alive then I might as well do so. Stands to reason, don't it?'

'You're right there,' I replied. 'But tell me what 'appened, I mean happened, to you?'

'Knocked off me blinkin' motor bike, mate. That's what 'appened. Then I appeared 'ere,' he looked around. 'These are all my mates in the biking club but none of 'em can see me so I suppose I must be dead. Don't feel it, mind you.'

'Then don't be dead,' I replied. 'Come with us and we can get you out of here.'

'Is there a way out of 'ere?' he asked. 'Before you arrived I'd only met one geezer I can talk to and 'e says that 'e 'as been 'ere a while and 'e can't find 'is way out.'

'I can help you both,' I looked round. 'Where is the other guy?'

'Probably by the food, mate. 'E's always 'ungry is that one.'

I looked over to the end of the laden food table. There was somebody busily eating his way through a pile of sausages. A large hairy man who looked vaguely familiar. Then I realised who the man reminded me of. He looked just like an older version of Peter the Werewolf who had assisted Lady Aradel and myself when we were on our former quest. Could this be Peter's father, Ard, the King of the Werewolves? I had heard a lot about Ard from my wife, Sienna, and from my two lads. If so, what was he doing here on the banks of the River Styx? Had he died?

*

'I'm here to see my son,' said Sienna as she hammered on the outer door of the police station. There was no response although she could see people moving around inside the building.

Sienna knelt down and shouted through the letterbox.

'This is Sienna Scott. I am here to see my son Joshua Scott.'

A uniformed policeman came to the door and let her in.

'I am Sienna Scott. I am here to see my son Joshua Scott,' she repeated quickly to the man. 'I couldn't get here before now because I needed someone to look after my younger son.'

'OK madam. If you could just, sit over there, fill out this form and then the Chief Constable would like to speak to you,' the policeman at the desk passed her a piece of paper and then glanced at the clock as he spoke to Sienna. Nine thirty on Sunday morning.

Sienna looked around. Something strange was going on. The whole police station was milling with plain clothes men and the outer door had been locked. There was tape across the door to the basement area and a sign saying "Crime Scene ...keep out."

After sitting for a few moments a grey haired man in a smart police uniform walked towards her. Sienna recognised the policeman ... this was Maxwell Devonport, the chief constable of Avon and Somerset Police.

The distinguished man came over and shook Sienna's hand.

'Please to meet you, Mrs. Scott,' said the chief constable. 'Thank you for coming in. I will take you to your son.'

'Is he in trouble?' asked Sienna.

'No, no. Not at all. The boy's a hero. He's just had rather a shock,' replied the Chief Constable Devonport. 'Mind you, so have I.'

Wondering what could possibly have shocked both a senior policeman and her son, Sienna stood up and followed Maxwell Devonport.

*

I went over to the hungry man who had been pointed out to me by the cockney biker. He was busily feeding himself from the various wakes on the banks of the River Styx . After introducing myself, I asked the pertinent question.

'Is it possible that you are Ard, the King of the Werewolves?'

'I am indeed, ' replied Ard, 'And you are the famous Lord James also known as Jimmy Scott. How do you do?'

We shook hands and I could not help but notice how hairy his hands were, even on the palms.

'How are your boys and your lovely wife?' asked the werewolf. 'And of course your redoubtable mother-in-law, Mary?'

'Sienna and the boys are very well,' I answered. 'But Mary has died. Not long ago, in fact, from cancer.'

'I'm sorry to hear that,' replied the werewolf. 'My condolences to the family.'

The werewolf's accent was clearly that of a well-educated gentleman, probably upper class Oxford, something that initially surprised me since the family had not explained that to me. Then I remembered how well spoken his wife and children had been and I also recalled how they had saved my life.

'I believe that condolences are due also to you, Ard,' I said. 'I met your wife and family and they were wonderful. Without their efforts Lady Aradel and myself would have failed and we would already be doomed.'

'Thank you, Lord James,' Ard replied in a whisper and I was shocked to see small tears form at the corners of both of his eyes. 'I miss them every day and that is the reason I am here.'

'Have you died, Ard?' I asked. 'I had not heard the news before I came here.'

'No, but like you I have travelled through Hades,' came the reply. 'I have been looking for Celestia, Era, Cinder, Arth and Jangle. They all died. Peter, my youngest, is looking after affairs until I return. If I ever manage to do so.'

'And you have not found them?' asked Vole who had joined us, having eaten her fill at the feasting table of the next funeral wake.

'No, I'm afraid not,' answered the werewolf. 'I was certain that I could find them if they were in the Domain of Hades but I now believe that they may not be there.'

'Did you meet Hades himself?' I asked worriedly.

'I did and passed the judgement of the scales.'

'Did you ask whether or not your family were in the Domain?' asked Vole.

'I did ask and the Devourer of Souls, who has even keener senses of smell and sight than myself, told me that they were not there.'

'Then they are definitely not in Hades,' concluded Vole. 'The Devourer is always right and never lies.'

'Where can they be?' asked Ard. 'My quest has failed and I have not even got as far as Orpheus did. At least he found his love Eurydice even if he did not manage to take her out of the Domain.'

'There are more places to look yet, Ard,' I countered. 'You can't give up until you have visited Valhalla, the Elysian Fields, Paradise, Heaven, Asgard. You name it you have to go there if you think that their souls are still alive.'

'But how can you get to those places?' asked Ard. 'I've been stuck here for at least a month. I can't seem to progress.'

'It can be difficult to see the ways out of here apart from going back over to Hades,' I answered waving my hands and pointing. 'But there are ways. More than one. I was lucky enough to pass the test of the sphinx. I know one chap who climbed up the cliffs.'

'Which cliffs?' asked the king of the werewolves. 'I only see darkness. No cliffs.'

The cockney, who told me his name was Harry, ('Arry), also stared at the blackness and then exclaimed.

'Blow me down mate, I can see them! There are cliffs there.'

Ard continued to stare but in the end gave up. 'I still don't see them. It's just blackness.'

'Perhaps you could see them if you were in your wolf form,' I suggested.

'Wolf form,' said Harry the cockney. 'Are you sayin' that Ard 'ere is a blinkin' wolf?'

'I'm a werewolf, Harry,' explained Ard. 'I am a magical creature both man and wolf and I suspect that Lord James is right. I would see better in my wolf form. For some reason I have felt constrained from changing here on the shores of the river.'

As he said that Ard discarded his clothes watched by an amazed Ard and astonished Vole. He stretched up as if starting some arcane exercise programme and then reached his hands down onto the ground and stood with his back arched. His strong muscles started to ripple and deform, his nose grew longer and hairier, his ears sharpened and his canine teeth became long and pointed. Next a tail apeared and thrashed around wildly for a few moments. Finally we were looking at a huge wolf.

'Stone the bleedin' crows,' said Harry. 'That's a turn up for the book.'

I had to stop myself from laughing. Harry's cockney accent reminded me of Dick van Dyke in Mary Poppins .... an American playing the part of a cockney .... and the accent was endlessly funny. Every time Harry spoke I had to stop myself from chortling. I thought all Londoners now spoke with a Del Boy estuary twang but Harry had a much older accent. Perhaps he was more ancient than he looked? Perhaps he had been riding motorbikes since the 1950s? Perhaps he has been here on the shore of the River Styx for a very long time?

I must get over it, I told myself. *You can't go round laughing at the way someone else speaks. Ignore it and pretend that you can hear all the consonants. Just do it.*

Taking myself firmly in hand I turned back to Ard. The wolf form of the lycanthrope was looking towards the cliffs.

'It's as plain as day now, old boy,' said the wolf, his accent still Oxbridge. 'I can see the cliffs and the narrow path up between the cliffs. Is that the way we have to go?'

'Yes Ard,' I replied. 'That is the way to go. But I have to warn you that the path is guarded at the top by an animated statue.'

'A sphinx?' asked Ard.

'Indeed,' I replied. 'And we must prepare to be questioned. The sphinx will pose some riddles.'

'That's great, mate,' said Harry. 'I'm really good at riddles. I love crossword puzzles. It should be a doddle.'

I had resolved to ignore Harry's accent and just listened to the content.

'Well, I know a few of his previous riddles so we could do some practice,' I suggested.

'Let's do it,' Harry concurred.

Vole nodded her head and Ard shook his large grey muzzle up and down in agreement.

Chapter 12

'We are Gog and Magog and we are the chosen of God.'
'We are Gog and Magog and we are the chosen of God.'
'We are Gog and Magog and we are the chosen of God.'
'We are Gog and Magog and we are the chosen of God.'
Habakuk's eyesight was slowly returning.

I'd rather not see my God if it means going completely blind again, thought the priest...*and now where are they carrying me?*

The vast mob of undead followers were surging like a sea up the slopes of a mountain side. At least that was how it appeared to Habakuk although it was very difficult to see due to the sheer numbers of followers. Millions upon millions of them.

Surely the Church of Armageddon Prophets doesn't have that many followers? queried the priest to himself but he then reflected that many churches in the United States had been forced by legislation to at least give lip service to the new denomination and the President's election had, of course, been by an overwhelming majority. Moreover the Church had rapidly spread to all parts of the globe.

Habakuk realised that the followers were completely surrounding the mountain, not just on the side he was on but also on all other approaches. Quite how he knew this he was not sure but he was totally convinced that it was the case.

As they all neared the top the press of the undead became tighter and tighter.

People could be killed by a crush like this, thought the priest and then he realised the foolishness of his thought. All these bodies, these followers, these sheep...... they were already dead, probably most of them at their own hands or at the hands of other Armageddon Prophets. The crowds were climbing on top of each other in their haste to reach the top and Habakuk became worried that he might be submerged by the hordes. He struggled, pushed and virtually swam to the top of the pile then looked up towards the peak. The apex was invisible due to a covering of fluffy white clouds but he could tell that it was not a sharp peak.

They were approaching a huge plateau and they were doing so from all sides.

*

As the chief constable walked down the corridor to the interview room where Joshua was sitting he outlined to Sienna what had been happening to her elder son and the role Joshua had played in saving his life.

'So is he in trouble with the law now?' asked Sienna when Chief Constable Devonport had stopped explaining the situation.

'No, not at at all. But he is very shocked and he is also worried about what you might say to him,' answered Devonport. 'He's a very brave lad but he's gone through some terrible psychological trauma.'

'He had enough of that when the Devil tried to sacrifice him and his brother,' said Sienna as they stood outside the door of the room. 'There are some people who don't even believe that it happened.'

'Well I know full well that it did happen,' replied the chief constable. 'I was there at Stonehenge.'

They walked into the room and Sienna could see Joshua sitting very quietly, his face ashen with shock. Someone had given him a blanket and he had wrapped this round his body which somehow served to make him look smaller and even more traumatised.

'I didn't realise how dangerous they were, Mum,' he started to explain but Sienna rushed in and hugged him.

Joshua burst into tears.

'It was awful Mum,' he said between tears. 'It was worse than when the devil tried to kill us. That didn't feel real. This time the acolytes tried to get me when I was talking to Rupert. He was my friend. You remember Rupert don't you Mum?'

'Your friend from the primary school?'

'Yes Mum. He tried to kill me. Then I was arrested and they all killed each other. Then the sergeant tried to kill the chief constable. I had to throw the knife at the sergeant. I didn't want to touch the knife but I had to stop the sergeant,' a large sob came from the boy.

'Don't worry, Josh,' Sienna hugged him even tighter. 'You're not in trouble.'

'But that's just it, Mum,' he countered. 'I am in trouble. We're all in trouble. The Church of Armageddon Prophets has gone mad and I think they will start World War III. They really want a final war to end time or something like that.'

Chief Constable Devonport had walked into the room with Sienna but had kept quiet up until that moment then he spoke.

'I'm afraid that the boy might be right, Mrs Scott,' Devonport spoke in hushed tones. 'The sergeant talked about a final assault on heaven. I don't know whether you have been listening or watching the very latest news?'

Sienna shook her head.

'Well, Israel and the USA, led by President Armstrong, have attacked a Syrian force in Megiddo,' explained the chief constable. 'Iran has launched a retaliatory nuclear strike on Israel. Israel has fired missiles at Iran. North Korea has launched an ICBM. China, Russia, India, Pakistan are all on a war footing.'

'What does it all mean?' asked Sienna, bewildered.

'Put it this way... they've started World War III and they've started it in Megiddo.'

'Is the place particularly significant?' asked Sienna.

'I certainly think so,' replied Chief Constable Devonport. 'A cursory search on Google will tell you that Megiddo witnessed more battles than any other location on Earth. It hosted the armed struggles of Assyrians, Canaanites, Egyptians, Greeks, Israelites, Persians, Philistines, and Romans.'

'...And now maybe the beginning of World War III,' Sienna nodded. 'I think I understand.'

'There's more to it, I'm afraid,' said the chief constable.'

'What?' said Sienna. 'What else is there about Megiddo.'

'It has another name,' the chief constable paused before continuing. 'The Mount of Megiddo witnessed all those wars but in the Book of Revelation of Saint John the Divine it will host the final battle of good and evil. ... the Mount of Megiddo is also known as Armageddon.'

★

'OK,' I said. 'The most famous riddle from the sphinx is: What has four legs in the morning, two at midday and three in the evening?'

'Right,' said Harry. 'The answer is man.....baby, adult and old age. Surely it won't still use that old chestnut?'

'No, it didn't when I went through,' I replied. 'It was more into wordplay. It asked me: Who put the frivolity into murder?'

Harry stood thinking for a moment. 'Not easy but what about the geezer who put the laugh into slaughter.'

'Brilliant, spot on,' I laughed. 'You've got that right first time.'

Vole laughed as well.

'I was just about to get that. I'd worked out that it was something hidden in the spelling and I was just behind Harry.'

'I'll give you another,' I thought for a moment, recalling what the sphinx had asked me. 'Right... Who put the monster into evolution?'

'Got it,' shouted Vole. 'Ogre into progress. Whoever put the ogre into progress.'

'That was quick,' remarked Harry ruefully. 'You beat me there. I was still working through words like advancement, development, growth. I hadn't got to progress. But it's a good riddle.'

I looked round at our group. Ard had switched back into his human form and reclothed himself. He looked completely confused.

'Are you alright, Ard?' I asked.

'I'm sorry old chap,' the werewolf replied ruefully. 'I've been listening to you but I haven't the faintest idea what you are talking about. Didn't come into my education for some reason.'

'It's like the cryptic clues in the Times crossword,' I explained and then nudged Vole. 'Do your one. Your name.'

Vole loudly proclaimed.

'Timid creature out of love.'

'Vole,' cried Harry triumphantly. 'L O V E twisted around makes Vole. A timid creature made out of the letters of love.'

'Which is the only cheese that is made backwards?' I asked, firing off another riddle.

'Edam,' answered Harry. 'That was easy.'

The werewolf sighed. 'I'm sorry. I still don't see them at all. My brain doesn't work that way. Why do they make Edam cheese backwards? Do they start with a packet on a shelf and end up with milk?'

'No,' I replied. 'That is being too literal. It's simply that the word MADE spells Edam when turned backwards.'

'I'll never manage it,' growled Ard. 'I'm doomed to stay here for ever.'

The werewolf disconcertingly turned his hairy human face up to the sky and let out a doleful howl.

*

'We've got to stop our Government from going to war!' exclaimed Joshua suddenly. 'If we're not careful they will join in on the side of the USA and we don't even know if they are the good guys or the bad guys. They may not realise that this is a religious war to end wars.'

The chief constable laughed cynically. 'I'm sure that they know it's a religious war but will we be able to sit this one out?'

'We must try to stop them,' agreed Sienna. 'Joshua is right. The Government is already suspicious of the new president. They think that Armstrong is a religious bigot and I know that Darcy Macaroon is worried about him. He sent Jimmy off to the USA to investigate.'

'Do you have many contacts in the Government?' asked Devonport.

'A few,' answered Sienna, taking out her mobile phone. 'Jimmy is now part of the Government in an advisory role so we've met most of the cabinet. I'll start ringing straight away.'

'It's a pity Granny is not here still, isn't it Mum?' said Joshua. 'I'm sure she would sort this out.'

'I reckon you are right, Josh,' replied Sienna, her ear pinned to the phone. 'It's a real pity she's not here. She'd have relished every minute of it.'

*

'We are Gog and Magog and we are the chosen of God.'
'We are Gog and Magog and we are the chosen of God.'
'We are Gog and Magog and we are the chosen of God.'
'We are Gog and Magog and we are the chosen of God.'

Habakuk was fighting hard to keep his head above the rabble of zombie Church followers. At the moment there appeared to be some sort of barrier around the top of the mountain but he could not see what it was. Then the clouds parted and he could see more clearly the plateau at the apex. It was truly gigantic, stretching for many, many miles in all directions. Near to where his own horde of undead acolytes were pressing forward, Habakuk could see two enormous gates that stretched upwards so that the tops were lost in the mists. Standing in front of the gates were two huge double-winged men. The angels, for that was what they surely were, glowed with a warm, bright light but they each held a large shining sword in their right hand. The light of the swords was not a warm glow but was instead a cold, whirling pattern of confusion that spread fiery lines across the portal, preventing access from below.

Some of the horde had already reached the angels and the fiery swords had halted their progress. But the hosts of followers kept coming like a plague of locusts, unstoppable. Habakuk reckoned that, although the gates were high, eventually the bodies would be piled even higher and the zombie acolytes would be able to gain access by spilling over the top. That, for now, was just a guess.

*

'Ard, don't give up,' I told the king of the werewolves, who was slumping onto the ground. 'There must be a way.' Then it came to me. 'You passed the test of truth, didn't you?'

Ard nodded.

'So your heart was weighed against the feather and found to be true?'

Ard nodded again.

'Did Hades tell you that you had a place in Valhalla or in the Elysian Fields if you so wished?'

Ard found his voice again.

'Indeed he did. He commended me for being a true and valiant soul. But the sojourn in the Slough of Despond has weakened me.'

'Then the Sphinx has no right to debar you, or me, or Vole,' I reasoned. 'The only one who is in danger is Harry ... and he's brilliant at riddles. He's proved that to us.'

Heartened the werewolf bounced up again.

'Then we should be on our way, don't you know?' said the werewolf king. 'Anywhere but this limbo land. It saps my will to live.'

I led the way and we were soon at the foot of the cliff pass. The going was steep but not treacherous and we soon found ourselves at the top of the passage. We neared the gateway that I knew led to the Inn at the Very End of the World. That, in turn, led to

Valhalla and the Elysian Fields. But before we could reach these fabelled places we had to pass through the gateway and guarding it was a gatehouse. In front of that was the huge, marble form of the sphinx.

The statue suddenly came to life and jumped in front of us preventing our access to the gate.

'Halt. Who goes there?' it demanded.

'Lord James Scott, Lady Vole, King Ard and Lord Harry,' I retorted.

'Lord James Scott can pass but the others must answer my riddles,' replied the sphinx, chomping and grinding its marble teeth.

'I don't believe that is correct,' I argued. 'Lady Vole and King Ard have been granted passage to Valhalla. They, and myself, have stood at the seat of judgment, been weighed in the balances and found to be true. You may not bar their passage.'

The sphinx ground its teeth, looked around as if seeking advice and then replied.

'I have checked with the Devourer of Souls and that which you say is true. However, Lord Harry has not stood at the seat of judgement. Lord Harry's heart has not been weighed against the feather of truth. Lord Harry has to guess the answer to my riddles if he is to pass through the gate that leads to the Inn at the Very End of the World. The Inn which is also the portal to Valhalla and to the Elysian Fields.'

'OK mate. Let's get on with it,' said Harry.

'The others must pass through first,' said the sphinx. 'I have had too many people listening, noting down my riddles and helping other people to get them right. So now I don't allow anybody to listen except the person being tested.'

I reluctantly passed through the gateway followed by Ard and Vole. We stood just inside and watched Harry as he answered the questions posed by the huge, animated statue. We could watch but we could not hear.

*

'I managed to get through to the deputy prime minister, Sidney Fence,' said Sienna to the chief constable, after talking on the mobile for some considerable time.

'How did he respond?' asked the chief constable.

'He wants all three of us to go up to Downing Street as soon as possible,' replied Sienna. 'I'm going to take Samuel as well. I'm not going to be split up from my children at a time like this.'

'That's not a problem, madam,' replied Maxwell Devonport. 'I will get my official driver to take us up to London with police motorbike escorts. We'll pick up Samuel on the way ... but first we must have a cup of coffee and some sandwiches from the canteen. They taste foul but we do not know when we will get another chance to eat and Joshua and I have been up all night.'

'You could say the sandwiches are not much cop,' remarked Joshua, cheering up for the first time.

The chief constable gave him a withering, contemptuous look but then could not help but laugh.

*

'We are Gog and Magog and we are the chosen of God.'
'We are Gog and Magog and we are the chosen of God.'
'We are Gog and Magog and we are the chosen of God.'
'We are Gog and Magog and we are the chosen of God.'

For the moment the gates to paradise were still holding. The angels guarding the gates stood impassively whilst their swords spread a whirling barrier of fiery light debarring any illicit passage. But within the gates Habakuk could see that there was considerable consternation. Such a full blown attack on paradise or heaven, whichever it was, did not appear to have been predicted. Habakuk remembered the Apocalyptic verses of Revelation and he did not recall that a large scale battle was to occur at the gates of paradise. On Earth, yes, at Armageddon and at Jerusalem to name two likely hotspots but not in heaven itself.

There was an elderly, bearded, bluff-looking gentleman with a craggy face who had been sitting at a table just within the gates. He was now gathering up his robes and collecting several huge tomes .... leather bound books by the look of it. He and his helpers were retreating to a walled area that was apparently made of pure white marble. This looked to be the inner sanctum of heaven and also had a gate on it. It was surely just ornamental? The gate shone with an iridescent, multicoloured light and looked to be made of a single enormous pearl. Carved on the gate was the Roman numeral XII.

That must be gate number twelve, thought Habakuk staring as hard as he could at the sight. *There are supposed to be a dozen gates to heaven. That is right.*

The path from the outer gate, guarded by the angels, to the inner pearly gate was made of pure gold, shining like glass.

If this assault does not succeed, thought Habakuk. *This may be my only sight of the true heaven. And if we do get in there it is bound to be spoilt so I better just enjoy what I can see.*

'We are Gog and Magog and we are the chosen of God.'

'We are Gog and Magog and we are the chosen of God.'

'We are Gog and Magog and we are the chosen of God.'

'We are Gog and Magog and we are the chosen of God.'

The countless masses of undead followers of the Church of Armageddon Prophets seethed up to the outer gate, continuously chanting, and Habakuk struggled to keep his place, riding atop the growing mound of zombie bodies. As he did so he rose higher and higher and could see further into the heavenly sanctuary.

This is not the right way to get into heaven, thought the twice dead priest. *But at least I have had a look at Glory Land.*

*

I watched closely as Harry was questioned by the sphinx. I'm pretty good at lip reading so I could just about make out Harry's answers but I could not see the face of the sphinx.

Harry set off by asking the sphinx what the rules were. I could not see the answer but Harry was surprised. I think Harry then said "I thought it would be best of three questions but you say it is just two and both must be correct." The sphinx nodded. "But I get three goes at each question?" Again the animated statue showed his agreement. "And if I get them wrong you eat me?" Once more the huge marble structure agreed.

The sphinx then asked the first question and Harry answered correctly. His reply was "aroma" if my lip reading was correct.

The second question did not go so smoothly. I thought that Harry answered "Ends" and the sphinx shook its massive stone head. Harry looked surprised and then said "Sandwiches." Again the sphinx disagreed. Harry looked very worried and took his time before finally saying, tentatively, "Lasagne?"

The sphinx shook its head again and I could tell that it had opened its massive mouth. It advanced on Harry.

'.... 'Ang on, 'Ang on,' cried Harry, jumping out of the way. 'You 'aven't told me the answer yet. You can't eat me until you tell me the answer.'

The sphinx stopped and said something that I could neither hear or see. Harry went ballistic.

'You cheating stone robot!' he screamed. 'You blinkin' marble muppet. That's what I said at the beginning. Damned if I'm going to let you eat me when you're cheatin'. You've got to play fair.'

The sphinx was chasing Harry round and round.

Harry finally screamed. 'I demand arbitration from a higher authority. Ask the Devourer of Souls. You're a blinkin' cheat!'

The sphinx stopped chasing Harry and stood with its head cocked to one side. It was clearly consulting someone, maybe the Devourer. Then it nodded its stone head and let Harry through the gate.

A very sweaty Londoner, born within the sound of Bow Bells, joined us on the road to the Inn at the Very End of the World. When he had regained his breath I asked him what had happened.

'The first one was easy,' replied Harry. 'The marble muppet asked me: What is scent from far Oman?'

'Anything could be sent from far Oman,' growled Ard, still not understanding the nature of riddles. 'People, ships, camels. Anything. That's like asking How long is a piece of string?'

'No, I realised it was scent with a c,' replied Harry. 'So the answer was AROMA.'

'I still don't get it,' growled the werewolf. 'How did you know that it was not frankincense? Oman is famous for it...... It's the second oldest precious commodity in the world after gold so surely that is the answer?'

'Nah. It's a riddle,' Harry retorted. 'A cryptic clue. So the answer's either 'idden in the clue itself or it 'as a clever twist.'

'I still don't get it,' growled Ard, shaking his head. 'I must be stupid.'

'Nah,' replied Harry. 'I didn't know all that about frankincense. That's proper knowledge, that is. I could tell that the words "far Oman" had the word "aroma" in the middle.'

'Good lord!' said the werewolf. 'It's as simple as that but I couldn't see it!'

'So what happened next?' I asked, dying to find out what had gone wrong with the second riddle and why Harry had succeeded in the end.

'Well,' said Harry, gathering his thoughts, 'The sphinx just said "Layers of Food" so I replied, quick as a shot 'ens. But 'e disagreed. So I said sandwiches and then lasagne but I knew I was right first time.'

'Then he chased you?' asked Vole.

'Yeah, then 'e chased me and I said 'e 'ad to tell me the answer,' replied Harry. 'And the sphinx replied in 'is posh voice, marble in 'is mouth, "The answer to the riddle is Hens, Hens are layers of food when they lay eggs," which is what I told 'im at the beginning!' Harry turned round triumphantly. 'So I 'ad got it right all along and 'e 'ad to let me through the gate!'

I said not a word and just about managed to stop myself from laughing. Harry's accent had almost been his undoing but he had succeeded.

We walked towards the Inn at the Very End of the World. Next to it was a church but I was damned if I was going there. I wanted to sup the ale in the tavern which stood on the edge of the enormous cliff overlooking the Vale of Styx.

Chapter 13

Habakuk was being pushed higher and higher up the outside of the gates to heaven. The highest parts of the gates were still shrouded in mists but he could, intermittently, make out that there was a top. Either side of the gates there were walls that surrounded the heavenly plateau. He could see no end to the walls ... they appeared to rise endlessly up into the sky.

'We are Gog and Magog and we are the chosen of God.'

'We are Gog and Magog and we are the chosen of God.'

The chanting went on endlessly. Habakuk was tired of hearing it but the mindless masses just kept going. Then just faintly he could pick up a chant from round the other side of the mountain.

'Great is Diana of the Ephesians.'

'Great is Diana of the Ephesians.'

What is going on now? wondered Habakuk. *It's like a rival football crowd.*

The masses kept surging forwards and on top of one another in a stinking pile of bodies and Habakuk rose higher and higher. Then from round the other side of the mountain came the cry.

'There is but one God.'

'There is but one God.'

Well that one's wrong, for sure. I've met two .... Hades and our own God......... and in addition there are creatures like the Devourer who could be likened to a demigod. And I'm pretty certain that there must be another God inside the pearly gates of heaven. Quite which one I am no longer sure.

The disparate chanting continued from all sides but the common thrust was upwards towards the beautiful walled and gated plateau. The plateau that housed Heaven.

The police car sped along the M4 with motorbike outriders front and back. The traffic was unusually low. The earthquakes and hurricanes nineteen months previously had destroyed many cars and disrupted transport generally but the main routes had been repaired and on a working day the traffic would have been considerably worse. This was a Sunday and traffic was usually less than on a weekday. In addition the news from abroad was frightening people. Everybody was wondering whether Britain would be dragged in to a third World War and each further announcement made the likelihood seem greater.

The Chief Constable sat in the front passenger seat of his official car. He normally sat in the back working through paperwork but today Sienna, Joshua and Samuel were in the back seats. The radio was tuned to BBC World Service and the latest bad news was that the conflict in Megiddo had spread to Jerusalem.

North Korea, having successfully invaded South Korea, had now declared war on the USA, China, Ireland and Switzerland. Quite why Ireland and Switzerland had been singled out was beyond everybody including the Irish President, who was in a funk about the whole thing. The European Union had immediately pledged support for both of the countries as had NATO, the North Atlantic Treaty Organisation. Ireland and Switzerland were traditionally neutral but had signed up to NATO's partnership for peace. NATO was also trying to decide what to do about South Korea, having previously signed alliances with the country. When the car had reached Reading a report came through on the radio that the North Korean President had meant Australia and New Zealand not Ireland and Switzerland. In a rabid speech the man had stated that despite his mistake the war footing would still stand with the addition of Australia and New Zealand.

The car reached London with no further changes in the news reports. Taking the priority lanes the police car raced towards Downing Street where they expected to meet Sidney Fence, the wishy-washy deputy Prime Minister of the UK who lived up to his nickname.... Sid "on the" Fence.

★

The Inn at the Very End of the World had changed very little since the time that I had been there before. Just like previously there were hordes of people making merry. The area around the fire was still dominated by a big bunch of rugby players who would intermittently burst into song and strip off another item of clothing.

> *Haul 'em down!*
> *You Zulu warrior!*
> *Haul 'em down*
> *You Zulu*
> *Chief, Chief, Chief!*

I looked very closely but could not recognise any of them from the last time I had been there but the scene was identical in form.

I ignored the people in the public bar and led our group to the staircase. Upstairs, in the quieter room, I found the publican, Good Will, who expressed surprise at seeing me again.

'We don't normally get repeat customers but it is a pleasant change.'

'We're passing through,' I replied. 'But we would like to stay overnight if we may.'

'You've already paid for your board and lodging,' said the inn keeper.

'That was last time,' I replied, not wanting to cheat the man.

'One time, all time,' replied Good Will. 'Time stands still here so I can't distinguish between one day and the next. You've already paid as far as I'm concerned. '

So it is like Groundhog Day, I thought to myself. *You have to be very careful not to get stuck in a time loop.*

*

The Right Honourable Sidney Fence, Deputy Prime Minister of the United Kingdom, Sid for short, met the Chief Constable and the Scotts at the door of 10 Downing Street. Chief Constable Devonport's car had driven right up to the front door, outriding motorbikes screeching ahead all the way through London.

'This had better be worth it,' said Sid Fence, looking more careworn than usual, a little threadbare and lacklustre. He spoke with his usual ineffectual mumble, his mouth barely opening. 'The Prime Minister has a lot of respect for your family but you always seem to be mixed up with the most strange happenings.'

The Deputy PM led the family inside Number 10. The outer hall was a large affair with a red patterned carpet over a black and white floor. The house was clearly much larger inside than it looked from outside. Joshua remarked on this to the Deputy PM.

'You are, of course, right,' replied Fence, 'Your mother has been here before and I expect the Chief Constable has done so as well. It's Devonport isn't it?'

The policeman nodded and Fence continued his explanation.

'So it's no surprise to them. The house is actually linked to a much bigger house behind it and by a passageway through number eleven to number twelve. So it feels huge.'

He led them though a maze of corridors and up several flights of stairs to a back room, which appeared to be part of a separate flat.

'People are not normally admitted to the holy of holies,' Fence explained. 'But this time we thought it was important.'

They entered the room with some trepidation as it was clearly a bedroom. Lying in the bed attached to a bundle of wires, with tubes coming out of several orifices and limbs, and looking extremely ill, was Darcy Macaroon, the current Prime Minister of the United Kingdom.

'Hello Sienna,' said the ailing man. 'We met when I first

appointed your husband to his roving ambassadorial role.... and hello to your children how do you do?'

Chief Constable Devonport entered the room behind the three Scotts. Darcy noticed him.

'Hi Maxwell,' said the PM. 'Come to lock us all up have you? Still doing your paintings in your spare time?'

Chief Constable Devonport nodded and smiled wryly.

'What has happened to you, sir?' he asked politely. 'And yes, I'm still daubing away.'

'Mysterious illness' answered the PM. 'Might be the Norovirus, which was the quack's first suggestion.'

'Are you getting better or worse?' asked Joshua.

Almost simultaneously Samuel asked.

'Are you going to die?'

'I'm pretty stable. My condition hasn't changed much but they don't know what is wrong with me.'

'Why has your hair fallen out?' asked Samuel bluntly.

'Good question,' answered the PM. 'I've always been a bit proud of my hair. It was one of the first signs that anything was wrong. I got D and V then my hair started to fall out in handfuls.'

'When did this start?' asked Sienna. 'Does the press know about this? I've not seen or heard any mention of it.'

'It started when I was over in the USA,' sighed the PM, weakly.

'Give me all the details,' commanded Devonport.

'I had tea with the new president of the USA,' answered Macaroon. 'I was invited over to the States just after he was inaugurated. I told him that we could not support his ideas for theocracies throughout the world. I explained that the Queen was our Head of State and was also the leader of the Church of England and that was as theocratic as we wished to be. I also said that we were very happy with that state of affairs.'

'And when did the symptoms start?'

'The very next day when I travelled back to the UK. I travelled secretly on an RAF plane and felt sick on the plane.'

'And the alopecia?'

'Started the following day. Also shooting pains down my legs and arms. I've been like this for a week.' Macaroon took a long breath in and continued. 'We are trying to keep it a secret. The world is in a mess right now and we don't want to add to it. Sidney has had to do all my work for me. It's most inconvenient.'

'Tell me what happened when the President served you tea,' Chief Constable Devonport suggested.

'Not much, he served me a cup of tea, rather weak and dilute if I recall properly. Then I left. Next thing my hairs falling out and I've got this dreadful virus.'

'Have you thought of poison?' asked Devonport.

'Who for?' replied Macaroon with a slight smile.

'For you,' answered the chief constable.

'Well, they're pumping a whole load of fluids into me and they're probably poisons,' said the PM in a weak voice.

'No, I meant that somebody might have poisoned you or still be doing so,' suggested the policeman.

'Nobody has come near me except my wife and the deputy PM,' said Macaroon. 'Except the doctors, of course.'

'President Theodore K. Z. Armstrong came near you,' said Sienna. 'And they don't call him Crazy Kayzee for nothing.'

'Thallium,' said the chief constable. 'Most likely poison if he is not getting any worse. Usually kills immediately if the dose is big enough but makes the hair fall out if it is at a lower dose. They call it the poisoner's poison. '

'What about Polonium,' asked Joshua. 'I've read about that and that also makes the hair fall out.'

'Yes but the patient gets progressively worse and from what Darcy has told us he is staying pretty much the same,' replied the policeman. 'Both are colourless, tasteless and odourless.'

'Is there an antidote to Thallium?' asked Sidney Fence, standing quietly to one side. 'Or for Polonium for that matter?'

'Prussian Blue for Thallium and chelating agents for Polonium,' answered the policeman. 'Did the President serve the tea himself, pass you the cup with his bare hands etcetera?'

'Yes he did,' replied Macaroon. 'He certainly was not wearing gloves.'

'Then I'm sure it's Thallium,' said the chief constable. 'Polonium is too dangerous to administer in that way. We must get you to hospital.'

'No,' replied the PM. 'I'll be treated here.'

'Fence,' said the chief constable, taking charge. 'Call the doctors in. I'm not impressed that they did not think of poison and we need them to move quickly.'

'Certainly chief constable,' replied the Deputy PM, who had been fidgeting and fretting like an old mother hen.

He now appeared glad to have been told what to do.

*

Mercy, the barmaid, served us breakfast and we ate the repast heartily.

'Now we must go immediately,' I said to Harry.

'You've said that at least ten times already,' replied the East Londoner.

'Have I?' I answered, bewildered. 'Then it really is time to move. We won't do any further planning. We move now.'

'Just finish this plate of food, old boy,' said Ard, the king of the werewolves, who seemed to have an unquenchable appetite.

'No,' I responded. 'We won't wait. You must leave the rest of the plateful and come right now.'

'Oh, I say,' replied the werewolf. 'That's a bit harsh. I was enjoying that steak.'

'But you are constantly eating and we are not moving,' I explained.

Ard shook himself and stood up. 'I will have a better view of happenings if I change into my lupine form. Could you please look away.'

He took off his clothes and changed into the enormous wolf that his other shape resembled. He sniffed around and then changed back into a man and dressed himself.

'You are right,' he said. 'We have certainly been here for several days. But the local time is peculiar and does not directly relate to the outside world. You are right in saying that we must move now as now is all that we have.'

'That's true everywhere,' said Harry. 'The now is just a bit longer 'ere than elsewhere and it is 'arder to see the past and the future.'

I led the team over to a different stairwell. When we reached the ground floor from the second staircase we were amongst a group of Greek warriors and gentlefolk. Through the open door I could see beautiful fields of wild flowers stretching into the distance.

'Wrong staircase,' I explained to the team. 'These are the Elysian Fields.'

As I turned to lead the team back upstairs a slightly portly but very attractive middle-aged lady floated over to me. She hovered above the ground, maintained at the height by fluttering wings. I immediately recognised her.

'You are the fairy godmother!' I exclaimed. 'I thought you were the ambassador for Oberon and Titania, the King and Queen of the fairies.'

'I was,' replied the fairy. 'But I died in the battle with Lucifer and Parsifal X.'

'You were at Stonehenge?' I asked.

'I was indeed.'

'I did not see you,' I said . 'I looked out for any faerie folk that that I thought I knew but I must have missed you.'

'Good gracious me,' replied the godmother. 'I didn't look like this. I wore a much more appropriate illusion.'

Suddenly standing in front of me was a formidable Boudicca figure, still with wings but now wearing battle gear and waving a gigantic axe. I took a step back.

'How did anyone manage to kill you, godmother dear?' asked Ard.

'Oh, Ard. It's good to see you,' said the fairy Boudicca. 'How did they kill me? A lucky strike on their part I suppose. I had despatched ten of those dreadful cyclops monsters when one caught me from behind with a swipe of his iron sword. Just one blow was all it took and I ended up here. Well, to be exact, I appeared at the seat of judgement and then came here.'

'We are not staying, ambassador,' I said when she had finished telling us her story. 'We are trying to follow the weak trail left by a priest judged to have failed on the scales of truth but whipped away from the Devourer by his own god.'

'Where do you think they went?' asked the fairy.

'Out of this reality, across my own real world and into the far realm. The eternal kingdom,' I replied.

'I can smell the trail of corruption,' added the werewolf. 'When I heard the story I sniffed the air and the corruption was clearly present. I can help lead the way.'

'And how do you intend following?' asked the formidable warrior figure.

'Via the Bifrost Bridge, if we can find it,' I answered.

'Then follow me,' cried the winged warrior. 'I have been there before and I know the route.'

The fairy fluttered powerful wings and glided back towards the stairs. We followed in her wake.

*

Habakuk reached the top of one of the huge gates and climbed off the pile of bodies onto the upper surface of the structure. Several of the zombie followers tried to do the same but none of them appeared capable of passing over the   threshold. Habakuk looked at them in amazement. Apparently entry into heaven was debarred for the hordes but not for himself. He looked down into the outer rim of heaven. The gold path, shining like glass, did not just look a few feet below him .... it looked miles. It was as if he was standing on the top floor of the Empire State Building and looking down at Fifth Avenue.

He could see Saint Peter, at least that was who he supposed it was, and the man was staring up at him and gesticulating. Saint Peter was like a little speck but Habakuk's eyesight, having been blinded and then cured, was better than it had ever been in life. He could see that the saint was trying to encourage him to come down from the gateway and enter the kingdom of heaven.

How am I supposed to do that? pondered Habakuk as he sat down on the metalwork. *I'm damned if I'm going to jump.* Then Habakuk started laughing ... the first time he had laughed in a long time. *Damned if I'll jump into heaven. That's ironic surely?*

So he stood up and flung himself off the barrier towards the heaven he had fought so hard to reach and away from the zombie hordes he now abhorred.

*

Three doctors hurried into the bedroom behind the deputy PM.

'Of course we thought of poison,' said the most senior doctor. 'But we did not believe it was very likely.'

'So you didn't test for it?' asked Maxwell Devonport sarcastically. 'That was clever!'

The doctors looked suitably chagrined and the most junior in the team was prevailed upon to take some blood for toxicology.

'Get it done immediately and get the results back here within the hour,' ordered the chief constable in his grandest manner.

'Oh come now,' replied the most senior doctor. 'It takes weeks to get toxicology results back not minutes and it is a Sunday.'

'Take the samples directly to the laboratory yourself and wait until the tests are done,' replied the policeman.

'We're busy people,' protested the doctor.

'You won't be if you don't get the results back immediately,' replied Devonport. 'Because I shall arrest you all for aggravated and reckless negligence.... and the maximum penalty for that is twenty years in the clink. So get moving.'

The gaggle of Harley Street specialists scurried out of the building with their metaphorical tails between their legs.

'They'll be back very soon and we'll know the answer,' said the policeman. 'In the meantime we can explain to the PM and his deputy why we are here.'

The chief constable turned back to speak to the Prime Minister but Darcy Macaroon was fast asleep.

We followed the warrior fairy up the stairs, across the bar and down another staircase. There was a huge room at the base of these stairs. Gigantic beams crossed the room holding the ceiling up. A huge fire roared in an open grate in the middle of the room. Very large men, all wearing bicornuate helmets, were drinking mead from vast tumblers and were being served by a bevy of blonde, scantily clad, Scandinavian girls.

We were in Valhalla.

The fairy Boudicca led us past all the singing and quaffing Vikings to the huge oak front door. This swung open at her touch and we followed her into the cobbled courtyard. To one side of the yard we could see a small arched doorway and we all walked through it. There in front of us, was the Bifrost Bridge, stretching out to the stars in all the colours of the rainbow plus a few more !

Chapter 14

'I have the results,' shouted the senior doctor as he entered the bedroom.

'One hour and ten minutes,' replied Chief Constable Devonport, consulting his watch.

'Now we're not going to quibble about ten minutes, are we?' responded the consultant physician. 'I've never got toxicology results so quickly.'

'And the results?' asked Devonport impatiently.

'Thallium, just as you said,' replied the doctor. 'But strangely I got some results on a previous blood sample we had taken and stored. That also had thallium in it but at a lower dose.'

'So somebody here is still poisoning him and increasing the dose!' exclaimed Sienna.

'That would seem to be the inference,' Devonport agreed and then turned back to the doctor. 'When was the first blood taken?'

'Just after he got off the plane, I believe,' said the doctor.

'OK, so the USA angle is pretty well established. So who has been in a position to poison him over here and if they wanted to kill him why did they not give a larger dose?' asked Devonport.

'Perhaps they just wanted to keep him quiet for a while?' suggested Joshua.

'I think it was you,' said Samuel pointing his finger at the Deputy PM in the blunt way that children have.

'Me?' retorted Sidney Fence. 'Why would I do a thing like that and why would I invite you up to London if I had done so? I would hardly invite a policeman here, would I now?'

'But maybe you didn't expect the policeman to come,' said Sienna, agreeing with Samuel. 'It's either got to be you or the doctors.... and they wouldn't have returned with the results if they had done it.'

'I'm not the only one here,' blustered Fence. 'And anyway, you have no proof.'

'I did notice that your hair is falling out just a little,' said Devonport. 'And that could be because you accidentally contaminated yourself.'

'Don't be ridiculous, man,' retorted Fence. 'I would hardly lead you all up to see the Prime Minister if I was poisoning him.'

'You might have felt obliged to act as normal as possible,' said Sienna. 'And you might not have had a plan B when you saw the chief constable with us.'

'Why would I have invited you up here to London at all?' asked Fence.

'To neutralise us, maybe? Or so that you could hold us captive and intimidate Jimmy, my husband. There are many other possible reasons...'

'And there's the thing about the tracts,' Samuel interrupting his mother.

'What thing about the tracts?' asked Fence, angrily.

'I've been collecting "The End is Nigh" leaflets,' said Samuel. 'It's my hobby.'

Sienna looked on rather worried, wondering what they would think of her for allowing Sam to have such a strange hobby.

But Samuel continued unabashed. 'There are loads of people out on the street giving out these bits of paper. Some are glossy and on card. Others are flimsy sheets.'

'So?' interjected Fence.

'I put them into groups originally based on colour. Then I realised that they all had little logos on them,' Samuel showed the chief constable and Fence a scruffy example he had in his pocket. 'There were three different logos so I put them in groups based on the logo. One logo was a bible group that had been around for a long while. They were the nice ones that said things like "Jesus loves You". The other two logos took me a long time to find on the internet.'

'And you think that's important?' Fence interrupted again and slammed his hand down on the table. 'Let's stop this nonsense right now!'

Samuel looked over to his mother and to the policeman rather worriedly.

'Go on,' urged the chief constable. 'Don't let Fence stop you. Tell us what you found.'

'The two logos belong to one company and that company belongs to Sidney Fence,' said Sam and pointed at the Deputy PM. 'Your company prints all the horrible tracts that say "The world is going to end right now" and that say "The war to end wars must start now." The ones that tell us to join the Church of Armageddon Prophets.'

'That doesn't prove a thing,' Fence was blustering again, very loudly. 'Absolutely nothing.'

He bent down and stared at Samuel.

'And you are just a nasty little boy who should not accuse adults of things you have no idea about.'

Sienna's hackles rose. *How dare this man treat her child like that?* She stepped between Samuel and Fence.

'I don't care how important you are,' she yelled at the Deputy PM, jabbing him in the chest with her finger. 'You do not shout at my child.'

Darcy Macaroon had slept throughout the discussion but the final shouting woke him.

'Is that you Sidney?' asked the Prime Minister. 'Is it time for the special tonic your own doctor suggested I should have.'

'Not now, PM,' replied Fence, 'I think we have run out.'

'There's still some in the cupboard by the sink,' replied the PM. 'I saw you put it back a few hours ago. I'll have it with whisky this time.'

The chief constable stepped over to the cupboard before Fence could move.

'I think that this is what you wanted, PM?' suggested Devonport, holding up a bottle of clear, colourless liquid.

'That's it,' said the PM. 'Half full. Can't taste the stuff and I'm not convinced that it does any good but Sidney swears by it.'

Sidney Fence ran for the door but Joshua, having learnt the trick from the policeman who tripped him up during the night, stuck out his foot. Fence fell right over and cracked his head against a chair. He lay motionless on the floor and a physician ran over and felt his pulse.

'He's OK,' said the doctor, moving him into the recovery position. 'He's just knocked himself out.'

'There's something I would like to see,' said Devonport, striding over to the fallen man.

The chief constable bent down and pulled at the Deputy PM's lips revealing his dentition. Sidney Fence's teeth were filed to points.

*

Habakuk fell from the top of the gate down into heaven but it was a strange dream-like descent. He did not crash to the ground accelerating under the effects of gravity. No, he was a leaf falling from a tree in the autumn, fluttering down to the ground below, his job was done in the tree of life and he was now joining the loam of paradise.

As he slowly descended a transformation occurred. His filthy mire-soaked clothes disappeared, replaced by shining white raiments. His nails became manicured, clean and tidy. The hair on his head regrew to a perfect length and all the various scars around his body disappeared.

He landed on his feet and walked over to Saint Peter, who was observing him with a tinge of amusement in his kindly, bluff, twinkling eyes.

'I'm glad that you made it at last, Brother Andrew,' said the saint who stood in one hand holding the keys of heaven and in the other a huge leather-bound book. 'Or would you prefer to be called Habakuk?'

'Does it matter,' asked the dead clergyman.

'No, not at all,' replied St. Peter. 'Choose whichever name you like. Or a new one if you wish.'

'I've got used to Habakuk,' answered the priest.

'Habakuk it is then,' said Peter, his craggy face breaking into a smile. 'Welcome to Heaven.'

✶

'We've brought some Prussian Blue,' said the senior physician. 'It's the antidote to Thallium.'

'But you really should be in hospital so that we can perform hemodialysis and hemoperfusion,' said a second physician accompanying the senior consultant. 'I'm a toxicology specialist and we should take you to our ward.'

'Can I take the Prussian Blue here?' asked the Prime Minister.

'Certainly but it could have side effects,' said the toxicologist. 'And you must carefully dispose of your faeces as they may be toxic.'

'Then I shall stay put and rely on the Prussian Blue and my strong constitution,' said the PM. 'And flush my number two down the loo as usual.'

The Deputy PM started to stir on the floor. The chief constable took a pair of strong handcuffs from his pocket and locked them round Fence's left wrist. The other part he attached to a solid cast iron heating pipe.

'Can't allow him to get away,' explained the policeman. 'And I've seen what these chaps are capable of.'

The PM had swallowed the first dose of Prussian Blue and sat up brightly.

'I'm feeling better already,' he announced to the company in the room.

'I expect that is a placebo effect,' said the toxicologist. 'It is unlikely to work for some hours.'

'Don't knock it, doctor,' answered the PM. 'If I tell you that I feel better then I really do feel better. Now what is all this that you Scotts have come up here to tell me about?'

*

The Bifrost Bridge stretched out in front of us in full rainbow glory. The bridge glimmered in all colours imaginable and looked insubstantial, like a mist glittering in a valley on a summer's morning or the Milky Way observed on a very clear and starry night. All around the celestial bodies stood stationary as if held in position by their connections to the bridge. The rings of Saturn, the moons of Jupiter, the constellations of stars ... all were touched by the bridge. Earth itself could be seen as a spinning blue orb with patches of white cloud and occasional touches of green land. The bridge dipped to touch the Earth and then swooped back up into the firmament to finally reach a golden castellated structure.

Distances were strangely deceptive and by staring hard it was possible to make out small details at the place where the bridge touched the various realities. I could see that the bridge was attached to Earth, or Midgard, somewhere in Scandinavia. It was attached to a moon of Jupiter and swept past a ring of Saturn.

'What is the golden castle?' I asked.

'That is in Heaven at Himinbjorg,' replied the armoured fairy godmother. 'Heimdall lives there and guards the bridge.'

I looked into the distance and fancied that I could see a tall viking warrior standing on the bridge in front of Himinbjorg. In his hand he had a large horn.

'So where is Asgard?' I asked.

'Technically we are already in Asgard,' replied the fairy. 'When you walked down the stairs and into Valhalla you passed through a space/time portal much like the fairy bridges that link faerie with

Earth. Valhalla is one part of Asgard and you can enter the rest of Asgard if you leave Valhalla by one of the other gates.

As we talked a large, blonde warrior appeared. He was wearing the requisite horned viking hat and armour and carrying a huge hammer.

'Freya,' shouted the warrior. 'Where are you going?'

'I am leading these warriors over the Bifrost Bridge,' replied the fairy.

'But that is forbidden, dear Freya,' said the warrior. 'You cannot do that. Heimdall will not permit it.'

'Thor,' smiled the fairy who in this aspect was clearly doubling as Freya .'You are such a stickler for protocol. I will persuade Heimdall. I can bend him round my little finger.'

'Then I shall come with you,' stated Thor. 'What is your quest?'

'Let the mortals tell you,' replied the fairy Freya. 'I shall attract Heimdall's attention whilst they do so.'

So the fairy godmother doubles as the Norse Goddess of Love and leader of the Valkyries, I pondered. *And could this giant warrior be the noble Thor, God of Thunder? Oh lummy, we're playing with heavyweights here. But how did it work? How could Freya have been killed at Stonehenge?*

I decided that the ramifications were too difficult to work out but I did remember from somewhere in my reading of mythology that Freya was to die at Ragnarok. So maybe Ragnarok had begun and this was Freya, resurrected simply to die once more?

'I am waiting,' said the huge warrior who was called Thor. 'What is your quest?'

I explained about the new church on Earth and that they were calling for Armageddon.

'Which is equivalent to Ragnarok to Asgardians,' added Thor with a nod.

I talked about the escape to the Domain of Hades.

Thor laughed.

'A noble and brave way of escaping. Putting yourself in the arms of the Devourer of Souls.'

I told Thor about the judgment and how Vole and I had passed the test and been judged honest and noble but that the priest had failed.

'So he was swallowed into the oblivion by the Devourer?' surmised Thor.

'No,' I answered. 'Not at all. His own God from the Eternal Kingdom removed him from the Devourer's clutches thus denying the judgement of Hades.'

'But that breaks all the laws!' exclaimed Thor. 'That risks ending the balance of reality and destroying time and space.'

'Yes,' I answered. 'That risks Ragnarok, Armageddon and Gotterdamarung rolled into one. But that, unfortunately, is what they want. That is what they say their god demands and what their church is preparing for.'

Chapter 15

'The followers of the Church of Armageddon Prophets are trying to cause a Third World War,' explained Sienna to the Prime Minister. 'And they are also committing suicide in their droves.'

'We think that they are planning an assault on heaven,' stated Devonport. 'In fact they say that the assault has already begun.'

'But I can't see what I can do about it,' replied Darcy Macaroon, the British PM. 'I can hardly stop an assault on heaven. Not really within my remit.'

He gave the company in the room a weak grin.

'No, that's obvious,' retorted Devonport. 'But you can try to stop World War Three from happening. Mobilise the United Nations, ring the President of Russia on your hotline. Get in touch with India, China, Pakistan, North Korea, Israel and finally the USA. Anybody you can think of. Britain is uniquely regarded in the world and our recent problems at Stonehenge received huge coverage worldwide. They'll believe you if you say that there are supernatural forces causing the war in Jerusalem and Megiddo and may take heed if you tell them to stay out of the conflict.'

'The President of the USA won't take any notice of me,' replied Macaroon. 'Especially not if he has tried to kill me.'

'I don't think he wanted to kill you,' interrupted Sienna. 'Judging from the toxicology he was just trying to make you ill to get you away from the press and from your contacts. Possibly so that Sidney Fence could take over temporarily.'

'Get in touch with some of your other contacts in the USA. Get the Senate or Congress to impeach him. Get our secret service agents to contact the FBI and CIA,' the chief constable finally ran out of breath and sat down exhausted.

'Yes,' agreed Darcy Macaroon after a long pause. 'I will do all of that. Bring me the telephone .... the red one.'

*

'I will ask Saint Paul to show you round Heaven,' said Saint Peter in a very pleasant tone, taking Habakuk's arm and steering him towards the inner pearly gates . 'I have to stay near the outer gate most of the time otherwise I would show you around myself.'

'I don't quite get all this,' replied Habakuk. 'I really don't think that I deserve this treatment.'

'Anybody who thinks that they deserve good treatment in Heaven is probably deluded,' replied St. Peter.

'But I followed a false god,' Habakuk whispered. 'With all due respect, you must have made a mistake. I should be down in Hell. I don't deserve Heaven.'

'We don't make eligibility mistakes in Heaven,' replied Saint Peter. 'Infallibility comes with the territory. When we decide a person should be permitted to enter Heaven we are correct. So don't worry, you are definitely supposed to be here.'

'But I must tell you how I went wrong,' Habakuk responded. 'I was led astray by the Antichrist or something much like it. I thought the acts of God I saw on Earth were signs from Yahweh, Jehovah, the mighty God, the King of Kings. But now I realise that I was wrong.'

'And yet you were baptised?'

'Yes, St. Peter, I was definitely baptised.'

'And you followed the Lord?'

'I did but as I am saying, I went astray.'

'We all stray from the paths of righteousness, Habakuk,' replied St. Peter, softly. 'There is not a day goes by that I do not regret denying my Lord. Even here in Heaven I hear the cock crow and I shudder to recall my sin. But then the next moment I realise that I'm here and remember that Heaven is a great place, it's another day in Paradise and all is well.'

'All is not well down on Earth, St. Peter,' countered Habakuk. 'Things are going badly.'

'Tell me about it Habby,' said St. Peter. 'You don't mind if I call you that, do you?'

'No, not at all,' replied Habakuk. 'In fact I would count it as a signal honour.'

'Well Habby, let us sit down again and you can tell me what is going wrong on Earth,' suggested St. Peter. 'You are obviously worried about it and it is entirely possible that I can help.'

*

We walked out onto the ethereal, polychromatic Bifrost Bridge and I gazed into the distance.

'The castellated heaven must be many miles away over the bridge,' I surmised.

'It is,' replied the fairy Freya. 'Thousands of miles.'

'Then how can we see Heimdall so clearly?' I queried. 'We shouldn't be able to see him at all.'

'The bridge itself endues us with perfect sight wherever we look,' replied Freya.

'If we are walking there it will take forever,' I mused. 'Perhaps Thor could fly us there, dragged along by his hammer, Mjolnir.'

'I don't think I could do that,' replied Thor with his musical Scandinavian accent. 'Not really.'

'Against the 'ero's code I expect,' laughed Harry, wryly. 'Rule number ten, no givin' lifts to 'itchers.'

'Sorry?' replied Thor. 'I didn't quite get that.'

'Harry thinks that giving lifts to hitchers was against the hero's code,' said Vole dryly.

'No, no,' replied Thor. 'I'd help if I could but my powers are very limited. I can draw a bit of lightning and thunder and throw the hammer fairly accurately. It always comes back to my hand!'

He finished the sentence with a triumphant grin.

'But I thought the Norse god Thor was the most powerful god

apart from his father Odin,' I protested. 'You should be able to do a lot more than that!'

'Agreed, agreed,' said Thor spreading his hands placatingly. 'But then I've only been a god for a matter of weeks and I'm still learning.'

'If you've only been a god for a matter of weeks what were you doing before that?' asked Vole.

'I was an estate agent and surveyor in Stockholm,' replied the huge warrior. 'But I did a great act as Thor at enactments .... basically, plays in the park and mock battles.'

'Then how come you have ended up here in Valhalla?' I queried.

'I fell off a ladder inspecting a loft, broke my neck and woke up in the Domain of Hades,' answered the new god Thor. 'He sent me straight to Valhalla saying that it was about time that we had an active Thor again.'

'What about you, Freya?' asked Vole.

'Lord James knows that I was previously the fairy godmother,' replied Freya. 'And you saw me in the Elysian fields in that guise. I had often used the Boudicca entity when I needed to but when I died I appeared here as Freya. I can turn back into the godmother if I wish to but Freya seems to suit me and the Valkyries all follow me without a shadow of doubt.'

'So that's all sorted,' I concluded. 'We are a party of two new gods, one dead cockney, a witchdoctor or shaman, and one sceptical electrical engineer who doubles as a spy. Have I left anybody out?'

'What about me?' asked Ard, who was standing behind me. 'The king of the werewolves looking for his dead wife and children.'

'Fine. Six of us and we've got to hike thousands of miles across an admittedly beautiful but insubstantial cosmic bridge to prevent Ragnarok.'

'That's about it,' agreed Freya. 'But if we can convince Heimdall to help he will blow his horn and summon to our   assistance the heroes of Asgard and the heroines of the Valkyries.'

✷

'The Russians don't want any involvement on either side,' reported Darcy Macaroon, putting the red phone down. 'They say that they are only posturing and that in any case they have sold most of their nuclear warheads to America to be used in nuclear power stations. Apparently their spare bombs generated ten percent of the electrical power in the USA over the last twenty years.'

'Interesting,' said Chief Constable Devonport. 'What about the Chinese, India, Pakistan, North Korea...'

'Yes, yes. I'm coming to that. Don't be so impatient Maxwell,' replied the PM. 'I'm   not   one   of your junior colleagues or a criminal like our Deputy PM.'

They all turned and looked at Sidney Fence, handcuffed to the pipe. The man had fully woken now but was saying absolutely nothing.

Macaroon continued.

'So I have spoken to the Indians and they are trying to cool things with the Chinese and the Pakistanis. I've managed to get through to the Deputy President in Pakistan and he is an ardent Islamist, keen to take on India. I did extract a promise that he would tell his boss that I rang.'

'The Chinese?' queried Devonport. 'What are they doing?'

'Yes,' replied Macaroon. 'I spoke to a politburo member. He sounded very frightened and was not sure that he should speak to me at all. Luckily he spoke good English and after a while he began to realise that I was not phoning to threaten him or any such thing. He was surprised that we were not automatically endorsing the stand of the US President.'

'And the Secretary General of the United Nations, will he call a meeting of the Security Council?' asked the chief constable. 'If we can get them talking we might cool things down... and we might get it debated in the General Assembly.'

'He's missing,' replied Macaroon. 'Absolutely nobody knows where he is. He may have gone into hiding or he might have been abducted. He hasn't been seen for a couple of days.'

'Why hasn't a fuss been made of that?' asked Sienna.

'His staff at the UN thought he was having a few days off but he did not turn up to make a speech at the International Potato Week celebrations.'

'That is unlike him,' remarked Devonport. 'He usually puts out a press release and takes photo opportunities at any event that he can.'

'That's what his office said,' concurred Macaroon. 'So they have become very worried about him.'

'Any others?' asked Devonport.

'No, that's all the folks that I've managed to get hold of so far,' answered the British PM. 'Now if you don't mind I need a bit of time to recover my strength. That has taken more out of my poisoned body than I expected.'

'I don't want to leave you unprotected,' said Devonport. 'Where are your secret service men who are supposed to be guarding you?'

'Oh, they're in the house somewhere,' answered Macaroon. 'I expect that they are in their staff room playing cards. That's where I usually find them.'

'Then I shall locate them, check their identity cards and dentition and send a couple up to keep you company,' replied Devonport and pointed at the Deputy, Sidney Fence. 'Then we will leave you for a while and we'll take this monstrous traitor with us.'

✶

Habakuk had finished hesitantly telling St. Peter about the rise of the new god who claimed to be the god of the covenant.

'That is fascinating, Habby,' the saint looked pensive. 'Do you now think that Lucifer was behind the deception? Is this new god our old foe Satan?'

'I really don't think so,' answered Habakuk. 'Lucifer appeared on Earth about two years ago.'

'Really?' replied Peter. 'I didn't know about that but then I am out here on the edge of Heaven away from the hub and hubbub, so to speak.'

'Yes, he tried to sacrifice two innocent boys at Stonehenge,' answered Habakuk. 'And he had forged an alliance with a powerful elemental from Faerie.'

'An alliance between Faerie and Lucifer?' the saint was amazed. 'That's a new one. I don't think that has happened before.'

'They were defeated,' replied Habakuk. 'But the new god did not act or look like Lucifer.'

'He is the master of deception,' replied St. Peter. 'So maybe it was our old enemy, the serpent from Eden.'

'Maybe,' agreed Habakuk but he was not convinced.

Chapter 16

We set off across the Bifrost Bridge. With every step we took the bridge rang like a bell.

I'm going to get really fed up with this chiming, I thought. *And the journey will be endless.*

But it was not the case, not at all. After just a few minutes I no longer noticed the ringing tones. They were still there if I concentrated but were not a problem if I just walked and talked .... and sang! As we walked Thor led us in marching songs and we soon all joined in. I remembered one that I had heard the British Army sing:

> *Way hey rock and roll,*
> *Way hey rock and roll,*
> *A little bit of rhythm and soul,*
> *A little bit of rhythm and soul,*
> *Early in the morning,*
> *Early in the morning*

I sang this once through and immediately all of us were singing it together. I then improvised on the army marching song and the others came in on the repeat words.

> *Marching o'er the Bifrost Bridge,*
> *Marching o'er the Bifrost Bridge,*
> *Hope we don't fall off the ledge,*
> *Hope we don't fall off the ledge,*
> *Early in the morning,*
> *Early in the morning*

The time spent marching across the Bifrost Bridge was like a very pleasant dream. It was impossible to judge how long it took but we did not stop to eat or drink and required no physiological stoppages. As we neared the abode of the ever-watchful Heimdall I reflected that the time on the Bridge was one of the most relaxing periods I could ever recall. It had the same, slow, satisfying feeling of achievement that one has when taking a holiday on the canals with the added aspect of surreal space travel

Maybe one day I could take a holiday on the canals of Mars, I thought to myself as we passed the Red Planet but then recalled that the canals were a myth. *Were they always a myth?* I asked this of myself, not expecting an answer.

I thought I hear a faint reply from my friend Lady Aradel who always seemed ready to answer such questions, like a walking, breathing Wikipedia.

There were no canals as such, dear James, but there were a lot of lakes and seas. Now sadly gone.

Had she really replied? I decided that I had imagined the response due to wishful thinking. Certainly Lady Aradel, Queen of the Elves, would have been a very useful addition to our party. Both a beautiful female elf and a full magical, golden dragon, she was a formidable foe and a wonderful ally. I had last seen her at Stonehenge when the dragons, fairies and elves responded to the call of the MacLeods of Skye and helped defeat the forces of Lucifer and an evil elemental called Parsifal X.

This reminiscing brought us to the very feet of Heimdall, a god who seemed to have grown in stature and brightness as we approached him. He stood at least twenty metres tall, his feet were planted on the bridge and his left hand held a huge horn. More worrying was the enormous sword in his right hand.

'That is an enchanted Uru sword,' explained Freya, almost as if she was a guide on a tour of a stately home run by the National Trust. 'The sword permits Heimdall to disguise himself as an ordinary human being.'

'And the horn?' asked Vole. 'What sort of animal is it from and what does he use it for?'

'The horn is from a mythical goat that lived with the ice giants. Heimdall can summon the gods with it,' replied Freya. 'It is part of an endless cycle. When Ragnarok approaches, Heimdall summons the gods. We fight, eventually the gods win but all is destroyed including Midgard. Heimdall always dies fighting Loki. It has happened many times before and will happen again. Very soon.'

'Unless we stop it,' I remarked.

'If we can,' interjected Thor. 'And even then it will happen eventually so we will only be delaying the inevitable.'

'During which time many people can live and die,' I answered. 'Life can go on and evolve. I do not hold to this idea that the future is already predestined. I believe that small changes can be wrought that result in massive alterations further down the line so it may not all be inevitable.'

'Ah, yes,' replied the blonde Scandinavian neo-god. 'Chaos Theory. The butterfly's wings causing a hurricane in Brazil. The scenario seems unlikely but I agree it is worth trying to change things.'

Suddenly the huge god defending the bridge stirred from his motionless pose.

'Thor and Freya you must explain why you bring mortals across Asbrú, the Bifrost Bridge,' his voice was like thunder. 'And the explanation must be good or they will have to forfeit their lives.'

*

'Come with me now and we will find Saint Paul,' said Simon Peter. 'He likes showing people around.'

St. Peter took Habakuk by the arm and led him through the pearly gates. Habakuk was flabbergasted with what he could see. The outside gates and walls gave a completely wrong impression of the size of the paradise. It was huge. Habakuk could see it stretched out below him, shining clean and brightly with the most wonderful fields of flowers, trees in blossom whilst also fruiting, white marble buildings like Greek Temples and several crystal flowing rivers.

People and animals sat down contentedly by the riverside and some bathed in the pure waters. A few angels could be seen playing harps and the air was filled with celestial music. This was all happening nearby but heaven stretched for miles into the distance. Just the section that the priest could see covered many square miles.

'How big is Heaven?' Habakuk asked.

'About ten million square miles at the moment,' replied St. Peter. 'But it is always getting bigger.'

'Always getting bigger?' queried Habakuk. 'Why and how?'

'Heaven cannot be permitted to become overcrowded,' replied St. Peter. 'And souls are constantly arriving. Very few souls leave, so Heaven has to constantly get larger.'

'And how can that happen?' asked the priest.

'His Nibs simply deems it so and it happens,' replied a twinkling Simon Peter, the rock on which the Christian Church was founded.

*

Sienna, the two lads and the doctors waited with the Prime Minister while the Chief Constable took the cowed figure of Sidney Fence with him to find the security staff. He returned a few minutes later with two tall secret service agents and the party bade farewell to the Prime Minister.

'We have to return to Bristol to sort out the mess there,' explained Devonport. 'But we will return at any time if you should want us.'

'You've done very well. Very well indeed!' exclaimed Darcy Macaroon. 'You've saved me from poisoning, discovered the traitor and alerted me to the danger of Armageddon.'

'I wish we had heard back from Jimmy,' said Sienna. 'Have any of your staff heard anything at all?'

'Not that I know of as yet,' replied the PM. 'But I will chase them first thing after I have had a short nap. I'm feeling a lot better and I will get on top of all of this.'

Chief Constable Devonport led the party out of the room leaving the PM lying relaxed on the bed. Two doctors were sitting in the room with him and the security staff were sat outside the room on guard.

They walked downstairs and Devonport spoke to the policeman on guard outside the door of Number 10, explaining to him what had happened. The official police car and outriders were still waiting outside the PM's house and the party from Bristol sat back inside the vehicle.

'Bristol please, Matthews,' said Devonport and they pulled away from the kerb.

*

Freya replied to the gigantic figure of Heimdall.

'Please Heimdall. Talk to us on our scale.'

'For you, Freya, beautiful goddess, I will oblige.'

The huge figure waved its massive sword and the god instantly reduced in size to about the same dimensions as Thor.

'But I warn you all that the explanation for your presence on the Bifrost Bridge must be good.'

'We are trying to prevent Ragnarok,' I explained.

'Tell me more little mortal,' ordered Heimdall.

As he said this I could tell that he was listening to something far off.

'It is said that he can hear grass grow,' whispered Freya.

'I can, dear Freya,' Heimdall responded. 'And it is not the quietness of grass growing that is interesting. It is the quality of the sound when it does so.'

'A priest was judged wanting by Hades but removed from his Domain of the Dead by another god whose name we do not know,' I explained. 'This usurped Hades judgement.'

'Troublesome but is there more about Ragnarok?' asked Heimdall.

'The priest was part of a new religious group on Earth called the

Church of Armageddon Prophets and they are actively   promoting the idea of Armageddon and Ragnarok.'

'And you wish to follow the priest by using the Bifrost Bridge. Is that right?' asked Heimdall.

'We believe that he came over into the eternal realm,' I expounded. 'If so we need to follow him and make sure that the judgment is executed.'

'He did not come this way and...' intoned the god.

'... I can smell the trail of corruption,' interposed Ard. 'It is either from the priest or his god and it passed near to here and into the eternal realm.'

'The king of the werewolves!' Heimdall nodded his head. 'I do not doubt your word and yet I saw and heard nothing of this god or priest.'

Heimdall moved his head to one side in a quick gesture of surprise.

'But as you speak I have been picking up sounds of a disturbance at the base of Jacob's Ladder.'

'That's the way up to heaven,' whispered Freya. 'It is a metaphorical set of gigantic steps set into the mountainside leading to the plateau of paradise.'

'Freya dear, there is no need to whisper,' stated Heimdall. 'I can still hear you, loud or soft. And it is beginning to annoy me.'

'Sorry Heimdall my loved one,' crooned Freya. 'Let me calm you by massaging your shoulders. You are so tense.'

'Time for that after I have decided about the mortals,' said Heimdall, still irritated about our incursion.

'My life can't be forfeited as I've already died,' laughed Harry.

'But your afterlife can easily be destroyed,' remarked Heimdall and Harry's mirth evaporated.

'We have been sent by Hades and he awarded Vole, Ard and myself a place in Valhalla,' I argued.

'A place in Valhalla does not mean that you can wander across the Bifrost Bridge,' retorted Heimdall.

'What if we can prevent Ragnarok and prevent Loki from fighting you?' I suggested.

'To do that you would have to interfere with the supernatural cycle by which all is controlled,' answered Heimdall.

'Not necessarily so,' I replied. 'Chaos theory combined with quantum mechanics would lead me to believe differently. We might cause a very small change now but this may prevent the final battle from occurring later.'

'It maybe too late already to prevent Ragnarok from starting,' replied Heimdall. 'I will permit you to travel further on the Bifrost Bridge but I can hear a huge rabble of people trying to gain access to it and they seek to go in the same direction as yourselves.'

'Can you not prevent them?' asked Vole. 'Why not blow your horn and summon the Norse gods to our assistance?'

'I will summon the Aesir if we fail but we will first try to prevent the incursion,' replied Heimdall. 'I repeat, if we fail I will summon the Aesir.'

*

The police car with outriders had reached the M4 when Joshua spoke up.

'What I can't understand is how we didn't spot that they had such weird teeth before they revealed them?' he asked.

'That they were filed to points?' said his mother. 'Yes that is odd.'

'Perhaps they had something over them,' suggested Samuel. 'You know like the cap Dad had put on his tooth when he broke it.'

'Turn the car round as soon as possible,' ordered Devonport, who had been listening to the conversation.

'Certainly sir,' replied Matthews the driver and he spoke into the two-way radio to inform the outriders.

'We must go straight back to Downing Street,' said the chief constable to the driver and then explained to Sienna. 'Your son has just pointed out how my plan was flawed. I checked the dentition of the security staff but they could have had prostheses over their teeth. Some sort of gum-shield or removable veneers. They could all have been as monstrous as Deputy PM Fence.'

'So Darcy Macaroon is in danger,' conjectured Sienna.

'Yes,' replied Devonport. 'And although he may not be the world's greatest leader he is the best we have got right now.'

The car turned off at the next exit preceded and followed by out-riders. It would take at least twenty minutes to reach Downing Street even with all sirens blaring and the driver doing his very best to weave through the London traffic.

*

Heimdall moved us to the apex of the Bifrost Bridge. From there I could see that the bridge was a multidimensional domed disc rather than simply a rainbow arc. I could also see that where we were standing was defending the connections both to Heaven and Asgard and that from Midgard or Earth a huge number of creatures were invading the bridge. Most of the creatures were human but they were all maimed in some way or other. They were missing a hand or a foot, an eye or an ear. One poor creature appeared to have been decapitated but the body still stumbled on with a mass under its left arm. As it got closer to us I realised that the bundle was its severed head.

These were the embodiments of people who had died serving the Church of Armageddon Prophets.

'How can we defend the bridge against these creatures?' I asked. 'I'm unarmed and so are Vole, Harry and Ard.'

Ard growled and changed into his enormous lupine form. He was clearly indicating that he did not need to be armed.

'Where is you favoured weapon?' asked Heimdall.

'It was taken off me and left in Midgard in a place called New York,' I replied.

Heimdall stood still and looked towards the Earth fixing his vision on North America.

'It is a sword called the Morning Star,' said Heimdall. 'And I have located it.'

'That's good,' I nodded. 'But we don't have time to go and get it.'

'Your companion Lady Vole can bring it here,' replied the ever watchful Aesir god.

'I can?' asked Vole, surprised. 'How can I do that faster than any of the rest of you?'

'Link your vision with my own and use your power of telekinesis,' answered the god of the bridge.

'My ability in the field of telekinesis amounts to moving sheets of paper from a distance of fifteen feet,' replied Vole. 'That can be useful at times but it does not prepare me for moving a lump of iron thousands of miles through space.'

'You underestimate your power,' replied Heimdall, watching and seeing everything as he spoke. 'Here on the Bifrost Bridge you will manifest the full extent of your unusual strengths and can attract the sword to your hand. In truth you will be able to move the weapon to any place you wish.'

'OK,' agreed Vole. 'I'll give it a try but don't expect too much.'

So saying she concentrated hard looking in the direction that Heimdall indicated. At first she could discern no more than she had done previously and then she gradually became aware of an improvement in her vision. It was as if she were peering through the very strongest binoculars coupled with penetrating X-ray vision.

Finally she was looking into a locked room in a police station in downtown New York. She really could see the sword. Now to try shifting it. She gave it a mental push and the sword fell off the dusty shelf it had been consigned to. Then suddenly it had disappeared from the floor. Simultaneously it appeared in my right hand and I nearly dropped it off the Rainbow Bridge.

'Bingo!' I cried and Vole looked round in surprise.

'It worked! It really worked!' she exclaimed.

'Indeed,' Heimdall agreed in an understated way. 'Now Lady Vole, do the same for Harry and yourself.'

Vole looked around with the enhanced vision lent to her by Heimdall and teleported swords for Harry and herself.

'Why couldn't you get me a submachine gun, Vole?' asked Harry.

'I have a feeling that guns wouldn't work here but I may not be right,' Vole replied.

'Guns, bombs, gunpowder, dynamite and any ordinance of that nature will not work on the Bifrost Bridge or in Heaven, Asgard, Faerie, Valhalla, Elysian Fields or even in Hell,' answered Heimdall. 'It has been decreed so and thus shall remain.'

'Blinkin' 'eck,' groaned Harry. 'So its only on Earth that we 'ave guns. Weird or not?'

By the time we were armed in this way the vanguard of the advancing army had reached us and Thor, Heimdall, Freya and Ard were already in the thick of the fighting.

The three of us piled into the fray and initially we all did very well. In our favour was the absolute lack of discipline of the zombie hordes. They had one purpose and that was to invade the Eternal Realm and to do so the army of undead Armageddon Prophets piled upwards onto the Bifrost Bridge and tried to move to their heavenly goal. We were inexplicably in their way, pushing them back.

As they advanced we tipped them off the Bifrost Bridge.

'Where do they go to when we push them off the bridge?' I asked Freya, panting for breath as I did so.

The goddess, who seemed to know most of the answers to my questions, replied.

'I believe that they are either suspended in space or fall towards Hell.'

'So is that a different hell from Hades?' I asked, trying to get my theological geography right.

'Of course,' she answered, deftly avoiding a thrust from one of the cleverer zombies as she did so and pushing the poor ex-human into the void.

'So where did that spring from?' I asked. 'Who created Hell?'

'Can't say,' she said springing onto the shoulders of a huge troll, chopping off its head with her battle-axe and then taking down three adjacent zombies as the body fell. I continued with my best fencing style, parry, thrust, parry, thrust.

'So you don't know anything about Hell?' I asked.

'I didn't say that,' she countered, kicking a goblin-like soldier into space. 'I know who is in charge there and where it is.'

I swung my left fist into the face of a humanoid that had crept up behind the goddess. Simultaneously with the Morning Star in my right hand I took out two zombies with one thrust.

'Thanks,' said Freya as we gathered our breath. 'Yes, Lucifer is in charge of Hell and it is there.' She pointed with her axe over the edge of the bridge and I took a second to lean out and down whilst she held on to me to prevent me from falling. Below us I could see a gigantic hole, a frightening maw in the fabric of space. It looked red and angry. That was Hell.

*

A small, bald-headed man was walking towards Saint Peter and Habakuk. *Love is All* was emblazoned on a T-shirt he was wearing but otherwise he was clad much like Saint Peter with white robes and sandals. Habakuk assumed that this was because the two saints originally came from the Middle East.

'Let me introduce you to St. Paul,' said Simon Peter. 'Otherwise known as Saul of Tarsus, writer of numerous epistles and a founder of the early church.'

Habakuk bowed deeply.

'No need to do that, young fellow,' said St. Paul with a grin. 'We are very happy people and don't need obeisance.'

'Perhaps for Yahweh himself?' suggested Habakuk.

'If you like but he doesn't insist,' said St. Paul.

'I need to talk to His Nibs,' said Simon Peter. 'Habakuk has brought disturbing news.'

'The wars on Earth and the hordes at the gates of Heaven?' queried St. Paul.

'Told you,' grinned Simon Peter, digging Habakuk in the ribs. 'Those who are nearer to the hub of immortality know what is going on.... But do you know what is behind it?'

Simon Peter directed the question back to St. Paul.

'The usual human perfidy, lack of love and ability to go wrong?' suggested the small, epistle writing saint.

'Partly, no doubt,' agreed Simon Peter. 'But Habakuk has told me about a new god who works miracles and walks the Earth claiming to be the Lord of the Covenant.'

'Is it Lucifer?' asked Saul of Tarsus, shocked. 'Has he loosed his chains and started walking the Earth again.'

'He may have done so two years ago according to Habakuk but he does not believe that Satan is behind this God,' explained Simon Peter.

'Then it must be the Antichrist,' stated St. Paul. 'Yes, Yahweh must be informed.'

'Doesn't he know it all already?' asked Habakuk. 'I thought Yahweh was immortal, invisible, omnipotent, omnipresent and omniscient.'

'He is, He is,' answered both saints together and Simon Peter continued the thread. 'But not necessarily all at the same time.'

'So He might not be listening or aware of the situation?' asked Habakuk.

'True, true,' agreed St. Paul. 'If we were not in Heaven we might find it slightly irksome but we don't. We love Him for it.'

'So what happens if you tell Him something?' asked Habakuk, bemused. This was all like Quantum Physics to him. Baffling confusing.

'Then He has always known it because He is omniscient,' said St. Paul.

'And if He wishes to do something?'

'Then it is done simply because He deems it so,' answered Simon Peter.

'But if you don't ask Him?'

'Then it may not be done but we don't know because we did not ask,' explained Saint Paul.

'And can He be everywhere at the same time?' asked Habakuk.

'Definitely. Unless He is there with you of course because then He is with you,' said Simon Peter trying to clarify the situation.

'And is He all powerful?' asked Habakuk.

'If He decides to be,' said Saint Paul. 'At least we believe He is.'

'Although that one is harder to judge,' replied Simon Peter. 'How do you know if you are all powerful until you come up against an almost as powerful foe.'

'Such as the Antichrist?' suggested Habakuk and for the first time the two saints were not smiling.

'You are right,' said Saint Paul, and turned to address Simon Peter. 'We do need to talk to "His Nibs" as you insist on calling Him. We need to inform him of this news.'

'He will, of course, already know,' said Simon Peter. 'But we won't know that until we speak to Him. Where is He at the moment?'

'In the bosom of Abraham discoursing with Moses,' answered the small saint.

'He's been doing that for some time,' said Simon Peter.

'Many days,' added Saint Paul.

'Could that be why we haven't lately seen much of His activity on Earth?' asked Habakuk. 'Given that a thousand years is like a day here, supposedly.'

'It is, it really is,' agreed Simon Peter.

'What century is it on Earth?' asked Saint Paul.

'The twenty-first century,' replied Habakuk.

'Twenty-first?' Saint Paul whistled through his teeth. 'I thought it was the twelfth or maybe thirteenth century. What about you Simon?'

'Sixteenth,' said the Saint. 'I've always been very good with names and faces but not so good with dates. Perhaps the seventeenth but certainly not the twenty-first century. That does probably explain the strange clothes some people wear when they arrive at the gates. Still, they are all in the book. Their names are all there.'

He clasped his large book firmly against his side with his right arm as he said that and held the keys of Heaven in his left.

'I better disturb Him then and tell Him that we have a problem,' said Saint Paul.

'Indeed,' agreed Simon Peter. 'But He will know that already.'

'Inevitably,' Saint Paul nodded. 'Once we have told Him.'

Chapter 17

Thor, for a rookie god, was doing extremely well. He summoned lightning and thunder, swung the hammer to create tornados and pushed thousands back at a time. Heimdall's sword turned out to be as mystical and magical as Freya had said. Heimdall could appear in one place, disappear and reappear behind his enemy. He could wave a fiery barrier to prevent egress. But slowly we were pushed back, hacking and thrusting as we went.

Eventually Heimdall cried out. 'Enough!'

His very cry halted the advance and in the momentary pause he blew the horn. The sound was numbing in volume and quality. The swarming mass at the back of the army that had not been stilled by his voice stopped their incursion onto the bridge.

Perhaps he could just keep sounding his horn and the invasion would be forestalled?

But a voice louder than Heimdall's by some magnitudes came from the rearguard crying out "Forward!" and the crowd surged towards us once more.

From the back of the crowd we could hear chanting.

'We are Gog and Magog.
We are the chosen of God.'
'We are Gog and Magog.
We are the chosen of God.'

The sound was as endless as waves crashing on a pebble beach. Heimdall looked stunned at this latest assault. But then he peered into the distance, having observed something invisible to us behind the advancing army.

'Has he seen the Aesir? The hero gods and goddesses,' I quietly asked Freya.

'Not from that direction,' replied the warrior goddess of love and former fairy godmother, ambassador of the fairies.

'There are Ice Giants behind the army,' Heimdall announced. 'Someone has resurrected the Ice Giants.'

'How many?' asked Thor.

'As countless as the grains of sand on the seashore,' replied the guardian of the Bifrost Bridge.

'And was it an Ice Giant that shouted for the army to advance?' asked Vole.

Heimdall laughed despite our predicament.

'No Lady Vole. Something far worse. Behind the Ice Giants there is a God. I can discern his shape despite all the hordes in between.'

'What is the god?' asked Freya. 'Do we know it? Is it Loki?'

'It is not Loki and I can just about hear his name despite the chanting,' replied Heimdall. 'It is a God more ancient than myself. He is called Dagon, Hadad or sometimes Baal. It is he who recreated our nemesis, the Ice Giants.'

'More ancient than yourselves?' I queried.

'Dagon is a myth older than time itself,' answered Freya. 'He first appears in human records in Sumerian texts of four thousand and five hundred years ago. He was initially a god of agriculture but in various forms was considered the god of gods, lord of lords.'

'And Lord of the Covenant, I believe,' added Heimdall.

'So he may have been the God of the Israelites?' I queried.

'That much is disputed but Baal was sometimes worshipped by the Israelites and was occasionally indistinguishable from Yahweh,' agreed Freya. 'It's a long time ago.'

'So how could this ancient and forgotten god have become so powerful so quickly and who is the God in Heaven?' I asked.

'The Judeo-Christian-Islamic heaven?' asked Freya. 'That is definitely Yahweh.'

'So the God trying to invade Heaven and the one in   Heaven could both be considered as Yahweh, the God of Gods,' Vole concluded.

'That's right. Confusing isn't it,' said Freya chopping the heads off a particularly troublesome trio of cyclopean monsters. The fray had restarted and there was no more time for discussion.

'One last question,' I shouted. 'Who is the son of god?'

'There are many sons of god,' came the reply from Heimdall over the din of battle. 'Which son do you mean and which god.'

'The son of the God of gods, perhaps?' I asked but I could not catch the reply due to a troll-like Ice Giant trying to thump me with a club.

*

The chief constable was fretting all the way through central London.

'I left Sidney Fence with the Downing Street police,' he grunted. 'I telephoned the local police and instructed them to pick him up but Lord knows who I spoke to. Fence is a murderous liability and I left him with police staff who might well have been his accomplices. I've been such a fool.'

'That's how you feel when you've been up all night,' commiserated Joshua who was also feeling the lack of sleep and finding it hard to concentrate.

The chief constable was fiddling with something in the glove compartment when the police car turned into Downing Street. It pulled up outside Number 10 and Devonport, Sienna and the boys all leapt out.

'Back so soon?' queried the uniformed policeman on duty outside the door.

'Yes,' answered Devonport shortly. 'Have there been any disturbances and has anybody come out?'

'No sir,' replied the policeman.

'Good,' replied Devonport. 'Now we just need to get into Number Ten and check up on the PM.'

'I'll speak to my counterpart inside,' suggested the duty policeman, bringing out his radio.

'Good,' said Devonport. 'Tell him to hurry.'

The chief constable, Sienna and the two boys waited outside Number 10. After five minutes Devonport impatiently asked the constable what was happening.

'I don't know, sir,' came the constable's worried reply. 'He usually answers immediately. I've never had to wait more than thirty seconds before now.'

'Is there another way to get in?' asked Devonport.

'There is an internal link door between eleven and ten, sir,' replied the constable.

'But how can we get into number ten?' asked the chief constable. 'We don't want to have to break the door down.'

'I wouldn't let you do that, sir. With all due respect,' replied the constable. 'But I can let you in to Number 11. I don't have keys to 10 but I do have keys to 11.'

'Do it man. Just do it,' ordered Devonport becoming more and more impatient. 'And after you have let us in call for back up. I have a nasty feeling that we may need it.'

'Certainly sir,' answered the constable, feeling nervously and unsuccessfully in his pockets for the keys. 'That's strange, I can't find the keys.'

'Come on, man. Get a grip,' the chief constable spat out the words.

The man continued to search through all his pockets and then finally said.

'Ah, ha! They might be in my coat.'

The uniformed man looked down behind a pillar and retrieved a greatcoat that was hidden from view.

'Yes, here they are,' he remarked. 'Lucky I hadn't lost them!'

Devonport was going red with the effort of stopping himself from exploding. The agonising waste of time was torturing the poor chief of police.

The constable left his guard post and led the way to number eleven. Then he sorted through all of the keys and, as usual, it was the last key to be selected that fitted. Dealing with the dead lock and the latch the policeman let the party into number eleven.

'The communicating door is over there,' he said pointing to the back of the hallway. 'I cannot come with you. I must stay on my post outside the doorway.'

'I may need your back up at some point soon,' suggested Devonport.

'I'll send for help right away,' said the policeman. 'I'm sure that they won't take long in coming to your aid.'

'No longer that it has taken your colleague inside Number 10?' ventured Devonport, sarcastically.

'And he still hasn't come,' muttered Joshua.

*

I avoided the giant's club and we managed to push the army back temporarily.

'If the Aesir do not arrive soon we will be overwhelmed,' said Freya.

'They are coming,' replied Heimdall, listening and watching with his supernatural senses. 'But they will be too late. They are scattered presently and will take time to arrive. There is only one way to protect the heavens.'

'Destroy the Bridge?' surmised Freya.

'Yes. Destroy the Bifrost Bridge,' agreed Heimdall. 'We must do that or all is lost.'

'And the only one who can do that is Thor,' said Freya.

'That is correct,' Heimdall concurred. 'Thor must destroy the bridge.'

'Me?' said Thor. 'How can I destroy the Bridge and what will happen to us if I do?'

'You can destroy it with a couple of blows of Mjolnir, your

hammer, ' replied Heimdall. 'And we shall be suspended in space and have to take our chance with whatever befalls us.'

'You're sure that the Aesir can't hold back the hordes?' I asked, very worried about the talk of destruction. Vole and I were human and still alive. We needed air to breathe and ground to stand on. The fabled Rainbow Bridge was providing these but if it was destroyed I suspected that we would indeed die.

'If we do not destroy the bridge Valhalla, Asgard, Elysian Fields and the divine Heaven will be invaded and destroyed,' replied Heimdall.

'Then I shall try,' said Thor.

'And you shall succeed,' replied Heimdall.

*

Saint Paul scuttled off towards the centre of Heaven.

'All we can do,' explained Simon Peter. 'Is wait for their return. It will be a very pleasant wait but a wait nevertheless.'

Then in an apparent non sequitur he turned to Habakak.

'Do you play Bagatelle?'

'You mean the pinball game?' queried Habakuk.

'Yes,' answered Simon Peter, 'It's like pinball but it's non mechanical. Perhaps it was a precursor to pinball.'

'I used to play when I was a kid,' added Habakuk. 'Usually on a rainy day when I was bored.'

'We've got an enormous bagatelle board here,' said Simon Peter. 'I play it whenever there is a spare moment from allowing souls to enter the heavenly kingdom.'

Saint Peter led Habakuk over to a domed, white marble building. Inside was a bagatelle board five metres in length by two in diameter.

'That's more than five times the size of the one I played on,' said Habakuk. 'But I'll give it a go.'

The balls were the size of large golf balls as opposed to the marble-sized ball bearings that Habakuk had played with when he was young. Simon Peter took the first ball and put it into the slot on the right hand side of the board. He then gave it a thump with an instrument like a snooker cue. The ball shot up, round the inside of the top of the board, hit against a pin and dropped into a cage marked fifty.

'That's all there is to it,' said Simon Peter. 'I just keep hitting the balls round until I've finished them all then I count up my score. You can have a go first.'

He retrieved the ball from the "fifty" cage and put it back to the start.

Habakuk lined up the first ball, ready to hit it with the cue.

'.....And we could have a little bet on it, if you like?' suggested Simon Peter. 'Best of three?'

'OK,' said Habakuk. 'But I don't have any possessions to wager.'

'No, but if you lose you can take one of my turns at the gate whilst I have a rest,' replied Peter.

'And if I win?' asked Habakuk. 'What do I receive if I win?'

'You get two turns on the gate,' laughed Simon Peter.

'OK,' replied Habakuk, also chortling, all fears about the Antichrist momentarily expunged from his happy heavenly mind.

*

Once inside 11 Downing Street the chief constable, Sienna and the boys quickly found their way through to number ten. Nobody was visible on the ground floor so they ran up the stairs towards the "holy of holies" as Fence, the Deputy PM, had called it.

There were no staff outside the room and the party from Bristol barged straight in. Sidney Fence was in the room on the far side with one of the security men. They were both trying to open the door to the lavatory.

It was clear that the PM was ensconced within.

'It's no good Macaroon, you can't get away,' Fence was shouting through a small key hole.

'Nor can you get in here, Fence, you murderous weasel,' came a faintly heard reply. 'I had this important little room strengthened with steel plates. It's a safe room.'

Fence and the security policeman turned when they heard the Scotts and the chief constable enter the room. The security policeman went to take a gun from his belt but the chief constable cried out an order.

'Drop the gun and don't move.'

The security policeman laughed and started to point the automatic at Devonport. Two shots rang out and the policeman fell. The chief constable had shot the security policeman in the arm and leg and he had fallen in a crumpled heap.

'Get the gun, quickly,' ordered Devonport, talking to   Joshua who, acting as told, flung himself forward to grab the fallen automatic before Fence could get to it. The Deputy PM had also jumped for the gun and the two met in mid air. Joshua, although the smaller of the two, was used to tussling at judo and when playing rugby at school. He smacked into the Deputy PM and had the satisfaction of flooring him for the second time. The elder Scott son grabbed the gun and stood up triumphantly.

'Sienna,' suggested Devonport. 'Could you and Samuel tie up these felons?'

'I think we could just about do that,' replied Sienna with a somewhat grim grin. 'Tightly, I suppose?'

'Very tightly, madam,' replied the chief constable. 'As tightly as you can possibly manage.'

Chapter 18

Thor thumped his hammer down onto the Rainbow Bridge. The mystic structure doming the firmament and joining the heavens and Earth let out a loud ringing tone "CLANG" but it stood firm.

'Hit it as if you mean to break it,' ordered Heimdall, the defender of the Bridge. 'Don't tap it as if it's a xylophone.'

With a measure of irritation Thor swung his hammer down onto the celestial bridge. This time he had really put in some effort and the Bifrost Bridge cracked along its length. But still the hordes were coming and they were trying to bypass us.

'Hit it again Thor,' cried Heimdall, holding back several hundred zombies with his mystic sword.

Thor smashed Mjolnir, the sacred hammer, down onto the mythical bridge once more and a metallic shriek could be heard from the dome. A massive crack appeared in front of us and a large section fell away into the void of Space. The cracks zigzagged in several directions and the whole middle section of the bridge collapsed taking most of the invading swarm with it. A large groan went up from the remainder of the army and they tried to turn and escape from the collapsing remnants.

Our section stayed firm for a short while, attached as it was to the heavens, but it slowly keeled over and bent down towards the great red hole that represented Hell and abruptly the remaining parts of the Bifrost Bridge gave way. We were all flung into the void. I took a deep breath and held it, not knowing when I would be able to take another. I could see that Vole and Ard were doing the same.

Harry was grinning as we accelerated towards the giant mouth of the pit.

'Bloody amazing experience,' he shouted, not trying to save his breath at all. 'I'm dead already so I might as well enjoy it.'

How does he breathe and talk if he is already dead? And how can I hear him in a vacuum? I asked myself these imponderables as the last air burst from my lungs in the vacuum of space and I felt my eyeballs and ears expanding. *And what a pity that Lady Aradel isn't here. She took me through Space on her back and because of her magical abilities I was able to breathe.* That was the very last thing I thought before I passed out and it all went black.

*

'What you are doing is pointless,' cried Sidney Fence, sitting on the floor, trussed up tightly in torn sheets. 'You are going to lose. The end of the world as you know it has already been called and you are on the wrong side.'

'Let us be the judge of that,' replied Maxwell Devonport. 'And you shall go to jail for a long time.'

Fence burst out laughing. 'You just don't get it, do you? I won't go to jail for a long time because there won't be a long time. Time is coming to an end.'

'People have been saying that ever since human beings could talk,' replied Devonport. 'And they have always been wrong so far.'

Fence laughed again. 'You are all blind fools. You just can't see the signs.'

Devonport strode over and ripped a pillow case off the bed. He then gagged the deputy prime minister. He had a quick look at the security man who was bleeding from his wounds and used the rest of the pillow case to staunch the flow.

'I can't stand hearing him talk,' explained the chief constable when he realised that the others were looking at him in surprise. 'Fence may or may not be right but we don't need to listen to him and I couldn't bear to see the security policeman bleeding to death in front of me, even though he is a villain.'

Sienna had reached the bathroom door and shouted into the keyhole to the Prime Minister.

'You are safe now, Darcy. It is Sienna Scott here. You can come out.'

'How do I know it is you, Sienna?' asked the PM. 'The world's full of apocalyptic cannibalistic maniacs.'

'Have you got your mobile phone?' asked Sienna.

'Yes but it's not working,' answered the PM.

'Is there a landline in there?' asked Devonport.

'There is somewhere,' came Macaroon's distant reply. 'I don't normally use it. Yes, here it is in the airing cupboard.'

'Telephone the local police and you will find that we have sent for back-up then telephone Sienna or myself on our mobiles. We gave you the numbers earlier. Have you still got them?'

'Yes,' replied the frightened PM. 'Yes, I'll do that now.'

There was a pause of a few minutes and Sienna's phone rang. She instantly answered it.

'Hi, Sienna here.'

'Where's here?' asked the PM.

'Outside your bathroom,' replied Sienna.

'What are you wearing?' asked the PM.

'Black trousers and a pink top, then a pink fleece on top of that.'

'And when did we last meet?'

'About an hour ago, Darcy. For God's sake open the loo door. We want to see if you are OK.'

A rattling noise came from the door as the various locks were undone and a timid face peeped round the partially opened portal. Then came the scraping sound of a chair being pulled away and the door was flung open.

'Fat lot of good you turned out to be!' exclaimed the PM as he came out of the closet. 'You were supposed to protect me and you left me to the mercy of my murderous deputy!'

Devonport looked most sheepish.

'To be honest with you, sir, that is just how I would feel if I were in your shoes.'

'I'm not even in shoes,' shouted the PM. 'I'm in bare feet because this pig came back to finish me off.'

Macaroon took a feeble kick at the bound deputy PM who was sitting on the floor and caught the man on his shoulder. Sidney Fence fell over in a heap but the Prime Minister hopped around the room in agony.

'Now I've broken my bloody toe. Ruddy, ruddy hell!'

Joshua and Samuel couldn't helping laughing. Sienna tried not to join in but could not help herself. Eventually the chief constable, the three Scotts and even the PM, were all laughing.

The two trussed up traitors lay scowling on the floor.

*

"Ker....ching" went the ball and landed in the fifty yet again. Simon Peter was astoundingly good at Bagatelle. He had just played his last ball and he added up the score from the twenty objects. Not one of them had missed a pocket or cage.

'That's four in the 125, one in the 150, one in the 130, one in the 70, one in 100 and all the rest in the 50,' counted the twinkling saint. 'A total of one thousand, five hundred and fifty. Now what was your score?'

'Two hundred and twenty,' replied Habakuk.

He felt that he ought to be annoyed at being so comprehensively outclassed but it was as if there was a Happy Pill in the air, or some kind of heavenly Soma. He just smiled and enjoyed the game.

This is how all games should be played, thought Habakuk. *Just for the enjoyment and the thrill of taking part.*

'Best of five, shall we?' asked Simon Peter as he put all the balls back into the bottom cleft.

'Why not?' replied Habakuk.

'Using your saintly persuasion on the balls are we?' came the voice of Saint Paul, returning from conversing with his boss. 'Don't let him beat you, Habakuk.'

'I don't think I can avoid that, sir,' replied Habakuk as his first ball missed all the pockets and landed with a clunk at the bottom of the board.

'No need to call me sir,' answered the small, much-epistled saint. 'You can call me Paul or Saul. I don't mind.'

He then paused and studied the huge Bagatelle table. 'You are not guiding the balls into the holes.'

'How do I do that?' asked Habakuk.

'Just tell it that you'll be upset if it doesn't go into a nice pocket and it will oblige. The inanimate objects are not perfidious here in Heaven,' answered Saint Paul.

'So I just think at the ball and its trajectory will change?' queried Habakuk.

'That's right. It can't allow you to be upset,' Saint Paul added. 'Give it a go and your score will improve.'

Habakuk thought hard when he let loose the next orb and it sailed round into the 150.

'Is that what you were doing?' Habakuk asked Simon Peter.

'Of course,' replied the saint.

'Was that cheating?' Habakuk queried. 'Or was it just good heavenly sense?'

'I like to think the latter,' replied the saint.

'So do I,' replied Habakuk, smiling warmly. Even the knowledge that Simon Peter had been manipulating the scores could not expunge his good humour.

'We'll stop now. What news about Yahweh?' the saint who held the keys to the gates of Heaven, directed his question to Saint Paul.

'He will join us soon. He is busy walking in the fire with Shadrach, Meshach and Abednego,' replied the short saint. 'He wants to talk to both you and Habakuk.'

Yahweh is coming, thought Habakuk. *Will I be blinded as I was by the Antichrist or will He be a thoroughly decent person as I always imagined Him to be?*

★

I woke up in Hell. This was definitely different from Hades. For a start it was a lot hotter, it smelt of brimstone and the light was a deep red hue. Freya, Thor and Heimdall were nowhere to be seen but Vole, Ard and Harry were also there with me. Harry was already awake but Vole and Ard woke up at the same time as myself.

'How did we get here?' asked Vole.

'I watched it all,' replied Harry. 'Thor and Heimdall somehow cushioned the impact with their hammer and sword. We got here just in time or you would have suffocated.'

'It has got an atmosphere or I wouldn't be breathing,' I remarked.

'Unless you're dead like me then you don't need to breathe,' laughed Harry.

'We are not dead,' said Vole. 'At least, Jimmy, Ard and myself are not dead or we would have been transported to Valhalla.'

'I think that Vole is right,' I agreed, pinching my own arm painfully as I said it. 'But what we do now I have absolutely no idea.'

A sound made me turn round. Standing at a doorway was a huge distorted figure. It had two cloven hooves, the tail of a dragon, a hairy body, a goat's head. In its left hand it held a huge pitchfork.

'Who is first for the fire and brimstone?' asked a sepulchral voice which was strangely familiar and almost female.

'I suppose I should go first,' I said, standing up, my knees knocking as they had done when I'd met the devil previously . 'It's my fault the others are here with me. I dragged then along.'

'Always the bloody hero, James,' laughed the figure and in front of my eyes morphed into a good-looking, tall lady of indeterminable age.

'Mary?' I gasped. 'Is that really you?'

'Of course it is,' Mary replied between wheezing laughter. 'Oh God. I did enjoy that.'

'What were you doing looking like the devil?' I asked, totally confused.

'Trying to frighten you,' she gasped, red in the face.

'And you succeeded,' I said with a scowl.

'I know, I know,' she laughed again.

Being dead has not improved her one bit, I thought to myself. *She's meaner than ever.*

'Who is the bitch?' asked Vole with passion.

'She's not a bitch,' I protested. 'She's my mother-in-law. Like you, she's a witch.'

*

'Now I can get back to work,' said the Prime Minister. 'After you left me I closed my eyes for a few moments but I was too fired up to sleep. So I first telephoned our agent in New York to ask about Jimmy Scott.'

'Was there any news?' asked Sienna.

'What has happened to Daddy?' asked Samuel.

'The agent said that Jimmy is fine and has popped over into the alternative reality,' replied the PM.

'You mean Faerie don't you?' asked Samuel.

'Yes, that's right. The alternative reality,' answered the PM, not quite bringing himself to use the term "faerie".

'Any other news from the States?' asked Devonport.

'Yes,' said the PM. 'The FBI have been investigating President Armstrong and they are trying to get him impeached for electoral irregularities.'

'That's good news,' replied Devonport.

'And the Pakistani President rang me back,' continued Macaroon. 'He was very interested to hear that this conflict could bring on Armageddon. He is totally against that, even though he is a good Muslim. He believes that we deserve more time on Earth to sort out our problems.'

'So he won't nuke the Indians?' asked Joshua.

'I sincerely hope not,' said the PM flinching. 'But that's not all.'

'What else have you heard?' asked Devonport.

'Just before my murderously minded deputy appeared at the bedroom door I was speaking to the United Nations.'

'..And?' prompted Devonport.

'And the Secretary General has reappeared.'

'More good news!' exclaimed Sienna.

'I don't think so,' replied Darcy Macaroon. 'He wanted to give a speech in the Assembly Hall in front of all the delegates.'

'That's his right, isn't it?' asked Sienna.

'Yes, but his staff noticed that his teeth were filed to points and that he could barely string two sensible words together.'

'It's the former that is the new factor,' growled Devonport. 'So what did they do?'

'One of the members of staff sat on him and they called security,' continued the prime minister. 'Unfortunately two of the security men also had teeth filed to points and a fight broke out. The cannibals were eventually defeated but three staff are dead.'

'That's shocking news,' groaned Sienna.

'Except that all three staff had their teeth filed down.'

'So the people who died... were they the security men?' asked Devonport.

'Yes, and the Secretary General,' said the PM. 'The Secretary General of the United Nations has died in a fight at the UN. The very organisation that is set up to keep the peace.'

Chapter 19

'Whilst we wait for Yahweh perhaps you could show Habakuk around?' suggested Simon Peter to Saint Paul, 'I did promise him a tour.'

The holder of the keys to heaven smiled at Paul and added 'Pretty please!'

'Of course, of course. No problem,' replied the small saint with a slight laugh, not at all put out by the suggestion. 'Now where should we start?' He paused and looked around. 'I know, we'll go down to the crystal flowing river.'

Saint Paul led the way down to a clear stream. Habakuk followed.

'Are there people of different denominations here?' asked Habakuk, looking around at the inhabitants of paradise.

'Yes, yes, definitely' replied Saint Paul just a little impatiently.

'I expected that,' concurred Habakuk. 'What about good folk from different religions?'

'Yes, yes. Of course,' answered the saint. 'Faith, hope and love get you a long way.'

Habakuk looked round at the very Christian interpretation of heaven.

'But don't they find it a bit strange when they get here. It's not exactly as they expected is it?'

'Heaven very rarely disappoints,' replied Saint Paul. 'Give me an example religion and I'll show you.'

'OK,' said Habakuk. 'I'll bowl you a real googly....'

'A what?'

'It's a cricketing term for a mighty difficult and puzzling delivery,' answered Habakuk. 'I picked it up when I lived in

England.'

'OK, go on,' said the saint.

'Buddhists!'

'What's difficult about that?' asked Saint Paul.

'Gee, you must know what I mean,' replied Habakuk. 'There are loads of them, really gentle kindly folk, who don't believe in god or heaven but in reincarnation.'

'That is a common misconception,' replied the saint. 'Many Buddhists wish to be reincarnated in a Deva world, particularly in Tusita which is right here. Then they can sit at the feet of a master and hope to be born again on Earth to full enlightenment.'

'But, hey, it doesn't look like a Buddhist place,' protested Habakuk.

'Heaven rarely disappoints,' replied the small saint and turned Habakuk round to look behind him.

The scenery had completely changed. Habakuk could see that they were surrounded by a snow-topped mountain range and that the crystal clear waters did indeed flow from between the peaks. Nearby Buddhist monks sat around a guru, all of them wearing saffron robes. Even Saint Paul's robes had changed from bright white ... they had turned to a deep maroon colour.

'This is a heaven where divine beings dwell but is not the seventh heaven,' said the saint. 'That is the pure land reserved for the Buddha.'

'Could it also be the bosom of Abraham?' asked Habakuk.

'You're learning,' nodded Saint Paul, pleased with Habakuk's progress.

*

Mary led us along a corridor and into an utterly vast throne room. She then left us standing at the bottom of a tier of steps. The features of the room gradually came into focus. Centrally there was a huge pit from which smoke periodically erupted and occasionally red and orange flames emerged. There was a definite smell of rotten eggs also coming from the hole along with distant wailing and infrequent shrieking.

Vole was staring daggers at me and I felt obliged to ask her why.

'You said I was a witch!' she exclaimed in a high degree of dudgeon.

'That's what you told me when we first met,' I replied flinging my hands up in exasperation.

'I said I was a shaman, a witch doctor,' replied Vole. 'Not a witch.'

'Is there a difference?' I asked.

'Of course there is,' answered Vole. 'A witch is an old hag whilst a shaman is a healer.'

'Then my mother-in-law is a shaman, just like you,' I replied.

'She seemed more like an old hag to me,' said a marginally mollified Vole. 'But don't ever call me a witch again.'

'Sorry Vole,' I replied.

'I am a Cherokee Indian not a withered, evil old hag,' she continued.

'I'm really sorry Vole,' I repeated.

'Don't do it again.'

'I promise.'

We were silent for a few moments.

'So now what do we do?' asked Ard, having carefully kept out of the argument.

'All we can do is wait,' I replied. 'I expect that the evil worm will appear and torture us in some way. But, as I said, we just have to wait.'

'It's not a problem to me,' laughed Harry. 'I'm already dead. This is all an extra as far as I'm concerned.'

*

'OK, OK,' said Habakuk. 'An even harder one...Scientologists. There are plenty of them in LA even if there are not many in New York where I come from.'

'Not so difficult,' laughed the saint. 'It depends on the mind set. Some play games fighting aliens and others float around as spirit Thetans waiting to inhabit new born human beings as their souls.'

The saint paused and then added .... 'Or so they think.'

'So this isn't a Christian heaven,' mused Habakuk.

'It doesn't belong to any one religion but those who practice a particular faith often think that it does belong to them even when they are here.'

'Isn't that a little difficult sometimes?'

'Do you see that brick wall?' asked Saint Paul.

Habakuk looked in the direction that the small saint was pointing and could make out an area completely surrounded by a high brick wall.

'I do,' he told the saint.

'Within that brick enclosure are the Exclusive Plymouth Brethren.'

'Why?' asked Habakuk. 'Are they being punished?'

'No,' replied the saint. 'They just think that they are the only ones here.'

'But why the brick wall?'

'Heaven does not like to disappoint,' replied the saint, yet again.

*

'So what is going to happen at the United Nations?' asked Sienna.

'The Deputy Secretary General will take over temporarily, I expect,' answered the British Prime Minister, Darcy Macaroon.

'Is there one?' asked Sienna. 'I didn't know there was such a post.'

'There is,' growled Chief Constable Devonport. 'Has been since 1997 or 98. This guy isn't at all bad if he is allowed to act.'

'Do you think that there will be something about it on the news channel?' asked Joshua, looking over at the PM's flat screen

TV.

'There will be soon,' agreed the Chief Constable. 'But you must ask the PM's permission before you turn it on.'

'Go ahead,' agreed Macaroon, waving his hands in dismissal and then pointing at the deputy PM and the security policeman, trussed like mummies. 'But first take those murderous bastards out of my room and dispose of them as you think fit.'

Devonport nodded and spoke swiftly on his phone. He then looked over to the PM. 'The back-up will be here soon. I intend going down to Charing Cross Police Station with these guys.'

'How are you going to search out the murderous CAP followers in the police force?' asked Sienna.

'I have spoken to a contact in MI5 and he is coming here for further instruction from myself and the PM.'

'But wasn't that guy from MI5?' asked Joshua, pointing at the bound security policeman.

'No,' answered the chief constable. 'He was regular police.'

'How do you know that you can trust MI5?' Joshua questioned again.

'I'm convinced that my contact is OK,' replied Devonport. 'He's a confirmed atheist who won't even accept my own eye-witness accounts of Lucifer at Stonehenge. A profound sceptic. But he'll be convinced by the filed teeth of these two traitors.'

'So we wait,' concluded the PM, and then spoke to Joshua. 'You may as well put on the TV. Go ahead.'

*

The waiting in Hell was beginning to get me down and I was feeling hungry and thirsty. I had no idea what day it was or whether such concepts still applied. I was not really sure whether I was alive or had perhaps died and arrived in Hell the orthodox way. I sat down on the floor of the huge throne room and the others did likewise. I continued to contemplate my predicament. We had fallen off the smashed Bifrost Bridge into the gaping mouth of

Hell. It had looked like a volcano crater as we had fallen towards it but I had blacked out so did not know what happened on arrival. Then I had awoken in the company of Vole, Ard and Harry but also, inexplicably, my dead mother-in-law. She had taken us to this room and here we waited around a large, sulphurous pit.

That about sums it up, I thought. *And still I'm waiting.*

'I won't say I'm sorry to keep you waiting,' came a loud voice. 'Because I'm not. But then of course I might like to lie to you and I would be happy to do so. Sorry to keep you waiting.'

The voice came from a charming but sinister figure in a white dinner jacket and matching trousers. I recognised him despite the alteration in appearance. This was Lucifer.

'The only consolation I can give you,' said the figure, pausing for effect. 'Is that there is no consolation in Hell..... and that is where you are. In my domain.'

'What do you want with us Lucifer?' I asked.

'Want?' queried the frightening but strangely attractive man. 'Want from you?'

He then laughed out loud, looked around the throne room and spoke again. 'I don't need anything from you. The real question is what do you want from me?'

'We arrived by accident,' replied Vole. 'And we don't want anything from you.'

'Tell me another one,' said the Devil. 'I might just believe it. The bigger the lie the easier it is to believe.'

'She's telling the truth,' I stated baldly. 'We fell from the Bifrost Bridge.'

'You, Lord James Michael Scott, otherwise known as Jimmy fell, by sheer chance, into my domain. You Jimmy boy, the only creature to have dealt me physical pain in one thousand years, fell into my domain in the powerful company of Thor, Heimdall and Freya,' added Satan, Lucifer, the Devil.

'That's right. They were on the bridge when it collapsed,' I

replied.

'It didn't just collapse, old boy,' said the suave hell dweller. 'You collapsed it. You broke it.'

'Yes, we did do that,' I agreed. 'Or at least Thor did.'

'That's right,' said Lucifer. 'My dear brother broke the bridge with his mystic hammer Mjolnir to prevent incursion into Asgard by the Ice Giants and now I am supposed to fight Heimdall to mutual assured destruction.'

'Your brother?' queried Ard. 'How can Thor be your brother?'

'So the werewolf speaks,' said Lucifer. 'Because, my dear human form of a lycanthrope, I am also called Loki. The evil and mischievous Norse god.'

'You can't be 'is brother 'cos 'e was an estate agent until a couple of weeks ago,' laughed Harry. 'Unless I am very much mistaken.'

'Which of course you are, my old cock sparrow,' said Lucifer, alias Loki. 'He is the reincarnation of Thor and is already beginning to regain his memories. Which, unfortunately, include a considerable hatred of myself.'

'We had no desire to enter your realm,' I replied. 'That happened because we broke the bridge.'

'Then why didn't you break the bridge nearer to Asgard so that you wouldn't fall into Hell?' demanded Lucifer. 'You could have fallen back into Valhalla and still broken the bridge.'

Will he accept sheer incompetence? I wondered. Certainly I had never thought of moving closer to Valhalla.

'And I can see that you still have strapped to your waist the sword that bit me,' noted Lucifer. 'What a surprising coincidence.'

'I'm sorry,' I said as honestly as I could. 'We were not picking a fight with you. I did not even realise that you were both Lucifer and Loki.'

'The similarity of the name didn't occur to you?' asked Lucifer, incredulously. 'Loki and Luci. Or that I am the god of evil in all religions? That didn't occur to you either?'

'Not really,' I replied.

'Perhaps a little torture would loosen your tongue,' suggested Lucifer.

'It's pretty loose already,' I replied. 'It is just that I had never really given you two thoughts before you decided to try and sacrifice my innocent children. Which you were only stopped from doing by my mother-in-law.'

'Who is a witch,' added Vole. I looked at her with some trepidation.

'Yes, she is a witch,' added Lucifer. 'She is my witch. The bitch, as you called her, is mine now and I intend keeping it that way. You, with your powerful friends and biting swords, will not be allowed to stop me.'

✴

"There are reports from the United Nations that Secretary General Vesteymann has died in a shoot out between religious fanatics and the security forces at the UN building in new York.

Our reporter at the scene is Becky Underwood."

"Gee, thank you Andrew. Extraordinary events at the UN building on a day of developing tension around the world. Early reports indicate that Iain Vesteymann died a hero fighting two intruders, names unknown. The Deputy Security General, Balbir Chaturvedi, is due to give a speech in the UN Council Chamber any minute now. We will take you there just after this message."

" Why buy Gibson's feet powder? Because Gibson's make only the best and your feet deserve only the best. Don't forget .... your feet are worth keeping."

'Typical American TV,' remarked the PM who had been

watching the screen with rapt attention. 'They cut away from the story just when the action starts and torture us with a ghastly, stupid advertisement. Give me the good old BBC any day.'

'Shall I switch channels, sir?' asked Joshua, worried that his choice was annoying Macaroon.

'No, no. Leave it on. We might miss Chaturvedi's speech if we turn it over,' came the PM's reply.

Chapter 20

Could it be that Lucifer is actually fond of my mother-in-law? I wondered. *He certainly obeyed her at Stonehenge. He could still be besotted by her. Was that possible?*

'I shall invite Thor, Freya and Heimdall to come in here and then consider throwing you into the pit, one by one, until someone cracks,' Lucifer laughed.

'You'd be wasting your time,' shouted Vole. 'You are just a fool. A powerful fool but a fool nevertheless.'

'You shall go first,' said Lucifer. 'I will fetch the three godlings so contemplate your fate whilst I am gone.'

We sat down and waited for his return. Every few minutes a wild shriek and a horrifying cry would come from the pit and a puff of smoke would issue forth. The pit flickered with a red light and the smell of brimstone was almost overpowering. None of us had ventured to look into the hole due to the foul emanations.

After perhaps as long as an hour Lucifer returned with the three Norse gods. They were bound up and were being carried by enormous scaly demons.

The demons, taking their cue from Lucifer, showed the gods to the four of us and then walked over and casually threw our struggling companions into the pit.

The shrieking continued and Lucifer stood and questioned us again.

'So you see, resistance is futile. So tell me all you know and why you are here?'

He sounds like a Nazi left over from a cheap war film, I thought *He'll be saying next that he has ways of making us talk.*

'You really are wasting your time,' said Vole. 'We had no

intention of landing here and throwing our friends into your abyss doesn't win you any admirers.'

Lucifer went completely berserk. He burst out of his white suit and turned into a huge dragon-like creature and then into a snake.

The worm from the Garden of Eden, I pondered. *I wonder what other manifestations he has.*

'Asss I promisssed,' hissed the snake. 'You are next.'

'Stop, stop,' I shouted, holding up my hands imploringly. 'Please stop. Don't hurt Vole. I have thought of something.'

'Sssso,' the snake whispered. 'He ssspeaks up rather than sssee hisss girlfriend thrown into my pit. What issss your sssecret?'

'I don't know that it is a secret,' I replied. 'But I do know what or who is behind the new church on Earth and Ragnarok.'

'That I know already,' hissed the serpent. 'It isssss the ice giantsss.'

'But what's behind the ice giants?' I asked. 'Who leads them on?'

'Nothing and nobody,' replied Lucifer, reverting to his humanoid aspect, once again beautifully clothed but this time in expensively tailored black leathers. 'They have always existed and always been the enemy of the Aesir.'

'Now that is where I can help you,' I started to say.

'....You? Help me?' sneered Lucifer.

'Yes,' I said. 'Because this time there is someone or something motivating the ice giants.'

'Tell me more,' ordered Lucifer, who was now sitting, or more correctly lounging, on his enormous throne.

'His name is Dagon or Baal and he is an ancient god,' I answered.

'How do you know this, petty mortal, when even I do not?' asked Lucifer who had flicked into a Loki appearance, in which form he looked much like Thor but with black hair and beard.

'Via your supposed nemesis, a god who is your equal,' I

replied.

'If you mean Heimdall, I have thrown him into the pit,' sneered Loki. 'He is not my equal. He has failed.'

'Maybe for now,' I replied. 'But it was he who detected the god behind the latest Ragnarok.'

'Dagon? Baal?' mused Loki. 'I recall the names but only just. This will require thought.'

The lord of Hell looked down the room at the four of us and then glanced into his pit. A large smile played across his face and he vanished from sight.

*

'The Deputy Security General, Balbir Chaturvedi, gave a very short speech in the UN Council Chamber and we will hear what he said in just a moment. This is Becky Underwood reporting live from the United Nations Headquarters on Manhattan Island, New York, New York.'

'So we did miss the speech whilst the advertisements were on,' fumed the British Prime Minister. 'Turn it over to BBC.'

Joshua duly obliged, turning the television to the 24-hour BBC News Channel. A reporter was standing in front of a flooded street in Somerset and talking about the change in the weather due to global warming. Flickering across the bottom of the screen, rather like the old ticker tape, were various inconsequential, unrelated snippets of news. The Archbishop of Canterbury was seeking an audience with the Pope. The Queen was not keen on him going. Chelsea had beaten Arsenal in a local Derby. A man had fallen into a large hole in a Derby road after chasing a ram.

Then suddenly the messages across the bottom changed . BREAKING NEWS. SIEGE AT DOWNING STREET. PRIME MINISTER HELD HOSTAGE BY TEENAGE BRISTOL POLICE MURDERER. DEPUTY PM ALSO BELIEVED TO BE HOSTAGE. UNCONFIRMED REPORTS OF LOCAL CHIEF CONSTABLE ASSISTING THE MURDERER. BREAKING NEWS. SIEGE AT

DOWNING STREET...........

Maxwell Devonport, the Scotts and Darcy Macaroon looked on in horror. The two captives laughed, Sidney Fence almost choked as he did so, due to his gag.

'Fence told you that you were on the wrong side,' said the bound injured policeman. 'This place is probably completely surrounded now by our own people. The police force is dominated by CAP followers.'

'Don't be ridiculous,' countered Devonport. 'I'd be surprised if more than one or two percent believed in that rubbish.'

'The Church of Armageddon Prophets have taken over the Freemasons,' replied the policeman. 'That's how we've done it. The Masons were just perfect for the Church.'

'Yes,' growled Devonport. 'I can understand that. The Masons were always damned credulous.'

'I still don't see how a new church can become so powerful in such a short space of time,' said the Prime Minister. 'Even if the realities have been clashing and supernatural powers are real.'

He looked mystified and concluded. 'Not that I've seen any myself.'

'They're real enough,' said Devonport. 'As the Scotts can tell you having been at Stonehenge when Lucifer tried to kill them. I was also there, by the way.'

'We've seen the power of our own God,' said the captive policeman. 'And the Armageddon Prophets will be here soon to finish you off.'

'I'll see if the police are at the front yet,' said Sienna to Maxwell Devonport. 'You better keep away from the windows in case they recognise you. I doubt if they know who I am.'

Sienna ran through from the flat and looked out of a first floor corridor window. She counted six police cars and saw a dozen policemen outside close to the building and more than ten in the road, some in combat uniforms. Just entering the road were two television outside broadcasting vans. She ran back to the Prime Minister's private quarters.

'There are nearly twenty policemen outside,' she told the company. 'Possibly soldiers too and a couple of TV vans.'

'How do we go through to the back?' Devonport asked the PM.

'Through the link corridors on each level,' Macaroon replied, pointing the way. 'But why are they not inside already? And how come the TV knew about it so soon?'

'It would seem that my contact in MI5 was not as reliable as I thought,' said Devonport wryly. 'I told him that I was armed. That might be a reason why they have not simply broken in.'

The bound policeman laughed.

'Your man in MI5, Sir George Frampton, is one of the CAP leaders. You've got to face it Devonport, you're finished.'

'That's yet to be seen,' replied Devonport. 'What I am surprised about is that my driver hasn't radioed or telephoned me.'

Sienna returned from looking out of a window at the back of Number 10.

'Just as many police there,' she reported. 'Doesn't look as if we can escape that way.'

'Is there any other way out?' Devonport asked Macaroon.

'There is but it is classified information,' replied the Prime Minister. 'Only those with top level clearance are permitted to know about it.'

'Do the police know?' asked Sienna. 'Because if they do they will have sealed that off as well.'

'MI5 must know,' replied the PM. 'But whether they have the right codes is another matter.'

'Why is that?' asked Devonport.

'I had them all changed after our government was reinstated,' answered Macaroon. 'After the Stonehenge incident I got a private security firm to change all the codes on all the doors. Not even Fence here knows about the codes. Probably doesn't know where the doors are or where they lead to either.'

'So where do they lead and who does know?' asked the chief constable.

'Come into the bathroom, you and Mrs. Scott,' said the PM. 'And I'll tell you. Don't want Fence or that policeman to hear in case he gets loose again.'

The three walked into the small bathroom and shut the door. The bound policeman had started struggling with his bindings so Joshua picked up a bottle from the sideboard.

'If you think that this is a chance to escape,' he said in as menacing tone as he could muster. 'Think again. You see this bottle of wine in my hand?' The policeman nodded. 'I shall smash it down on your head if you don't stop wriggling.... and consider this if you think that I won't do it. I'm the teenager that they are calling the police murderer... So I've got nothing to lose by bashing you. In fact I would rather enjoy it.'

Both of the prisoners became completely still.

*

'I'm confused,' said Habakuk. 'I thought that Judaism didn't really include heaven and hell yet when I half-jokingly said that the seventh heaven was also the Bosom of Abraham you agreed. How can these things be so?'

'How can any of this be so?' replied Saint Paul. 'Is this a physical place in the same way as Earth?'

'No,' answered Habakuk. 'It sometimes feels as if it is but it can't be, can it?'

'No,' replied Saint Paul. 'It is a spiritual realm in eternity. These things can all happen in the same place because in heaven time is no more.'

'So anything can be anywhere if there is no time?'

'Not quite, dear Habakuk, not quite. May I give you an analogy? An allegorical parallel?'

'Please do,' replied Habakuk.

'If heaven is a sea and we are the waves there are many shores but just one sea. To each shore the sea feels as if it belongs to that beach and that the waves were made just for that beach and the beach was made just for those waves,' said Saint Paul. 'But the sea is universal and the waves may lap onto many beaches. Does that help?'

'I don't think so,' said Habakuk after contemplating the analogy. 'I find it easier to think that this is the Christian heaven and all the rest of the people here are just deluded.'

'So does St. Peter, I think,' said the diminutive saint, sighing. 'Perhaps that is why you were getting on with him so well.'

✱

'What happened to the doctors?' asked Joshua when the Prime Minister led Chief Constable Devonport and Sienna Scott out of the cramped bathroom.

'Good lord!' exclaimed the chief constable. 'I forgot all about them.'

'Fence dismissed them and another policeman led them away,' replied the PM. 'Where they are now I have no idea.'

'They have the evidence that you were being poisoned,' said Devonport. 'I doubt if the Church of Armageddon Prophets followers will allow them out of their sight. They're probably incarcerated somewhere.'

'If they're still alive,' said the PM, wryly.

'Wouldn't the laboratory have the information too?' asked Joshua.

'The followers will have been there too, I imagine,' retorted Devonport. 'It seems these religious madmen are everywhere.'

'We are and we'll easily deal with you,' said the bound policeman, cutting in on the conversation.

'You can keep quiet, my lad, if you want to live,' said Devonport, drawing his gun again. 'We are going to have to move quickly and if you are a nuisance I will have to shoot you again. I've seen what you people are capable of and I am happy to shoot any of you without a qualm. I'm going to untie the legs of both of you and take you with us. Your arms will still be bound up and I will gag you. If you try to run or make any noise I will shoot. '

'Go ahead and shoot,' said the policeman. 'We want to die and join the assault on heaven. Our god demands it.'

'It's not going to work,' said Sienna. 'They'll slow us up and purposely make a noise. And you can't shoot them without drawing attention to ourselves.'

'So it's plan B then?' asked Devonport.

'Go ahead and do it,' commanded the Prime Minister. 'Bind them up even tighter and gag them really well then push them under my double bed. They'll get out eventually but with a bit of luck we will be long gone.'

'OK. The decision is made. B for Binding here we come,' said the chief constable as he knelt down and wound more strips of bedding round the two captive CAP followers.

*

I stood up and, bracing myself against the onslaught of foul fumes, walked over and looked down into the pit. In the flickering gloom I could see coruscating red light in a huge fathomless void. I could see no sign of the gods.

'Our best chance is to jump into the pit before he returns,' I concluded after deliberating over the options.

'Won't that be taking a case of jumping from the frying pan into the fire almost too literally?' asked Ard in his beautiful Eton-style of English delivery. He also stared into the pit with me.

'Step back,' I replied, pushing him back with my hand.

We all stood back from the edge and there was a terrible shriek followed by a burst of smoke and evil fumes shooting up from the mouth of the pit.

'How did you know that was going to happen just then?' asked Ard.

'I timed it,' I replied. 'My watch is not working so I used my pulse as a timer. Just like Galileo did in the church timing the pendulum.'

'And the bursts of smoke are regular?' asked Vole.

'Yes and the accompanying shrieking,' I replied, triumphantly. 'So I reckoned it was all flim flam. Fake.'

'But the pit is real,' argued Harry. 'Either that or it is a bloody good 'ologram.'

'That's exactly what I think it is,' I concurred. 'A large hologram. A projection. Not a real volcanic pit at all.'

'But why?' asked Vole. 'This really is Hell so why have a fake pit? Why fake a volcanic crater?'

'That's what I intend finding out,' I replied. 'So anybody else coming with me? It can't be worse than falling off the Rainbow Bridge.'

I crouched down ready to jump into the frightening void once more. Harry instantly joined me.

'Can't 'urt me, can it?' he said. 'I'm already dead!'

Vole and Ard readied themselves also.

'It's a stupid idea,' said Vole. 'But no worse than any of your other plans and I've followed all of those.'

'What if you are wrong and it really is a volcano?' asked Ard.

'Then we land in the lava just a bit quicker than if we wait for Lucifer and his henchmen to throw us in,' I replied.

'OK,' agreed Ard. 'As long as there are no silver bullets involved I'm with you.'

'Right. On the count of three,' I cried. 'One, two, three. Jump.'

And we jumped.

Chapter 21

The Prime Minister led the company down by a small back staircase. This was out of sight from the grand front hall and led to another set of steps down into the basement.

'Now that we have left Fence and the security policeman behind I am happy to let your children also know where we are going,' said the PM.

'Where *are* we going Mr. Macaroon?' asked Samuel who had been keeping very quiet, feeling rather frightened by the changing events.

'Into the secret tunnels of London,' explained Darcy Macaroon. 'They were commissioned during the Blitz and link up Downing Street with Buckingham Palace and with Pindar.'

'I've heard of Pindar before,' said Joshua. 'I think I saw a question about it on QI. Isn't it a big bunker under the Ministry of Defence?'

'Clever boy,' remarked Macaroon. 'That's right. There are also several other tunnels joined to it. So that is where we are heading.'

'What if the horrible prophets are there already?' asked Sam. 'What do we do then?'

'I don't really know,' replied Macaroon. 'But we may be about to find out.'

The Prime Minister stretched his hand out and entered a code into a small pad on a low door. He then swung the portal open and they stepped into one of the most sequestered places in London. The secret tunnel from 10 Downing Street, dark, cold and smelling slightly damp, stretched out in front of them.

★

Saint Paul led Habakuk back to Simon Peter. The rugged rock of the early church was still busy playing Bagatelle.

'I just beat my best score,' Peter chortled with delight to the small, serious saint. 'I scored five in 125. I've never done that before.'

'Fine,' replied Saint Paul, 'That's very good. Business at the gate not very busy?'

'Nobody can get in,' said the rock. 'But listen to this. I got a total of 1700 from twenty balls!'

Habakuk was impressed but Saint Paul just nodded his head slightly and his smile was just a little forced.

'What do you think we should do about the problems at the gate?' he asked Simon Peter.

'Do?' queried the rock. 'We can't do anything until His Nibs gets here. No, nothing to do. But I can still improve on my score.'

'Sure you can,' said Saint Paul. 'You could pick them all up and stuff them straight into the 125. I reckon you could pack all twenty in there and get a score of two thousand five hundred.'

'What would be the fun in that?' asked Simon Peter. 'That would be cheating!'

Saint Paul, also known as Saul of Tarsus, looked at Saint Peter with a fond smile and sighed a deep sigh.

*

We fell a distance of about nine or ten feet, the height of a fairly decent room, and we landed on a carpeted floor. Thor, Freya and Heimdall were already there struggling with their bonds. Ard and Vole were the quickest to recover from their fall and ran over to the gods to untie them, followed promptly by Harry. The bonds were very tight but when I also was able to help I made short work of them with my Elfin sword, Morning Star.

'Why do you think they let you keep the sword,' asked Vole.

'The same reason that I still have my sword, Thor has his hammer and Freya her axe,' answered Heimdall. 'The weapons are magical and Loki would be damaged by touching them.'

'He would not even be able to lift my hammer,' explained Thor.

'It responds only to one with a noble heart,' added Freya, patting Thor on the back as she said it.

'Maybe the time has come for my final fight with the god of mischief,' suggested Heimdall. 'It has been a long time coming and I suppose if it must be, it must be.'

We all look at him in dismay. The outcome of the fight was supposedly predetermined. They both lost.

'That really is the point,' came the cultured voice of Lucifer, alias Loki. 'Does it have to be? I'm inclined to think not. Which is why I have been treating you so well.'

'Treating us well, brother?' asked Thor, looking around for the evil sibling. 'Dost thou think that gassing us and then binding us like hogs constitutes good hospitality and treatment worthy of the gods?'

Lucifer laughed.

'Listen to you, brother. You are already beginning to sound like the last incarnation of Thor, full of noble wind and indignation and what is more,' Lucifer strode into the room and continued his sentence. 'I do indeed think that I have treated you well.'

Heimdall stood up and started to increase his size, doubling, trebling. Out through the hologram his head and torso projected and into the throne room.

'Now try to treat me your form of "well", puny god!' echoed Heimdall's challenge.

'I don't think so,' Lucifer turned. 'Mary, you come and explain it to them!'

My mother-in-law entered the area below the throne room.

'I certainly will, dear, if Freya can persuade Heimdall to reduce his aspect to that of a mortal. It will make my neck ache looking at him the size he is right now.'

'OK,' agreed Freya. 'Heimdall!'

'Yes Freya.'

'So that we can have a sensible discussion with this lady could you reduce down to mortal scale again, please?'

'And be attacked by Loki in my weakened form? I think not.'

'Just for me?' asked Freya.

Heimdall paused and then replied hesitantly. 'OK. Against my better judgment.'

Is this wise? I thought. *At least if Heimdall is in his full god aspect he has an equal chance against Lucifer but now he is going to reduce himself and we may all be endangered. Is it the right thing to do*

*

The tunnel lights automatically turned on as the Prime Minister led the fugitives under Downing Street and towards the nerve centre beneath the Ministry of Defence.

'We're heading north for just a hundred yards at most,' explained the PM. 'Then we branch off and into the Pindar complex.'

'And this tunnel continues to where?' asked Sienna.

'Straight to the palace. Buckingham Palace, that is, abode of the Queen,' replied Macaroon.

'Will we go and see if she is alright?' asked Samuel, excited at the prospect.

'No. She isn't there old chap,' answered Macaroon in a friendly tone. 'She is at Windsor Castle. The last time I spoke to her she said that she had no intention of coming into central London until all this religious fervour had died down a bit.'

'She hasn't joined CAP then?' asked Joshua. 'It would be awful if she had joined them.'

'No,' replied the PM. 'She told me that they are a bunch of dangerous lunatics. She was the person who persuaded me to send your father over to America to investigate them.'

They walked on in silence for a few more yards and then turned into a very short tunnel that led them to the door of the underground defence complex. The Prime Minister thought for a few moments and then typed in the new code.

The door swung open. This door was not like that in the basement of Downing Street. It was a much larger and more impressive structure. Joshua looked at it with appreciation. This was some door!

'It's a very strong blast door,' explained the PM. 'It's a composite construction forty centimetres thick with steel plate on both sides, concrete in the middle. I've seen all the specifications.'

The Prime Minister spoke as if the building of the underground hideaway had been all his own idea although, in fact, the complex had been finished well before his time in office. He led the party into the side room and thence to the central control area.

The lights in the main room of the complex were already shining brightly before they even entered the area. Sat at the main control desk was a distinguished looking gentleman in a grey suit, his silver hair combed back in a Tarzan Heseltine style. He was busy dictating a letter to a secretary sitting to his left. As the party walked in the man heard the slight noise they made opening the door. He looked up and half-smiled, almost a sneer.

'Good day lady and gentlemen,' he glanced around to a few other personnel in the room and gave a command to them. 'Close all the doors please. Thank you. As I was saying, good day Prime Minister, hello Maxwell and welcome Scott family sans father Jimmy. I've been expecting you.' He glanced at his watch. 'You are a little later than I anticipated but only about five minutes.'

Damn, thought Maxwell Devonport. *MI5 did know the codes. That is Sir George Frampton and supposedly he is one of the Church leaders.*

'It's simple really,' said Mary, speaking in the most reasonable tones that I had heard her ever use, thus belying my thoughts that she was more of a witch than ever. 'Lucien wants to sit this one out.'

'What do you mean "sit this one out"?' asked Thor . 'It's not a game of cards or a round of golf. This is Ragnarok, Gotterdammerung. Nobody just sits it out.'

'But that is what he wants to do,' said Mary calmly. 'And I agree with him. The endless cycles of destruction are ridiculous.'

She's got something there, I thought to myself. *Why does it have to work like the prophecy predicts?*

'If that which is foretold does not happen,' stated Heimdall. 'Time will stand still and all will cease to be.'

'Who says?' asked Mary. 'On whose evidence-based authority do we have that nugget of wisdom?'

'I say,' intoned Heimdall. 'I, the ever watchful keeper of the Bifrost Bridge say and I know.'

'And yet the ever watchful keeper has not prevented the Bridge being destroyed this time or any time before,' replied Mary. 'Am I right.'

'It is so,' replied Heimdall. 'And each time when Ragnarok was called Loki and I have fought to the death.'

'And each time you have both died,' added Mary. 'Well this time he is not going to fight.'

'The coward!' Heimdall cried scornfully. 'The craven coward!'

'Of course,' agreed Mary. 'But he doesn't care what you call him. He does not intend getting involved. He is not going to storm Asgard, Heaven, Seventh Heaven, Paradise, Valhalla, Elysian Fields, Earth, Sheol, Faerie, Hades or anywhere. He is just not going to do it. Period. Full stop.'

'That won't make Ragnarok just go away,' interrupted Freya, the Fairy Godmother and Goddess of Love, War and Death. 'Others will fight the battles.'

'We know that but the outcome may be different. What is more Lucien, or Loki as you call him, will give you any information you require whilst not getting directly involved himself,' stated Mary.

'What has made him change his mind?' asked Vole.

'Love,' replied Mary.

'Love?' queried Heimdall. 'The god of mischief has changed his mind for love?'

'That's right,' said Mary, planting her self squarely in front of the watchful god. 'Is there something about that which you do not like?'

'No,' replied Heimdall hesitantly. 'No. I suppose not. It's just so out of character. The god of evil doing something for love.'

'OK then. Call it lust if you must,' said Mary.

'Lust?' said Heimdall, brightening up. 'Now that I understand. Many things are done for lust.'

*

Habakuk looked round at the group of saints sitting near Saint Peter. They all had very benign expressions on their faces. Some he thought he recognised from the Old Testament, the Jewish scriptures. Standing near the back was a semi-clad figure who looked more ancient than all the rest.

Is that Methuselah? thought Habakuk. *The oldest man who ever lived?*

Habakuk took another, closer look. The man's midriff was bare and Habakuk noticed with a shock that this fellow was not like any other human being he had seen. The skin of his abdomen was completely smooth. He had no navel, no belly button! There was no sign of an umbilicus at all. He also had a scar over his lower chest.

This must be Adam thought Habakuk. *Directly created out of the clay and then had a rib removed, hence the scar. According to the Bible Adam died at the age of nine hundred and thirty. So he was almost as old as Methuselah and he was definitely more ancient. I can see why he bares his midriff. It's a badge of office.*

Habakuk observed the rest of the group. There was Methuselah, long white beard looking even older than Adam, but not as ancient, not as much like the noble savage. There was Eve, still eating an apple, and David, playing a lyre. Habakuk recognised the shepherd king from the inspired sculpture by Michelangelo. Just as handsome and just as poorly endowed. A couple of ruddy looking men clad in gowns were playing with a fishing net down by the river and Habakuk assumed they were apostles. Then in a gaggle of haloed saints he noted Saint George in shining armour, Sebastian, still with an arrow through his neck, Francis talking to some animals, Saint Agnes of Rome carrying a lamb, Simon Templar looking one minute like Roger Moore and then the next like a stick man with a halo.

Habakuk felt moved to ask Saint Paul about Simon Templar.

'Can you see The Saint?' asked Habakuk, pointing towards Templar.

'Which one?' asked the small, serious saint. 'I can see several dozen saints in that direction and hundreds more elsewhere.'

'You know what I mean. *The* Saint ... Simon Templar.'

'Yes. I see him,' agreed Saint Paul.

'He's a fictional character,' protested Habakuk. 'He doesn't exist!'

'You have a problem with that?' asked Saint Paul.

'How can a fictional character get into Heaven?' asked Habakuk. 'He never existed!'

'Do you think all the other characters are real?' asked Saint Paul. 'Saint George, who fought dragons. Did he really exist?'

'He may have done,' Habakuk replied. 'I think he was a centurion.'

'That one?' asked St. Paul pointing to a saint with a human body but dog head.

'Is he from Egypt?' asked Habakuk.

'No,' replied the saint. 'He is Saint Christopher the dog head. But if you want Egyptian gods I can oblige. Just look behind you.'

Habakuk turned round and saw a huge mass of gods with

animal heads. Saint Paul pointed out who they were.

'Horus with head of a hawk, Thoth, head of Ibis, Anubis, jackal headed, Bastet with head of a cat.'

'Enough, enough,' said Habakuk. 'They are just foreign saints and gods. I expect there is an elephant headed god or saint somewhere. They are just foreign concepts.'

'OK,' replied Saint Paul. 'What about that chap?'

The serious saint pointed to a fat figure in red gown, matching red trousers and a hood edged with fur, sporting a beard and carrying a big sack over his shoulder.

'That's Santa Claus,' replied Habakuk.

'So do you still believe in Father Christmas?' asked Saint Paul.

'I didn't until I landed up here,' retorted Habakuk. 'But I do now. He is Saint Nicholas.'

'Why is he wearing a red gown?' asked Saint Paul.

'That's what he always wears,' replied Habakuk.

'But he used to wear green clothes and was tall and skinny,' said the small saint.

'But people prefer red and fat people are jolly,' Habakuk protested.

'Exactly!' exclaimed Saint Paul. 'Does that tell you anything?'

'I'm sure it should,' said Habakuk. 'But I'm not sure what.'

'Heaven does not like to disappoint,' replied Saint Paul.

Chapter 22

Maxwell Devonport had drawn his gun before entering the large underground room and he now fiercely stared at Sir George Frampton.

'I'm armed as you see, George, and I'm not afraid to use this gun,' he said to his old colleague who he had been told was now an Armageddon Prophets' leader.

'Do put it away, Maxwell,' sighed Frampton. 'We're all friends here.'

'That's not what we've been told, George,' countered Devonport. 'I understand that you are a leader of the new Church and I know that they are our enemy.'

'Right on both counts, Maxwell,' nodded George Frampton. 'Classic case of infiltration at the highest level possible. I am an agent, Maxwell, as you well know. When the chance came I was in like Flynn.'

'Did it require female conquest?' asked Devonport, marginally confused by the turn of phrase.

'Actually yes,' preened Frampton. 'I seduced the female leader of the North European branch of CAP. Quite a beautiful lady, in fact.'

'So where are your allegiances now, George?' asked Devonport. 'With the girl and the CAP followers or with us and the sane, silent majority?'

'The girl died with the first wave of suicides,' replied Frampton. 'Nothing I could say or do persuaded her to change her mind.'

'And your teeth?' asked Sienna. 'Are you another closet cannibal. A religious Hannibal Lectern?'

'All my own,' smiled the MI5 man, pointing to a set of pristine natural teeth. 'Didn't let anybody touch them and I have become a strict vegan. Nothing persuades you to become a vegetarian quite so quickly as seeing your own beloved eating the flesh of herself and her friends. Gross in the extreme I can assure you.'

'So what are you doing here?' asked the chief constable.

'Waiting for you, Maxwell,' replied Frampton. 'You called and I knew that the proverbial had hit the fan, so to speak. All hell was about to break loose. So I gathered the few I could trust and came down into the underground bunker complex.'

'But how did you know the codes?' enquired the Prime Minister. 'I hired a private security firm to change them all for me. How did you get the numbers?'

'That was easy, sir,' replied Frampton. 'That private firm you hired is one of mine. I'm proud to say that I own it.'

*

'So what does the Devil say we should do about the present predicament?' I asked Mary. 'And how come you are not in Heaven? That's where you said you wanted to go.'

'I'll answer the second question first,' replied Mary. 'After you've answered my question. Where did you pick your girlfriend up?'

'Bitch!' exclaimed Vole.

'Easy Vole,' I cautioned. 'Vole and I met in New York and she is not my girlfriend.'

'Timid creature out of love,' said Mary. 'She is a walking, talking crossword clue and the love she desires is yours.'

'Mary,' I said. 'You are upsetting Vole and myself. It is unjust and unfair. We have not been lovers.'

'How did she know my slogan?' asked Vole, crying quietly. 'How?'

'You're in Hell, marriage breaker,' said Mary. 'It's not a nice place and we can see all your hidden carnal desires.'

'Mary,' I said firmly. 'We have had enough of this. I answered your question so please do me the favour of answering mine in return.'

'OK,' said Mary in her nice tone again, her personality switching as fast as a logic gate. 'I am in Hell because I chose to come here and Lucifer will appear soon and discuss options and outcomes with you. It will surely be useful in your fight against the enemies of the Aesir.'

'Don't believe her,' cried Thor. 'She is talking about Loki and he is a master of deception and illusion. He will lie to you just for the sake of it. He is never truthful.'

'Never?' I queried. 'Are you sure.'

'Definitely and this, his consort, will be the same.'

'Oh I know her,' I answered. 'She is my mother-in-law, after all.'

'Was, darling,' replied Mary. 'There is no taking or giving in marriage at the resurrection. It says so in the supposedly good book.'

'I'm not resurrected,' I replied. 'I haven't died yet.'

'Are you really sure of that?' asked Mary, her personality switching back to that of bitch queen. 'You've been judged by the scales of truth and you are now in Hell. What makes you think that you have not already died?'

*

'I'm still puzzling about your analogy,' said Habakuk to Saint Paul. 'If we are the waves then we all wash up on different shores. Are you saying that we are all washed up?'

'In Heaven there is no time. Everything is happening now. We are the waves still in the sea. Not on the beach,' said Saint Paul.

'But why should that make us happy?' asked Habakuk.

'Because we are what we wish to be,' said the small, serious saint.

'So why is that woman looking so unhappy?' asked the ex-priest of the Church of Armageddon Prophets, pointing to a dowdy female who was scurrying around, dusting under the saints' feet.

'That's Martha. She always likes to be busy and to seem unhappy,' explained Saul of Tarsus. 'That is her sole happiness.'

'But she is dusting away when the place is spotless,' said Habakuk. 'She doesn't need to dust.'

'I believe you would call it Obsessive Compulsive Disorder,' suggested Saint Paul. 'That's what a psychiatrist told me once.'

'A dead psychiatrist,' said Habakuk.

'Resurrected,' replied Saint Paul.

A little cheer went up from the group watching Saint Peter play Bagatelle.

'He's got a new personal best, I expect,' groaned Saint Paul. 'We better go and congratulate him.'

'Why do some of the people in heaven have haloes and some not?' asked Habakuk.

'The ones with haloes are saints and the others are just resurrected souls,' replied Saint Paul. 'The brighter the halo the more important the saint.'

'So why have I got a halo?' asked Habakuk. 'I certainly don't deserve to be a saint. I left the Christian Catholic church and joined the Armageddon Prophets. I tortured people to interrogate them. One or two. I wasn't even any good at torture and interrogation if the truth be told.'

'Which it always is, here in Heaven,' added the small, bald saint. 'Truth is always told.'

'So why am I a saint?' asked Habakuk. 'I saw the reflection of my halo in the crystal flowing waters.'

'Firstly, you wanted to be a saint, didn't you?' asked Saint Paul.

'Yes. Yes I did,' replied Habakuk hesitantly, reluctant to admit it.

'And secondly, you died a martyr. You were killed for the Church.'

'But it was the wrong church,' protested Habakuk. 'I still don't think that I deserve to be treated well.'

'I expect Simon Peter told you that those who think they are saints rarely are? And that people who think they deserve special treatment, rarely do?' asked Paul.

'He did say something like that,' agreed Habakuk.

'So just enjoy being a saint. You don't get special privileges except to wear the halo and speak to "His Nibs" occasionally,' said Paul. 'But now we really must congratulate Simon. He thrives on the attention.'

*

'So we're just supposed to trust you, are we?' asked the Prime Minister.

The MI5 man shrugged his shoulders. 'Take it or leave it, PM. I'm all you've got.'

'There must be more people out there who don't like these cannibals!' exclaimed the Queen's first minister. 'They can't all have been taken in by these Armageddon Prophets.'

'I don't know that being taken in is quite right, PM. With all due respect,' argued Sir George Frampton, the ex-leader of the Prophets. 'I've seen people die, be eaten and return. I've seen it with my own eyes.'

'So how come you now expect us to believe you?' asked Sienna. 'If you've seen all that why are you now on our side?'

'Are you kidding?' asked Sir George. 'I saw it with my own eyes but it was the most hideous thing I ever did see.... and they wanted to kill me and eat *my* flesh!'

'But why do you say that you are the only thing we have got?' asked Maxwell Devonport.

'Because the whole world is in turmoil out there and we are not in a particularly good position to stop it. The Prophets are on the move and they number in their millions just in the UK alone.'

'Millions? In the UK?' The PM found the figure hard to believe and looked round at the others in amazement. 'Surely not in their millions?'

'After the appearance of Lucifer at Stonehenge...' started Frampton.

'When he tried to kill Samuel and myself,' interrupted Joshua.

'That's correct. After the guest appearance of Lucifer and the activities of that elemental Parsifal X, it was easy to recruit people to a church that preached about the end of days,' the MI5 man finished his point and shrugged his shoulders again. 'I was there at Stonehenge. I poked a monstrous cyclops right in his one eye using my umbrella. He squealed like a stuck pig.'

Sir George looked quite pleased with himself as he turned back to the computer and communication complex. He then looked up again and waved his hands.

'Coffee is over there, milk and sugar too. When you are feeling refreshed we will talk.'

The group looked over to the refreshment area.

'It's strange how these MI5 chaps always think they are in charge,' commented the Prime Minister, sotto voce.

'I was thinking just exactly the same thing,' whispered Maxwell Devonport, in a very quiet reply. 'The trouble is that at the moment he actually *is* in charge.'

'We'll see about that,' said Darcy Macaroon. 'Just as soon as I have had a cup of some reviving brew.'

The Prime Minister led the fugitive party over towards the coffee and as he did so the radio crackled into life.

"....The outcome of the Siege of Downing Street is still in the balance. The Deputy PM has been saved, praise be to the Church of Armageddon Prophets...."

'So they found the traitorous Fence under my bed,' whispered the Prime Minister, quietly and they continued to listen to the radio broadcast.

"....The Prime Minister has not been found but sources close to the Right Honourable Sidney Fence ......"

'Right Honourable, my foot,' whispered the PM but was

shooshed by the others.

"....say that the PM has been murdered by the teenage police murderer, who has now been identified as Joshua Scott. Scott was one of the boys involved in the mass hysteria at Stonehenge. We will bring you more news as it occurs. Praise be to the Prophets..."

'At least you're famous!' said Samuel to his brother.

'Not for the right things though,' squeaked Joshua, his adolescent voice affected by emotion. 'They'll be trying to shoot me on sight!'

'The sooner we get this all sorted out the better,' said the chief constable.

'And I'm restored to life.' added Darcy Macaroon. 'I don't like being declared dead. Anybody can take a pot shot at me and then shoot the young Scott here and declare that Scott was the culprit. But first things first. Let's brew some coffee!'

✱

Lucifer appeared in his "smooth human" mode with just a whiff of sulphur. I looked at him closely.

"If you sup with the devil use a very long spoon", this ancient proverb went running through my head constantly as I pondered our situation. *This one is very tricky. How can we trust anything he says? Thor can't be right that everything Lucifer says is a lie. At Stonehenge Mary made Lucifer bind the elemental to save the integrities of the world and he had kept to his word. Perhaps he only does so when he is asked by a higher authority or someone or something that he already has a pact with? Or perhaps he always lies to Thor on some matter of warped principle?*

I decided to put this to the test.

'Would Lucifer mind if we took it in turns to ask him questions and sometimes ask questions with you as our representative?' I asked Mary.

Lucifer immediately spoke to Mary in his guttural language and she relayed the message.

'He does mind but he will cooperate,' she replied.

'Could you ask him if he has knowledge that can stop the Armageddon?' I asked and Mary relayed the question.

His reply to Mary was very short and in the same language that only she understood.

'His answer is no,' she retorted.

'Then what is the point of this conversation?' I asked, exasperated.

Again the devil, Lucifer, replied and this time he laughed and the answer was longer. Mary translated for him.

'He says that once started he cannot stop Armageddon but that the exact start of Armageddon is debatable. Armageddon is the final war of the Apocalypse and is unstoppable. Such a war seems presently imminent but could be put off for a thousand years or a thousand thousand years. Or perhaps even indefinitely.'

'Could I now ask Thor to enquire whether Armageddon has started?' I handed over to Thor who immediately asked Lucifer the question I had posed.

Lucifer responded in English.

'Ragnorak has started and all will be laid waste!'

'See,' stated Thor. 'He cannot be trusted. He says one thing to her and another to me.'

'It's confusing I admit,' I whispered to Thor. 'But let me try..... Lucifer!'

'Yes, he who bit my heel. What do you want?'

'Did I really bite your heel?'

'No,' replied Lucifer. 'You cut me with your elfin sword. So, what is your question?'

'Are Ragnarok and Armageddon one and the same?'

'Possibly not,' replied the devil. 'On all other occasions they have been synonymous but that is not a prerequisite. If I don't take part then Ragnarok may falter. It is an unknown.'

'Mary,' I directed the next question via my mother-in-law.

'Does Lucifer hate unknowns?'

'I shall ask,' she replied. 'But my own answer is that he detests them.'

She again talked to the devil in the unknown tongue.

Perhaps the native language of Hell? I asked myself.

'Knowledge is all that is left to him,' replied Mary having listened to Lucifer.

'What does he mean by "all that is left to him"?' asked Ard. 'He has this entire realm and he strides the Earth and Faerie wielding enormous power so why is knowledge all that he has left?'

'Do you want to ask him yourself or shall I?' enquired my dead mother-in-law, the witch.

'You ask, please,' I instructed Mary.

Once again she talked to Lucifer in the evil-sounding, incomprehensible language she had used before. Satan replied in the same guttural tones.

'He is willing to show you the reality of his situation. And, of course, yours,' replied Mary. 'But be prepared. It is not as you think and he can only show you that which you will comprehend. Then perhaps you can ask him more useful questions.'

She paused.

'But first you must consent to him showing you even that which you are capable of understanding.'

Mary looked at the group of us. The three Norse Gods... Thor, Freya and Heimdall. Harry, the blue-tinged ghost of a motorcycling cockney. Ard, the king of the werewolves. Vole, a beautiful native-American Shaman and, of course, myself. A simple electrician with an education in Physics and Cosmology.

'I have no qualms about agreeing to it. As long as the agreement holds no hidden clauses,' I replied.

Vole, Ard and Harry agreed immediately. Freya and Heimdall nodded their affirmative. But Thor stood firm.

'Always the god of deception will lie to me. What he will show me will be a lie,' said Thor.

'But even that lie may tell us something of value' I argued.

'How can I know whether I should see the supposed reality of this world or not?' asked Thor.

'Ask him whether you should agree to see it and whether it will further our cause,' I suggested.

'That I shall. It shall be so,' said Thor and he turned to the manifestation of Lucifer. 'Should I, Thor, agree to see the reality, Loki, god of mischief? Will seeing the reality further our cause?'

A huge rumbling laugh emanated from Lucifer and he replied.

'Of course you should not agree to see reality, Thor, over-powered neo-god of thunder,' came the roaring reply. 'And seeing such reality will irrevocably harm your cause and not help it in the least.'

Then the devil laughed again with his horrible, insistent laugh. A laugh that was far too powerful for the small figure in front of us.

'That's settled then,' I stated. 'We must see the situation in its entirety.'

'Wait, thou, for my decision,' countered the hammer-wielding god. 'Loki has admitted that I should not see his reality and that it will harm our cause.'

'But he always lies to you. That means we must,' I concluded. 'So you also must consent.'

'Yes,' agreed Thor, after thinking about this for a few fleeting moments. 'Thou art right. The noble Thor gives his assent.'

'Hold onto your stomachs,' interposed Mary. 'Here we go.'

*

'I feel surprisingly tired, all of a sudden,' announced Darcy Macaroon, having just swigged down two cups of coffee.

'I expect it's because you are relaxing having been on the run,' shouted Sir George Frampton gleefully from the other side of the room.

'No. It's more than that I.......'

He did not finish his sentence before slumping to the floor unconscious. Maxwell Devonport was already snoring. Sienna looked round wide eyed and furious.

'If you think that you can.....' she started to say but also fell in a heap.

Joshua Scott looked at the adults, gave out a large groan and fell on top of Devonport, gave a few twitches and then lay still. Samuel Scott looked round anxiously, grabbed at his head and fell next to his brother, also twitched a few times and then was completely motionless.

'That's put them out for a few minutes,' said Sir George Frampton, putting down next to him a glass of whisky that he had been sipping . 'Dempster, go over and tie them up securely then we will question them using the truth serum.'

'Certainly sir,' said the sidekick, rising from his desk.

'I'll help him,' announced Frampton's secretary, also standing up.

'Thank you Rebecca,' said Sir George as the two set off across the room leaving just himself and a man at the computers.

Chapter 23

There was a sudden lurch and instead of a comfortable room carpeted with red shag pile there was no floor, there were no walls and there was no ceiling .... not even a hologram.

I grabbed Vole and she also braced herself against Ard and Harry. Beneath us really was a huge, huge pit. It was too large for the human mind to take in and seemed to plunge downwards for ever. If we had not been warned to hold onto our stomachs I would have immediately vomited due to the vertigo induced by the giddying height. Poor Vole was instantly sick but since we had not eaten for some time she was mainly retching on bile. Mary just laughed at Vole's predicament.

'This is the reality,' she said, still laughing cruelly. 'Lucifer was simply being kind to our immortal souls. He is not always that way. In fact, very seldom is he kind.'

She stopped talking as we took in our situation. We appeared to be suspended by some kind of force field and there really was no solid substance beneath our feet or around us. Mary spoke again.

'Now look into the pit. Really stare hard into the mouth of oblivion. What do you see?'

I stared down into the red hot magma. I could feel the heat beating at me as I did so and the smell was almost completely overwhelming. I felt my gorge rise but I was determined not to let go.

'I see the pit,' I stated. 'And something moving slightly within it.'

'Try to focus on the movement.' said Mary. 'What is moving?'

'It looks like a huge worm or scaly snake,' I suggested.

'Or the worm that encircles the Earth, perhaps?' said the mighty

Thor, overawed by the size of the creature.

'How big is that thing?' asked Vole, having recovered considerably. 'It is far, far away but still looks large. ... And what is it?'

'It is many miles in length,' replied Mary. 'It is the serpent.'

'The serpent?' queried Vole. 'But it looks to be bound to something.'

'It is bound by iron to the centre of Hell,' stated Mary.

'If that is the serpent then it must be Lucifer,' I concluded.

'Well done, James,' said Mary sarcastically. 'As bright as ever. Yes, Lucifer is bound in Hell.'

'Then how come he was able to appear at Stonehenge?' I asked. 'We all saw him and I slashed my sword into his heel.'

'That was purely a manifestation of Satan,' replied Mary.

'If he is able to do that then he can walk the Earth and other realms,' argued Ard. 'I was right. He is not really bound here.'

'You are wrong. This is Lucifer's reality,' contradicted Mary. 'He can only appear elsewhere as a feeble manifestation of his true self and he can only do that when he is summoned and then only for a short time.'

'The legends say the devil is bound in hell so I suppose we should believe it,' I accepted reluctantly. 'But how can it further our cause?'

A great moan came up from the pit. A cry of anguish that would have broken the hardest heart. The beast in the pit was in terrible pain. I looked down in horror and this time I could see that the serpent was wounded. A huge split was apparent along the length of his body and blood, guts and gore were weeping from the cut.

'He's wounded!' I exclaimed.

'Yes,' agreed Mary. 'He is mortally wounded but he does not die.'

'How did that happen?' I asked. 'What could wound such a creature? Did I do it?'

'Not your little slash at his apparition at Stonehenge,' replied Mary. 'No. This wound was made by the original bearer of your sword.'

'Who was that?' I asked. 'Who did my sword belong to?'

'Your sword was forged millennia ago by the elves before humankind could even make stone spears,' answered Mary.

'For whom?' I asked, trembling with anxiety. Whose weapon was I carrying?

'You carry the Star of the Morning. Forged to cut Lucifer,' replied my mother-in-law.

'Yes,' I replied.

'..... It was forged for Saint Michael,' she continued. 'The most powerful of the archangels and the most warlike of all heaven's creatures.'

Bloody hell, I thought, *I must give it back to him. I don't want it.*

'Destiny has given it to you,' said Heimdall, perhaps hearing my subvocalisation. 'And when required you must wield it.'

The ever watchful god stared down into the pit and spoke again.

'What or who are those tiny creatures writhing in the fire and brimstone with the worm?'

'They are the souls of the damned,' replied Mary.

'But I can clearly see myself, yourself and, in fact, all of us!' exclaimed Heimdall.

'Yes,' replied my mother-in-law. 'Look at us writhe. We are actually in the pit with Lucifer it is just that we don't experience that fact at the moment.'

*

'Don't come any closer and drop any weapons you are holding,' shouted Joshua, springing up from the floor holding a gun.

Frampton laughed. 'You won't shoot,' wheezed the MI5 man. 'You probably don't even know how to take off the safety catch.'

Kapowww. A shot rang out and the glass exploded close to Frampton's elbow, shards flying in all directions accompanied by pale amber liquid.

'Perfect shot,' shouted Joshua, still recovering from the loudness of the retort in the confined space. 'I am indeed the person who killed the policeman in Bristol so the next one will be between your eyes unless you obey me!'

'You can't stop all four of us and we're not afraid to die,' replied Frampton. 'There's only the one of you. You may as well give up now.'

'I doubt if you really are happy to die,' answered Joshua. 'Or you would have had your teeth filed. I've been looking closely at you and those are your real teeth, not veneers.'

'We can still outmaneuver you,' said Sir George, signalling to his companions, all three of whom started to move around the room.

Joshua stood still, not quite sure what he should do and a shot rang out from a different gun. He looked in surprise at his younger brother who was now standing next to him, holding a smoking weapon.

'The chief constable had two guns, Josh,' explained Samuel. 'And that man on the far side had drawn a weapon so I had to shoot it out of his hand.'

'Sam, how the hell did you learn to shoot like that?' whispered Joshua, looking at the man clasping his bleeding hand.

'Using my latest Wii shooting game,' replied Sam. 'The one you told me was for cissies. It even features realistic recoil.' He paused then continued. 'Mind you, it's nowhere near as noisy. Those two shots were dreadful. My ears are ringing.'

They stood staring at their opponents.

'I want all four of you to lie down on the floor with your arms stretched out,' ordered Joshua. 'Do it now you bastards or sprout a third eye.'

All the three men and the female secretary obeyed him immediately.

'How did you like that command I gave them?' whispered Joshua to Sam.

'Awesome!' replied his brother.

'I got it from a film,' explained Joshua.

'What do we do with them now, Josh?'

'We find out if they have got an antidote for the poison they have given Mum,' replied the older brother. 'And if they haven't I really will kill them. All four of them. They deserve to die.'

*

'Do you pity me, neo-gods?' asked the huge worm in a voice that made my entire being shake with its reverberation. 'Do you see what has befallen the creature that once was equal to the Ancient of Days? Do you feel compassion?'

I looked at this monster, the immortal being that had tried to sacrifice my sons to give himself more power and despite myself, I could not help but feel sorry for his plight. If I was in such a situation maybe I would also want to steal the lives of innocents. How could I tell?

'Yes,' I replied. 'I do pity you.'

A horrible, hollow laugh came from the pit.

'Then you are a fool,' said Lucifer. 'No-one should pity the devil.'

'You are right,' I answered. 'I have more reason than most to hate you and yet I do pity you. Nothing should suffer your fate.'

Another great moan and wail came from the pit.

For a moment the huge creature looked like a bound giant and tears could be seen falling from his eyes. Then it transformed back into the gigantic, wounded serpent.

'It is one of the Titans,' said Thor. 'Beaten by Zeus in the battle of ages.'

'Yes,' agreed Mary. 'You are right. Lucifer is also the Titan. That is just another name for him.'

'Which Titan?' I asked.

'He is Chronos,' replied the witch. 'He is Time itself.'

*

Habakuk and Saint Paul walked over towards Simon Peter, the rock. Martha stood in their way.

'Where do you think you two are going in your dirty robes and dusty sandals?' she directed the question to the small, serious and loving saint. 'Just look at you. It's a disgrace. You should be ashamed of yourself, Saul of Tarsus, leading this young saint astray. Let me clean you up.'

Habakuk looked at his spotless clothes and sandals and then at Saint Paul. Not a single dot could be seen.

'See it through her eyes,' whispered Saint Paul and Habakuk looked again.

His cloak was all muddy and their was golden sand encrusting his sandals ..... sand from the shore of the crystal flowing river. Saint Paul's garments were in the same condition.

Saint Paul took off his sandals and passed them to Martha so Habakuk did likewise. Martha then took the cloaks from the saints. Miraculously she handed back to the two penitent saints new spotless garments and new sandals. The old, dirty clothes and footwear were still in her possession.

'I shall clean them and return them when ready,' she told them in a triumphant voice. 'They are very dirty and I must get to work straight away.'

Martha walked off with a big, beaming smile on her overworked face, delighted to have some more tasks to perform.

'Now we go and congratulate Saint Peter,' said the small saint, a smile playing across his own face. 'It all oils the works and keeps the wheels turning.'

Habakuk could not help but smile also. They were in Heaven and why not be happy?

*

Sir George Frampton was very unhappy.

'You'll rue this, young lad,' said the MI5 man as he lay prostrate on the floor. 'I'll make you suffer.'

'Not as much as I'll make you,' replied Joshua. 'Now tell me straight away. Is there an antidote to the poison you have given my Mother, the PM and the chief constable?'

'There is no antidote ...' Frampton started to say.

'Then I'm going to shoot you right now,' said Joshua, aiming the pistol at Frampton's head.

'No, stop!' exclaimed the man from a position of complete surrender. 'You didn't let me finish. There is no antidote but it will wear off in about fifteen minutes. It's a fast acting hypnotic that our labs produced and has no harmful after effects.'

'That's better,' said Joshua. 'Now tell me the news from around the world while we wait for them to wake up.'

A scuffling noise caught Joshua's attention.

'Stop moving!' he exclaimed to the secretary who had started to get up into a crawling position. 'Lie down again and keep still!'

'You wouldn't shoot a lady, would you?' asked the woman.

'I threw a knife into a policeman's back,' stated the older of the two brothers. 'So why should I stop there? You're another of the mad cannibals so you are barely human and I hate you.'

The secretary slumped back onto the floor her resistance gone.

'We've been monitoring world news by assessing editorial spikes on Wikipedia,' said Sir George Frampton, presently resigned to his position on the ground. 'I have no doubt that the Armageddon prophets are winning and that your resistance really is futile. I was in two minds which way to finally fall but you are right in thinking that I am supporting the Church. My position in it is assured and I will have a place in glory at the end of days.'

'Which I hope will not be for a very long time,' came a deep stern voice.

Chief Constable Devonport had reawakened from the effects of the sedative. Sienna Scott and Darcy Macaroon were still snoring gently on the floor.

'Well done lads,' said Devonport. 'Have you collected their weapons?'

'No sir,' replied Joshua. 'We were just making them stay still. One of them has a bleeding hand because Sam had to shoot the guy's gun away but otherwise all we did was to make them lie down.'

'And you did that excellently,' said the policeman as he went round relieving the Armageddon Prophets of their hardware. Each of the cannabilistic religious fanatics snarled at the man as he did so but with the guns still trained on them by the young lads the acolytes were too scared to move.

*

'Could you please ask Lucifer if we could have back our comfy room with the red shag-pile carpet?' I asked Mary, plaintively.

She laughed.

'James,' she chortled. 'You are so predictable. You want to see reality but only for a very short time. You think you are so brave but you are afraid of everything.'

'I disagree,' I replied. 'I know that I am a coward and this coward's mind has seen about all it can take. If we are to think about this clearly I need to have a semblance of normality around me even if I know that it is completely false. Then I might be able to ask some sensible questions.'

'OK, I'll ask,' replied Mary and she looked down into the pit.

An exchange in the horrible, hellish language followed and suddenly we were back in the room beneath the throne.

Lucifer was standing in front of us in his humanoid form, a sinister smile playing over his face.

'Now,' he said. 'We can start again.'

He waved his hands around and continued to talk.

'This is all false but feels to you like reality.'

The floor disappeared again and we were looking once more straight down into the maw of Hell. Lucifer was standing next to us on a floor of nothingness.

'And that,' he pointed to himself, writhing in the lava. 'That is reality but seems completely unreal.'

The carpeted room reappeared and we all breathed sighs of relief.

'I created this room, the throne room above and a palace, just to please Mary,' said Lucifer. 'For the first time in centuries I have found a person who has given me some peace of mind, however fleetingly.'

Thor laughed a cynical involuntary laugh and Lucifer turned to stare at him with a withering contempt.

'God of Thunder how easy it is for you, ever noble, to laugh at me in my imprisoned state. To ridicule me as I receive my just deserts,' said Lucifer. 'I corrupted heaven by bringing in change. I spoilt Asgard with my mischief and condemned the Earth with my evil deeds, casting Adam and Eve from paradise.'

'For this you are being punished,' replied Thor.

'But consider this,' replied Lucifer. 'Without time there is no change. Without change there is no innovation. If Adam and Eve had stayed in Eden for ever there would be no race of men. Even the elves, werewolves and other inhabitants of faerie are but an echo of Earth and its human inhabitants. So without me you would not exist.'

Chapter 24

'Thank you,' replied Saint Peter when Habakuk congratulated him on his Bagatelle score. 'And it's good to see that your halo is coming along nicely. Is there any score that you would like to better? Any result you would like to improve?'

'Not really at Bagatelle,' replied Habakuk, then he remembered something. 'Perhaps skimming stones. I could better my best score at that. I've always wanted to.'

'You mean bouncing flat stones across a calm lake?' queried Simon Peter. 'I used to enjoy doing that at Galilee.'

'That's right,' said Habakuk. 'One calm day I drove down to a particular lake. The rock formation of the surrounding mountains was slate and there were huge numbers of perfect stones for skimming right there on the shore. I spent a good hour and a half skimming those perfect stones and reached my highest score ever.'

'What was that score?' asked the rock of the early church and first vicar of Rome.

'Thirty one, if I remember correctly,' answered Habakuk.

'And we always do here in Heaven,' interjected Simon Peter. 'We always remember correctly. So come with me and I'll show you the perfect spot on the perfect lake.'

'Aren't there any new folk who require admittance to Heaven?' asked Saint Paul in a worried tone.

'Not one,' replied Peter. 'Nobody can get past the crowd of Armageddon prophets.'

*

'Mary chose to leave Heaven to come to Hell so perhaps you can understand why this time I wish to sit out Ragnarok and to forego the dubious pleasure of Armageddon,' continued Lucifer as we all sat down on the red carpet.

'Could we have some furniture, Lucien dear?' asked Mary.

'Of course,' he replied. 'How thoughtless of me. What about this?'

Suddenly the room was furnished with leather-bound, studded chairs. It was just like a London gentleman's club and even had small coffee tables and a waiter, who offered us drinks. I could have sworn that I had been somewhere identical on Pall Mall.

'Can you tell us more about the reality of heaven and hell?' I asked as I sat back comfortably on the red leather. 'It might help us to avoid Armageddon.'

'Yes,' replied Lucifer. 'But be warned. I feel duty bound to always tell Thor lies. I don't know why. I think that it is his insufferably priggish nobility.'

'But he was an estate agent!' I protested. 'One of the least noble professions!'

'And surveyor,' stated Lucifer. 'And despite the opportunities for cheating he always refused to do so and kept to an honest and upright code. No, he was insufferably noble even in his last human manifestation. So I cannot help hating him and therefore will always lie to his face.'

Thor grimaced and would have risen to the bait but Freya calmed him down.

'More about reality please,' I pleaded, hoping to prevent a fight breaking out, one that we would inevitably lose.

'Let us start with a conception of heaven and hell,' stated Lucifer.

'Why just a conception?' ask Freya. 'Can you not do better than that?'

'Freya,' replied the devil, his eyes dancing mischievously. 'You are goddess of love and war. But does that equip you to understand all of quantum theory, the totality of tensor calculus, the theories of relativity and string theory ?'

'No,' admitted Freya. 'But I could try.'

'And yet those are just the simple concepts that I shall use to illustrate some of the realities of heaven and hell. They are but models but such analogies must suffice.'

The Prince of Darkness paused, sipped for a short while from a drink served by a flunkey, then addressed me.

'No doubt you are familiar with Quantum Mechanics?' asked Lucifer

'Just about,' I replied with a wry smile. 'I studied it extensively at University.'

'Yes I know that,' replied Lucifer. 'In Quantum Mechanics a photon of light can be set off from a source. Before it arrives at its destination it can be described as a wave function.'

'Do you mean a wave?' asked Vole. 'I know that light can be both a wave and a particle.'

'No,' answered Lucifer. 'You are right that light can be a wave and a particle, as can all of reality. But the wave function is more than that. It is the sum of all the probabilities of both the wave and the particle. The statistical reality of the wavicle....'

'....OK,' I said, cutting in on Lucifer's reply. 'I'm sorry to interrupt but it is better for you to continue with the description of our reality and I will explain all the simpler physics to the rest of them later. I have a terrible feeling that there is little time for all of this. Bringing everybody up to speed on a degree course in physics may take too long.'

'I agree,' concurred Lucifer. 'The ignorance is shocking.'

I twitched apprehensively. I did not want any of our party to become offended and hold things up further but luckily nobody became upset. They were becoming used to the devil and were keeping his constant barbs at a metaphorical arm's length.

'The wave function can be anywhere in the Universe as long as it has not collapsed,' stated Lucifer. 'But you cannot exactly know its parameters at the same time. For example, the more you know about its mass the less you know about its velocity.'

'Indeterminacy,' I explained. 'Having no definite or definable value.'

'Correct,' stated Lucifer. 'That is Heaven.'

'How can the wave function be Heaven?' asked Vole. 'That doesn't make sense.'

'Oh yes it does,' I disagreed with sweet Vole. 'Much as I love you, my dear shaman, I have to take issue with you there. I can sense where this is leading. What I am interested in is where this heaven is.'

'Tell me then, clever fellow, what I was going to say next!' commanded the devil sarcastically, in a tone much like those used to such great effect by my mother-in-law.

'Heaven is the un-collapsed totality of all wave functions,' I stated. 'That is the logical physics explanation for a heaven that could be all things to all people. For each person whatever they hoped for could be provided in such a heaven as long as the situation was not crystallised and as long as the wave function was not collapsed.'

'Yes, you are right,' agreed Lucifer and he turned to Mary. 'Not only has your son-in-law cut my heel he also steals my thunder.'

Thor, god of thunder, growled at this suggestion.

'Intellectual thunder, Thor,' murmured Loki-Lucifer. 'But I wouldn't expect you to understand a simple metaphor like that.'

'But how is the non-collapsed state maintained?' I asked. 'And what is Hell and how does it alter what can be done to stop Armageddon?'

'This explanation for Heaven is one that was not apparent even to myself until clever humans created the analogy of quantum mechanics,' explained Lucifer. 'I have amalgamated the idea with Einstein's theories of Relativity and utilised the direct assistance of his equal in intellect.'

'Who might that be?' I asked.

'Paul Dirac,' replied Lucifer. 'I have had long conversation with the brilliant Dirac.'

'Why didn't you speak to Einstein?' asked Ard. 'Get it from the horse's mouth, as it were.'

'Einstein is not available for me to speak to,' replied Lucifer. 'He is a shade in the bosom of Abraham.'

★

Sienna Scott and the Prime Minister, Darcy Macaroon, had completely recovered. They had been busy binding the four Armageddon acolytes with a roll of electrical flex that Samuel had found in a cupboard and the latter-day prophets were now lying immobilised on the floor of the large underground room.

It was several hours since the fugitives had left Downing Street and they wanted to catch up with the national and international news. However, the information coming out of the computers was not good. The warmongering in the Holy Land had reached fever pitch with conventional forces slugging it out in all of the famous places including, of course, Megiddo, where the battle had started, and in Jerusalem.

Intelligence experts were now stating that Iran was about to use chemical and biological warfare and that any use of force to oppose this was justified.

Sidney Fence had somehow arrived at the United Nations as the representative of the UK Government. He was proposing that the UN dropped its anti-war pledge and agreed to the legitimate use of nuclear weapons to wipe out the threat in Iran and Syria. He had already masterminded a political coup by arranging an emergency meeting of the assembly and then expelling all Arab nations from the UN Chamber apart from those with representatives who had declared allegiance to the Islamic Mosque of Armageddon, known as IMAM.

The strike on Iran and Syria was to be called a Multifaith

Crusade but first, Fence proposed, a neutron bomb should be set off in Jerusalem. This would kill all the occupying forces whilst destroying none of the holy buildings.

The likely fate of the civilians was not mentioned.

✶

Habakuk stood looking out over the beautiful lake. A small group of Heaven's elite had gathered to watch his efforts and he took a little time to select the correct stone. He soon found one that was beautifully circular, slim and very flat. The stone fitted into his hand perfectly and the weight felt just right. He flicked his wrist in the way that he remembered and off went the stone.

'Twenty, twenty-one,' counted Habakuk. 'Twenty-two. Not bad for my first attempt.'

'C'est bon. Bravo, encore!' shouted Joan of Arc. 'Try again.'

This time, thought Habakuk, *I'm going to use Saint Peter's trick of willing it to do better.*

He selected another perfect stone and let it loose across the lake, willing it to keep going and beat his record score. The stone flew out, just touching the surface and sending out little wavelets every time it did so before bouncing on to the next meeting with the crystal clear water.

On and on it bounced, past the twenty-two, past his personal best of thirty-one. Bounce, bounce, bounce.... and still Habakuk counted.

Fifty, sixty, seventy. The stone get bouncing. One hundred, one fifty, one hundred and eighty. One hundred and eighty!

The stone stopped and sank below the surface leaving barely a ripple, its energy completely spent.

The audience of apostles, saints and a few passing angels who had stopped to watch, burst into thunderous applause and Habakuk gave a little bow.

A perfect score at darts, thought Habakuk, *so perhaps it is also the perfect number for skimming stones?*

*

'So what else have you concluded?' I asked, impatient to hear Lucifer's theories about the reality in which he found himself bound.

'I shall endeavour to answer your three questions,' replied the devil. 'First you asked me how the wave function state is maintained. It is maintained in the eternal realm by the binding of time. It is physically present at the event horizon of the black hole. Hell is the singularity and as yet I do not know how the knowledge can help to prevent Armageddon. That is where your clever human and neo-divine minds may help.'

He paused and then continued with his explanation.

'Although Hell is the singularity it is not, as you can see, without dimension. That is a logical but incorrect interpretation of relativity. The Pauli exclusion principle prevents all of the matter that makes up the mass of a black hole from residing in one dimensionless point. Nevertheless, Hell is at the very bottom of a gravity well and escape is nigh impossible.'

'But which black hole is Hell and which event horizon is Heaven?' I asked.

'The black hole and the event horizon,' replied Lucifer. 'The black hole is at the centre of the Universe of the Eternal Realm and the Event Horizon is that which circles the Multiverse.'

'Does that include our Universe?' asked Vole.

'Of course,' replied Lucifer. 'And all other universes in the Multiverse.'

'I still don't get this wave function thing,' growled Ard. 'I may be an ignorant dog but I don't see how real objects can be in more than one place and why you can't know their mass and velocity at the same time.'

'Well that's quantum theory for you,' said Lucifer. 'It's not my theory it's your human theory.'

'It doesn't explain the whole of reality,' I objected. 'You are basically saying that time and therefore events are suspended in a form of eternal flux of infinite probability at the event horizon but how does that relate to reality and why are there so many different realities?'

'Theoretically you might expect there to be an infinite number of realities if there is more than one but that does not appear to be the case,' replied Lucifer. 'Many probabilities cancel themselves out and some just do not seem to exist. Another way of looking at it is to say that in the event horizon of the multiverse there are a myriad of multidimensional dynamic systems and that the various realities are the phase maps or perhaps holographic projections of those systems.'

'If they are phase maps then they would be fractal,' I protested. 'That would mean that our realities were made up of partial dimensions. How could that possibly be the case?'

'He's faster than I thought,' Lucifer said in an aside to my mother-in-law. 'I thought you said he was thick?'

'Not thick, dear. I think I said dull and unambitious,' replied Mary.

Thanks a bunch, witch, I thought to myself.

'He's catching on fast,' remarked the devil, Satan, Lucifer. 'Yes. What you term the real Universe is fractal as are all the universes in the multiverse.'

'So what is happening with the hordes of cannibal followers trying to breach the walls of paradise?' asked Freya, trying to get the conversation back onto a practical level that she could understand. 'Can they succeed and what would the result be if they do?'

'That, dear goddess of love, war and death, is the million dollar question,' replied Lucifer. 'What indeed will happen?'

✱

'How the heck did Sidney Fence get over to the United Nations building in New York so quickly?' asked Macaroon. 'He must have been there some time already or he would not have managed to get proposals passed by the Council.'

'It says here that he has been there for two and a half hours,' said Joshua looking at a twitter from someone actually at the UN in Manhattan.'

'That's not possible,' argued the PM. 'It must be someone posing as him. We only left him three and a half hours ago. No transport, not even an RAF jet, could get him there, touch down and then ferry him to the UN building in that time. No, it's got to be an impostor.'

'There's a picture of him at the UN right now,' replied Joshua. 'It's a live transmission. No sound.'

They gathered round Joshua's console and stared at the images of Sidney Fence in the council chamber of the United Nations. Suddenly it zoomed in on the man and they could see that he had newly made rough red marks on his face and wrists.

'That's him alright,' remarked Chief Constable Devonport. 'I'd recognise his ugly mug anywhere and he has marks on him from the places we tied him up. It's definitely Sidney Fence.'

'Then I must get to the UN and denounce him,' cried Darcy Macaroon. 'It is our only chance.

'You'd be lucky to get anywhere, PM,' stated Devonport. 'Look at the closed circuit TV!'

The group moved over to look at the panels of flat television screens that displayed the information from cameras all around the underground site and in the immediate vicinity outside. There were hordes of police everywhere, most of them wearing CAP armbands, and it was only going to be a matter of a short space of time before they reached the doors to the main underground bunker.

'As long as they don't have the codes to this part of the complex they cannot reach us bar using a thermonuclear device,' declared the PM. 'The walls and doors are blast proof against normal explosives. It is proof against nuclear weapons from above but not from inside the tunnels but I doubt that they would risk such a weapon right under the heart of London.'

'They might,' growled Devonport. 'But that is the relatively good news, that they can't get to us at all easily. The bad news is that we need to get out but we can't. We're stuck here. Really stuck.'

Chapter 25

'That was great fun,' said Habakuk, relishing his achievement at skipping stones and still looking out over the beautiful lake. Saint Paul was at his side again.

'Yes,' agreed the writer of epistles. 'Yes. You are right. Heaven is fun.'

'I have another question,' said Habakuk. 'When I was alive on Earth as a little child I would often look up into the heavens and see the stars.'

'Of course,' replied Paul. 'We all did that. Beautiful twinkling lights in the night sky.'

'Yes,' agreed Habakuk. 'And in my era we had discovered that the stars are like our sun. Huge balls of gas burning brightly due to nuclear fusion. They are millions and millions of miles away from Earth and some are even in distant galaxies.'

'Yes,' said the saint. 'I know that.'

'....And more recently the astronomers have discovered planets around those stars. What happens if intelligent creatures live on those planets? Can they go to heaven? Can they come here?'

'Of course they can, Habakuk,' replied Saint Paul. 'Of course they can.'

'But I don't see them.'

'The Messiah said those that have eyes to see, let them see,' replied the small saint. 'Turn round and look!'

Habakuk slowly turned himself away from the beautiful lake. Sitting at a bar behind him sipping steaming green liquid from long glass bowls were the strangest creatures he had seen yet. Vaguely humanoid they each had three heads.

'Tri-human from the planet Zorg,' explained Saint Paul. 'Each head takes it in turn to determine the gender.'

'Is that large one particularly special?' asked Habakuk, pointing to an individual who was surrounded by other tri-humans.

'Oh yes,' answered Paul 'That is mezcarto ß 2. She is a Zorgish saint, loved by everyone on the planet.'

'She looks pregnant!' exclaimed Habakuk.

'Of course,' replied Saul. 'She's always pregnant.'

*

'Tell me if I am wrong,' I said to Lucifer. 'But forcing all these new people into heaven may be a very bad thing.'

'In some ways that is probably true but in other ways it is not,' said Lucifer, imparting no information.

'Thor,' I said turning to the god of thunder. 'Could you ask whether heaven will survive if the walls are breached and all the souls of the Armageddon Prophets force their way in.'

'I will certainly do that, noble Scott,' replied Thor and immediately asked the question. 'Lucifer, will heaven survive a forced invasion by the hordes?'

'Of course it will, fool,' Lucifer laughed in reply. 'Heaven is eternal, the power is totipotent and all knowing. It will, of course survive.'

'I thought it would,' nodded Thor. 'The All-father cannot be defeated. Thank you for replying truthfully for a change.'

'Thor, Thor, Thor,' I implored. 'He is manipulating you again. Heaven would not survive the breach and I think I know why.'

'Why is that, clever boy?' asked Lucifer, sarcastically again.

'Because the wave functions of souls entering heaven have to be compatible with the overall gestalt,' I replied. 'The entry in by the gate assures this to be the case. Otherwise the wavelets could be out of phase and cancel each other out just like noise suppression headphones.'

'Curse you Scott,' cried Lucifer. 'That was the one piece of knowledge I was keeping to myself. But hear this. Without my help you will never succeed in countering this invasion of Heaven.'

'How can they invade Heaven?' asked Vole. 'Surely the one who commands Heaven can just decree that it remains   inviolable.'

'Yes, but he has given human beings and all other sentient creatures the dubious gift of free will,' stated Lucifer. 'And if the elected representatives of humankind decide to purposely wage Armageddon the walls of Heaven could be destroyed.'

'They would never do that!' exclaimed Vole in reply. 'The elected body you are referring to is the United Nations which is dedicated to peace.'

Lucifer laughed, a horrible sepulchral noise, reminding them all that he and they were actually in the pit in Hell and not in a cosy carpeted London club.

'The UN are voting right now as to whether or not they should neutron bomb Jerusalem and destroy the Wailing Wall. That would breach the integrity of Heaven without a doubt.'

*

'I think we are completely scuppered,' said Darcy Macaroon, looking at the closed circuit TV.

'Don't give up yet, Mr. Macaroon' said Samuel. 'We still might be saved by my Dad!'

'I'm sorry to say that it is very unlikely he can help us,' replied the Prime Minister. 'He was sent away on a mission and he disappeared into an alternative reality. We have not heard from him since.'

'He'll come and save us,' said Sam. 'So don't give up. He saved Joshua and me from the devil and from Parsifal X so saving us won't be that difficult.'

'He doesn't even know where we are,' said Sienna. 'So how can he save us?'

'Don't give up Mum. He will come,' replied Sam.

'It would probably help if we could let him know where we are,' suggested Joshua. 'So let's put something out on the internet. We'll tweet all our friends, put out on Facebook what has happened to us, send e-mails to him and text messages. That's probably the best we can do.'

'Good thinking, young lad,' agreed Macaroon. 'At least it will keep our spirits up if nothing else. We'll start straight away.'

★

'Are there other aliens here?' asked the ex-priest of the Church of Armageddon Prophets.

'Billions!' replied Saint Paul. 'Look back at the lake.'

Habakuk dutifully turned round and looked at the lake. Large dolphin-like creatures were leaping in and out of the water joyfully, great smiles on their beak-like faces.

'Dolphins?' queried Habakuk.

'Not quite but very similar,' replied Saint Paul. 'They are the entirely peaceable and intelligent inhabitants of a small planet near Betelgeuse. They all come to heaven when they die.'

Habakuk then jumped back in alarm having noticed scuttling movement close to himself. Saint Paul put a quietening hand on his arm.

'There is no need for fear in Heaven, brother Habakuk,' said the small saint. 'The spiders are completely harmless.'

'But they are enormous,' cried Habakuk, still shaking slightly. 'They must be two metres across, each of them. And they have got huge hairy legs.'

'Absolutely true but again, they are completely peaceful. Where they come from they live on nuts and berries and have huge communities. They have even developed space travel.'

'Where do they come from?' asked Habakuk, hoping that he would never have to travel there. Spiders were definitely not his favourite creature.

'Andromeda,' laughed Saint Paul. 'Don't worry. It is a different galaxy from the Milky Way and you will never be asked to visit it.'

The scene changed back to the familiar one of a beautiful

crystal-clear lake surrounded by trees and flowers in blossom and a shore of perfect skimming stones.

'It is time we went back and joined the others. Yahweh will be with us very soon,' announced Saint Paul and he led the small group of saints back to the earlier gathering point.

*

'Why do you say that we cannot do anything without your help?' asked Vole.

'How do you think that you can leave Hell?' asked Lucifer.

'Perhaps we can fly out of here?' suggested Vole.

'Fly?' laughed Lucifer scornfully. 'Fly out of Hell? What, on a scheduled BA flight or a cheap Easyjet overnight package?'

He laughed again. 'There are no flights out of hell.'

'Why not?' asked Vole. 'What is so ridiculous about saying that we might fly out of here? We fell in easily enough.'

'Of course you did,' wheezed the devil, still finding her answer risible. 'We are in a gravity well. In fact not just any gravity well but the gravity well to end all gravity wells.'

'What does that mean?' asked Vole. 'I didn't do physics at college so what does a "gravity well" mean?'

'We are at the centre of a black hole, Vole sweetheart,' I said, trying to soften the blow with an endearment or two. 'There is no climbing out of this well. Everything falls into it.'

'Yes,' agreed Lucifer. 'And your only hope is myself. Let me loose and I can help you out.'

'How can we possibly let you out?' I asked. 'You have been bound here by God Almighty. How can mortals like us help you?'

'Mortals?' sneered Lucifer. 'You are not mortals. Do you think I would converse with mere mortals?'

'Then what are we?' I asked. 'I realise that Freya, Thor and Heimdall are deities but what are you saying about the rest of us? What are we if we are not mortals?'

'I thought you knew that by now,' snarled the devil. 'It is pretty obvious. Mary!'

'Yes dear,' replied my mother-in-law, the witch.

'Tell them who they are. What form of being they have reincarnated into or always were but did not know it,' ordered Satan, Lucifer, Beelzebub, Loki.

'That's an easy task,' replied Mary. 'Ard is the jackal-headed god Anubis, who is also known as Saint Christopher the dog head and Vole is Venus, the goddess of love. Harry, who you all will have noticed has rather blue skin, is Krishna.'

'Strike a light!' exclaimed Harry, examining his hands as if he had never realised before that his colour was unusual.

'So whom am I, Mary?' I asked fearfully. 'What awful creature am I now?'

'And you, Jimmy Scott, are husband to my daughter Sienna.'

'Yes,' I replied dutifully. 'But what else am I?'

'You are the latest incarnation of Saint Michael, the Archangel. The most feared and the most powerful angel in the whole of the heavens.'

*

The Church of Armageddon Prophets' police had reached the blast doors of the bunker. There were two portals, one leading out to a short tunnel that itself opened into Westminster and the other to the tunnel by which the fugitives had entered. The police had broken through the entrance to these tunnels in Downing Street, Westminster and Buckingham Palace and advanced cautiously down the tunnels. This encroachment had been watched all the way by the Scotts, by the Prime Minister and by the Chief Constable of Avon and Somerset Police.

The Prime Minister was becoming angry.

'They are regular police who have betrayed their calling!' he shouted, slamming the desk with his open hand.

'You are right PM,' agreed Devonport. 'It is a disgrace. Of course you could say the same about Sidney Fence. He is a disgrace to the political world.'

The Prime Minister laughed ruefully. 'He always was. It was just convenient to keep him on our side.'

'It has come home to roost now, wouldn't you say?' added Devonport.

'No doubt. But we all make mistakes,' replied Darcy Macaroon, his anger turning to self-reproach. 'Let us hope that we can find a way out of this mess without everybody everywhere suffering from our various errors, eh?'

'I agree,' said Devonport. 'But it doesn't look very hopeful, does it?'

The likely truth of his reply was reinforced by a shocking clattering and banging noise emanating from the Downing Street end of the room. The besieging forces had started on the doors with pneumatic drills. The fugitives in the bunker could see on the TV screens that the attackers had brought acetylene cutters and other tools. It was only a matter of time before the Church-controlled police force broke into the bunker.

*

'He has come in His Messiah aspect,' remarked Simon Peter. 'That's how I prefer Him. Just as He was when we first met.'

Habakuk looked in the direction that Simon Peter was indicating and a tall, slim bearded man came towards them. He was dressed, like everyone else, in a long white flowing gown but like Saint Paul had a slogan emblazened across his front and this one decreed "All you need is Love."

For a moment Habakuk thought that the man was remarkably like John Lennon, or maybe even *was* the dead Beatle, but closer inspection revealed major differences. The man who was approaching had a kindly, gentle face, the nose was a little longer and he was not wearing Lennon's small round glasses. Perhaps the most significant detail in distinguishing between the two was the light that shone in a very bright halo illuminating the man's head from above and behind and extended down behind his body thus illuminating him in glory wherever he walked.

'Behold our Messiah,' cried Saint Paul and fell at the feet of the man.

'Oh get up, Paul and stop mucking around,' protested the Messiah and Saint Paul jumped up smiling.

'See,' said Martha, with a smile. 'Look at him! This is what you boys should look like. Not a spot of dirt on Him.'

Habakuk took a good look at the Messiah. He was exactly as pictured in stained glass windows, just perfect. Habakuk suddenly became worried.

'What about the other religions?' he asked Saint Paul. 'What do the Buddhists think when they see that the Messiah is, well, so Christian.'

'I thought you'd got that one sorted,' said the small saint. 'Take a look at what they are seeing.'

Once again Habakuk became aware of the monks in saffron robes and that Paul was wearing maroon. He turned back to look at the Messiah and saw instead of the tall, bearded figure a small, fat bald fellow with a jolly expression on his face... it was without doubt Buddha.

*

'So you say that we can help you to escape your bonds?' I asked Lucifer. We were sitting in the leather armchairs sipping drinks brought to us on a silver tray. Lucifer had his legs crossed in a very nonchalant manner.

'If you want to get out of here and stop Armageddon that is really the only way,' replied the devil.

'So you have the power to escape from this gravity well and you will take us with you,' said Heimdall. 'Then shall we fight to the death, once you are free?'

'Maybe a billion years from now, if you like,' agreed Loki, Lucifer, Satan, Beelzebub.

'I see,' said Heimdall musing on the problem.

'Thor,' I said turning to the blond Scandinavian giant of a man who was wielding the mystic hammer Mjolnir. 'Could you please ask Lucifer if he really can take us out of here if we let him loose?'

'Certainly,' replied Thor. 'Loki, can you take us out of here if we free you?'

'Not really,' replied Lucifer. 'I was lying to your friends. I do not have sufficient power to take you with me.'

'There you go,' said Thor. 'There's no point freeing him. He doesn't have the power. He has just admitted that he lied to you.'

'Thanks Thor,' I smiled at the blonde god of thunder.

He's a really nice guy is Thor I thought to myself *but he is rather thick. He still doesn't realise when Loki is manipulating him even though he told us that his brother always lies to him. Fascinating.*

'So this puts an interesting dilemma in front of us,' I explained to the gathering of gods. 'We have a duty as gods, and in my case angel, to act as guardians of the realities. But we cannot do so because we are trapped in Hell. Apparently the only way out is to free the master of evil, Lucifer. We probably can do this using all our combined might but we would be letting loose unbridled evil into the multiverse. But he does have the power to set us free once he has himself been set free.'

Thor looked puzzled at my resumé. The two goddesses of love, Vole and Freya, looked horrified at the idea of freeing the monster. Harry looked as if he thought it was all rather amusing and Ard looked anguished. Only Heimdall was looking forward to freeing Loki and I could tell that he was spoiling for a fight.

'There is just one thing that Lucifer has told us that I find puzzling,' I continued.

'What is that, Jimmy?' asked Vole.

'Why was he *really* talking to Paul Dirac, if indeed he was?'

★

'Your only hope is to give yourselves up now,' said one of

the bound MI5 men lying on the floor of the bunker. The MI5 contingent had kept quiet up until his utterance. 'Once they get in here you won't last two minutes.'

'Don't tell them too much,' countered Sir George Frampton. 'I don't care if the PM and his party are killed when they break the doors down.'

'I'm not too keen on being shot myself,' replied the MI5 man. 'And I'm getting pissed off with the noise of the drills.'

'Maintain discipline or I will have you shot the moment they do break in, damn you,' cursed the leader of the Church of Armageddon Prophets.

The MI5 man became quiet, but appeared very annoyed.

'No honour amongst thieves, old boy,' chuckled the PM, leaning down and speaking to the seething MI5 man. 'He'll probably have you shot anyway.'

'Aren't there any defences in this place?' asked Joshua. 'If I had set this place up I would have put in machine guns, gas. That sort of thing.'

'I don't think so,' replied Darcy Macaroon. 'The place is well protected from nuclear attack from above but ground forces were only a secondary consideration.'

'Are there any manuals about the place?' asked Devonport. 'The boy does have a point.'

'I agree it is worth thinking about,' said Macaroon. 'We could look through the specifications of construction. I have found those on one of the computers.'

*

'It's great to see you, boss,' said Simon Peter. 'How were the shades in the bosom of Abraham?'

'Happy,' replied the Buddha to Simon Peter. 'Definitely still happy.'

'And the prophets in the fire?' asked Saint Paul. 'How were they?'

'Making toast to go with their tea,' replied the small, jolly figure.

'We do have some serious business, boss,' interjected Simon Peter, interrupting Habakuk's reverie. The Buddha changed back into the tall bearded Messiah figure.

'Thank you, Peter,' replied the tall figure. 'You are right, indeed we do. You are still my rock.'

Saint Peter swelled with pride and spoke again.

'I think Paul told you about the hordes at our gates and the god-like creature that may be the Anti-Christ?'

'Yes, yes,' replied the Messiah. 'I knew about that. Does Saint Habakuk have any more to say about what is happening?'

He's talking to me! Habakuk was amazed. *I am the least of all and he is talking directly to me!*

Chapter 26

'We might have something here,' said Joshua. The fugitives in the bunker had copied the specifications and were studying them on different computers. 'It's not a weapon but it could slow them down for a short time.'

'What have you got lad?' asked the Prime Minister. 'Do you think it might be something useful?'

'There's a sprinkler system in the tunnels,' replied Joshua. 'Sam and I have been looking at it and Sam has made an interesting suggestion.'

'Tell us what it is then, don't hold out,' ordered the PM.

'Don't waste your breath you young tyke,' shouted Sir George Frampton from his position on the floor. 'The sprinklers only work when there is a fire.'

'Not completely true,' said Joshua. 'They work whenever the detectors believe there is a fire.'

'That's the same thing isn't it lad?' asked the PM.

'Not if we can convince the computer that there is a fire in the corridors,' replied Joshua. 'Sam thinks we might be able to.'

'Are you sure?' asked Maxwell Devonport. 'We don't want to find that you put some code in and it makes the blast doors swing open.'

'We've looked at the command program,' said Joshua. 'And we're sure that won't happen. What we are thinking of doing is more likely to make the blast doors stay jammed shut.'

'OK,' said Darcy Macaroon. 'You can give it a try.'

'I agree,' remarked Devonport. 'At the very least it will soak the attackers and it might muck up the electrics of their arc welder. They'll have to stop, get a change of clothing and some tenting or something similar to cover the equipment.'

Joshua and Samuel started playing with the computers. It was much like hacking their computer games, something they had done many times in order to get high scores.

*

'How do you think we could free you from your bonds?' I asked Lucifer, the Prince of Darkness.

'Thor could use Mjolnir to break the rocks I am bound to,' replied the devil.

'But you would still be enwrapped in iron bands,' I protested. 'You would still not be free.'

'You could then use your sword as Saint Michael, chief of the Archangels,' replied Lucifer.

'To what avail?' I asked him.

'To cut through the iron and flesh allowing me to wriggle out. I could discard my old skin and appear renewed,' replied Satan.

'There's just one problem with that,' I said raising my eyebrows. 'We would then be without doubt wreaking great havoc on the whole of reality.'

'It is your only hope if you wish to leave Hell,' cried Lucifer in a frustrated rage. 'I have already told you that!'

'But what you say is not always true, Lucifer,' I countered. 'And it may be better for the multiverse if we stay in Hell and don't let you free.'

'You are right, Jimmy,' cried Vole. 'He is evil personified. He must not be set free.'

'That's one aspect of the equation,' I said, my mind working with rapier-like speed. 'But I have discovered another which may be distinctly more important.'

'More important than the fact that this huge creature is evil?' asked Freya. 'What can be more important than that?'

'We are talking as if evil is an absolute concept,' I replied. 'And yet it isn't. One man's meat is another man's poison. What is considered as evil in one context may be considered as good in another.'

'No,' countered Heimdall. 'There really are such things as ultimate good and ultimate evil.'

'There may be,' I conceded. 'But I am not a good enough philosopher to argue the case.'

'Now you are being sensible,' said Lucifer urbanely, sitting back in his leather seat and calling for another drink. 'I'm sorry I was getting annoyed. I thought for a moment you were going to agree with the love goddesses. You must have realised by now that I am not all evil?'

'I have noticed that you can do good deeds,' I replied. 'But again this is a distraction from the main points. Why have you been consigned to Hell and why were you having long discussions with Paul Dirac?'

'I was just passing time pleasantly with one of the cleverer of the humans,' stated Lucifer. 'I am Chronos and I have so much time to pass.'

'There is more to it than that,' I replied to the monster who sat opposite me looking so comfortable and relaxed. 'I suspect that your conversations were much more significant.'

'Yes,' said Vole, picking up on my questioning. 'There are plenty of clever people in all walks of life. Many may have had more interesting lives than a physicist.'

'So why Paul Dirac?' I queried.

'Humans so often act stupidly,' replied the devil, shifting just a little uneasily and beginning to think that he might have given something away that he had not intended when he told us he had been talking to Dirac. 'But Dirac is intelligent. I valued his company.'

'But he is not here with you now,' I stated, looking around. 'Heimdall, did you see Dirac when you looked into the pit with your perfect vision?'

'No, Lord James Scott, I did not,' replied the ever-watchful god. 'Nor did I hear him crying out in torment amongst the many others I could hear.'

'So what?' replied Lucifer. 'No, Dirac is not here or I would still talk to him. He is elsewhere.'

'Then how did you talk to him?' I asked.

'When he was still alive someone summoned me and I had the chance to make his acquaintance,' replied Lucifer.

'And he did not realise that you were the very devil himself?' asked Freya.

'No, of course not,' replied Lucifer. 'He just thought I was a particularly bright student.'

'And you were interested in his line of physics?' I asked as innocently as I could.

'I've told you that already,' said Lucifer, getting impatient. 'We are going over old ground. If you want to get out of here I suggest you start breaking my bindings straight away.'

'I don't think we'll be doing that anytime too soon,' I replied. 'You see I think I have worked out exactly what you are and why it was important at the moment of the big bang for you to be confined in an inaccessible place.'

The club-like surroundings started to fade as Lucifer shook with anger at my reply and I could see the brimstone and fire of the pit beneath us through holes that were developing in the floor.

'So, clever dick,' muttered the devil in his most sinister voice. 'What have you surmised from your logical progression of thought? Or have you remembered why you, as Saint Michael, most powerful of the Archangels, originally bound me in this godforsaken hell-hole?'

'No,' I answered. 'I have no memories of my time as Saint Michael, if that is who I am. This is entirely conjecture based on my knowledge of Dirac's work.'

'Then it is probably wrong,' smiled Lucifer, relaxing again. 'The club surrounding reappeared intact and all of us sat back in our chairs.

'Part of the clue lies in apocalyptic religion,' I added. 'You see it says in Revelation that an Antichrist will rise against Christ.'

'Yes, it does,' said Lucifer. 'I can quote chapter and verse if you wish.'

'No thanks,' I replied. 'I've always heard it said that even the devil can quote scripture.'

'So what do you think you have learnt from all this?' asked the devil, with a faint smile on his face. He stroked his goatee beard as he posed the question.

'Well, it's quite simple really,' I replied. 'Paul Dirac was working through the mathematics of quantum theory and he surmised that antimatter should exist in the universe.'

'That's correct,' said the devil. 'And he was right. Within a couple of years they had proven him to be so by discovering the positron. Your clever scientists went on to find all manner of antimatter particles and they have even made antimatter atoms.'

'Yes, I know,' I replied. 'But Dirac was puzzled and so are many scientists. You see, there should have been an equal mass of antimatter to the amount of matter. As many anti-particles as particles.'

'So what?' said Lucifer, trying to remain calm but constant twitches betraying his increasing tension.

'Well there aren't,' I answered him. 'There are far too few antimatter particles. There don't appear to be any antimatter stars, planets or galaxies.... and this has always been a mystery. Of course we are very grateful that there is little or no antimatter unless we make it in the laboratory because antimatter annihilates when it meets matter. If there was an equal amount we would probably not exist, as all matter would be evaporated into energy waves by interaction with antimatter.'

'This is all very interesting but I don't see why you are telling me this story,' said Lucifer shifting nervously in his seat.

'Don't you?' I asked the devil. 'Doesn't it seem strange that the so-called Antichrist should be bound away from the normal Universe?'

'No,' said Lucifer. 'Not strange just unfortunate. It is my punishment for disobeying God.'

'It is more fundamental than that,' I replied. 'You may be evil or you may not. I suspect you are, as you tried to sacrifice my two innocent sons, but I am not in a position to judge you.'

'Judge not that ye be not judged!' intoned Lucifer. 'The Gospel according to Saint Matthew, chapter seven, verse number one.'

'Quite,' I said. 'But consider this. For every force there is an equal and opposite force. Yin and Yang, Good and Evil, Christ and Antichrist, matter and antimatter. You were bound here for one reason and one reason alone.'

'So what might that be?' asked Lucifer, leaning forward and leering into my face. 'What do you think I am, you speck of unimportant dust?'

'You are the missing antimatter bound here to allow the universe to exist. If we free you the matter/anti-matter reaction is likely destroy the entire multiverse.'

'Damn you, James Scott,' cried the devil. 'You are too clever by far. Mary lied when she said you were stupid. You are far too clever. May you all rot in Hell. My Hell!'

The club scene disappeared and we all fell down, down, down into the burning pit of Hell, Mary included.

'Look what you have done, James Scott, you meddling fool!' she cried as she fell. 'Look what you have done!'

✱

'Come on, Habakuk, say something!' exclaimed Simon Peter. 'Now is your chance.'

Habakuk fumbled for words but gradually managed to get through his narrative again.

'So people are worshipping this god,' summarised the Messiah. 'Even to the extent of cannibalising each other and suicide.... and trying to invade Heaven. Yes, I did know that. '

'Yes,' agreed Habakuk.

'That shows great faith on their part,' stated the Messiah.

'Yes, indeed,' nodded Habakuk.

'And considerable hopefulness.'

'Yes, yes,' agreed Habakuk.

'But little or no love, or love that is misplaced,' the Messiah looked sad and all around him Heaven dimmed. Then he brightened up and all was well again. 'But I'm sure we can sort it out somehow. Nothing is insurmountable.'

'And the false god claims that he is the true Lord of the Covenant, the Lord of Lords and that his name is Dagon.'

'.......Or Baal,' added the Messiah. He looked perplexed for a moment and then His frown disappeared. 'Yes. He is Baal. I know that too.'

I didn't realise that Dagon was Baal, thought Habakuk. *That does put a different light on the problem.*

'That he is Baal and Dagon does cause some semantic problems,' the Messiah stated. 'But we can overcome them.'

'What shall we do about the hordes at the gates?' asked Simon Peter, ever mindful of the integrity of the portal.

'Do we need to do anything?' asked the Messiah.

'Well, yes,' replied Simon Peter. 'Even our gates won't stand up to the pressure that is being put on them for ever and it is getting difficult for those who should be entering Heaven to do so.'

'Yes, that is correct,' replied the Messiah. 'It is easier for a camel to pass through the eye of a needle than for a rich man to enter the kingdom of heaven. Many on Earth are now very rich and will find entry into Heaven difficult.'

'But what shall we do about it?' asked Simon Peter again. 'I think that a breach is imminent and it would endanger our integrity.'

'Yes it would,' agreed the Messiah. 'We shall contemplate the problem and come to various conclusions. And then I shall enlighten you with a parable or two.'

*

'We've written a short sequence that will make the computer think that the corridors are on fire,' said Joshua. 'When we press return it will hack into the control program of the security system controlled from this computer.'

'Wouldn't it just be easier to burn a piece of paper near the fire detector?' asked the Prime Minister. 'All this talk of hacking makes me feel very uneasy.'

'That would set off the sprinklers in here, Mr. Macaroon,' said Samuel. 'Which would make us all wet. Unfortunately the ones outside are on a different system and would be completely unaffected.'

'OK, you have my support to go ahead. What do you two think?' Darcy Macaroon directed the question at Sienna and Devonport.

'If the lads believe it will work I'm sure it will,' replied their mother. 'They're good boys generally.'

'I say go ahead,' answered Devonport. 'It is certainly worth a try.'

'Don't do it,' cried Sir George from his position on the floor.

'You,' said Macaroon kicking Sir George very lightly. 'Don't get a vote. So shut up.'

'I'm starting it now,' declared Joshua. 'It should work almost immediately.'

*

I felt myself sinking into the fire and brimstone. I was up to my neck and in agony. Now I was almost completely under, submerged by the sulphurous magma. I tilted my head backwards and could just see a gigantic head coming towards me, breathing fire and flashing its teeth.

The creature put its head into the lava and closed its mouth around my torso. It then plucked me from the molten rock.

You do get into some difficult scrapes when I am not around, don't you, Lord James?

I could hear the thought in my mind, telepathically projected there by Lady Aradel.

The great golden dragon, the mystical magical creature that could teleport through space and dance amongst the dimensions of the multiverse had arrived in Hell.

Chapter 27

'Dagon was the name given to the Lord of Lords by the Canaanites and others around the land of Israel,' explained the Messiah. 'He was a god of agriculture and was also known as Baal and it became necessary to distinguish between Baal and Yahweh.'

'How could there have been two Lord of Lords and God of Gods?' asked Saint Paul. 'This is rather complex.'

'You are right,' agreed the Messiah. 'Although initially one and the same, Baal was being worshipped in bad ways. Human sacrifice, cannibalism and smiting babies. When the Israelites took over the promised land it was important that they chose between a loving, just God and a weird, cruel unjust one. So a distinction had to be made.'

'So was this God of Gods, Lord of Lords, a part of yourself, Lord?' asked Simon Peter.

'In my aspect of God of All, then he was and still is,' replied the Messiah. 'Everything in creation is one with God and part of God.'

'Even evil, lord?' asked Saint Sebastian, the arrow still firmly planted in his neck. 'What about Lucifer? Is he part of God?'

'In the beginning was God,' replied the Messiah. 'And then evil and good split apart as order was made from the chaos. So the answer is yes, evil was there but has been bound apart from God.'

'I still don't quite understand it,' replied Saint Sebastian.

'God moves in a mysterious way his wonders to perform,' intoned Saint Paul seriously.

'Thank you, Paul,' agreed Yahweh, smiling on the small, serious saint. 'That is correct.'

Saint Paul returned the smile. When the Messiah looked with approval on you the whole of heaven brightened.

*

A horrible grinding noise drowned out the sound of the pneumatic drills for a few moments and the blast doors shuddered.

'Good lord!' exclaimed Darcy Macaroon. 'What have you done? That didn't sound like sprinklers.'

Nothing had changed inside the bunkers so they rushed to look at the TV screens. They could tell immediately that water was indeed pouring down on the workers in the tunnels. In addition several metal doors had swung shut that had previously been open. One of these had crushed equipment left in its way.

'Fire doors I presume,' said Maxwell Devonport, the chief constable. 'Didn't notice them previously but they install them everywhere now. They're held open on large electro-magnets and swing closed with powerful springs.'

'I didn't see them on the specifications,' said Joshua, a little shocked by the result of their program. 'I don't think it can do us any harm, though. Do you?'

'No, not at all lad,' replied Devonport. 'Overall I'd say that it is having the desired effect. Look …. they've all disappeared, presumably to get rain gear!'

'The fire doors were a later modification,' said Darcy Macaroon. 'I remember reading about them somewhere. I agree with Devonport that it may hold them up for a few more minutes though I doubt that it will be more than an hour or so before they break through these blast doors.'

They all stood and watched the activity which was being relayed from the cameras outside the bunker.

*

The great golden dragon stretched its wings. All of the party were on her back. I sat at the front on her neck. She had very gently placed me there after plucking all of the group from the brimstone of Hell. Behind me were Vole, Freya, Heimdall, Thor, Ard and Harry. Sitting at the very back in splendid isolation was my mother-in-law, Mary, the witch.

The dragon hovered over the pit and looked down at Lucifer, the mighty worm bound down by cruel iron bands. I stared down also.

'Presumably the bands are made of anti-matter iron,' I said to Lady Aradel.

'Why do you say that?' queried Aradel, the golden dragon and one-time queen of the elves.

'Lucifer is anti-matter,' I explained. 'So he must be bound by a similar substance. Or perhaps by some sort of magnetic bottle, exotic force field or even optical trap.'

'So Lucifer is antimatter. Is that what he is?' asked the dragon. 'I always wondered why I felt weird when I was near Hell.'

'Can you actually get out?' I queried, beginning to get worried.

'Oh yes,' she answered. 'I've never had difficulty doing that. I teleport out by quantum tunneling. It's just that Hell being such a foul place I didn't look here to start with.'

'You were looking for me?' I enquired.

'I've been looking for you ever since you left Valhalla,' Aradel replied. 'I heard from the sphinx that you had passed through, just missed you at Valhalla and followed you to the Rainbow Bridge where I thought I picked up one of your thoughts about Mars and canals.'

'You did,' I said animatedly. 'I heard you. You said that there used to be many lakes and seas on the planet.'

' I was standing on the Bifrost when it collapsed,' stated Aradel. 'It was no problem for me but I had to spend some time saving the Aesir. When I had finished doing so, you had completely vanished.'

'Down into Hell!' I exclaimed.

'But your presence here was masked by an illusion of some kind. I kept seeing you in a London club a billion miles from here.'

'Yes,' I replied. 'It was quite an impressive illusion. So when did you spot where we were?'

'Only a few moments before I plucked you out of the pit. The illusion disappeared and I instantly recognised Lucifer's Hell,' replied the golden dragon.

'And you are still in it,' cried the huge, bound monster, the evil creature that was Lucifer. 'And I will never let you leave.'

'Time we went,' said Aradel. 'The big boy is getting fractious!'

As we faded from Lucifer's reality I could hear him cry out in anguish.

'It could have been different,' he sobbed. 'I could have been the totality of everything rather than be bound here. I could have been matter and energy, time and space. Instead I am less than nothing. Less than nothing.....'

*

'A sower went forth to sow,' said Yahweh, in his aspect as the Messiah. 'And in two fields he sowed his normal seed and in the third field he sowed genetically modified, GM, grain.'

Saint Paul, Simon Peter, Habakuk, Martha and the gathered saints and apostles pulled in closer to listen to His words. The Messiah continued.

'....And the scientists had wrought mightily with the GM seed and it sprang forth and produced great produce. The normal seed produced a normal yield.'

The saints moved closer still and a few more folk left their activities by the crystal river and also came and sat down to listen.

'....And the second year the farmer sowed two fields with GM seed and just the one with his normal grain. And there came a great plague and it wiped out half the crop in the field sown with normal grain and all the rest of that field grew only weeds. But the GM crop multiplied and produced a good yield, not as good as the first year but still a good yield.'

Habakuk wondered where the parable was leading. *Was the*

Messiah extolling the virtues of science? Was He mysteriously in favour of GM crops?

'....And the third year the farmer would have sown all three fields with GM seed but it was very expensive. So he again sowed two fields with GM seed and one with the normal seed. And there came a great plague, a different plague this time and again it wiped out half the crop in the field sown with normal grain. But it wiped out absolutely all the crop in the field sown with GM grain as this plague was not one that the clever scientists had predicted and protected against and there was no diversity in the seed.'

The listening audience looked very confused.

'.....And the half crop from the single field was enough to feed the farmer, and his family and his family's families.'

The Messiah stopped and looked around at the audience.

'...And the scientists were perplexed and studied the fields. They quickly understood why their crop had failed in the third year but did not initially realise why the yield of the GM crop was reduced in the second year.'

The crowd around the Messiah had now grown very large. He took a bread roll from His pocket and broke it into a thousand pieces, each of which was large enough to feed a person. The disciples issued them to the throng.

'Then they discovered that the weeds were important. They were fixing nitrogen from the air and the grain needed Nitrogen.'

*

'I suppose technically you could say he is right?' asked Aradel as we flew out of Lucifer's Hell thus making Vole's suggestion correct. 'If Lucifer is the opposite of all that is in the Universe then instead of one, he is minus one which is less than nothing.'

'Not really,' I pondered the question. 'In many ways he is exactly the same as matter but opposite polarity etcetera. It is only a figure of speech that he is less than nothing. But it is undoubtedly true that put the two together and you would have a repeat of the Big

Bang. Total annihilation into energy.'

'Could he also be dark matter and dark energy?' she surmised.

'Quite possibly so,' I conjectured. 'We would have to ask cleverer cosmologists and physicists than myself.'

'I'm not sure that there are any, Jimmy,' replied the golden dragon. 'I think that you are the best we have got.'

'Not unless they have all died,' I answered.

'Many have,' she retorted.

As we left Lucifer's Hell, that gravity well at the centre of the universal black hole, seated behind me on the golden scales of the dragon's back were all my companions. Vole was right next to Freya, then Heimdall, Thor, and Ard. Harry was in animated conversation with my mother-in-law, Mary, having inched towards her as the beast flew high over the pit and away.

But when I turned back to talk to them after telling Aradel the saga of our adventures they had all disappeared. Gone!

'Aradel,' I cried in dismay. 'Lady Aradel, we have lost them!'

'Lost who?' she enquired, talking straight to my mind with her amazing telepathic ability.

'My companions,' I wailed. 'They must have fallen back into the pit, the maw of brimstone and fire. We will have to go back and find them.'

'No, dear heart,' she answered. 'They have gone back to the places where they need to be.'

'Where?' I asked, confused. 'Where, how and why?'

'Your fight with Lucifer is over but they have further deeds to do and we need to get back to Earth or Midgard as Heimdall would call it.'

'Where is Heimdall now?'

'He is back on the Bifrost Bridge, guarding the way between the heavens,' replied the dragon.

'But the bridge is broken,' I countered. 'Thor smashed it.'

'And your successful tussle with Lucifer has mended it,' she

replied.

'How could my arguments, my conversation with the devil, have mended the bridge?' I asked.

'The bridge is metaphysical and so were your arguments,' answered Lady Aradel, golden dragon, Queen of the elves.

'So more was going on and more was at stake than we could tell?' I queried.

'Of course and other aspects of yourself were at work,' replied Aradel. 'You knew that you were fighting to prevent the hordes from gaining access to heaven when their roll had not been called up yonder?'

'Certainly,' I answered. 'That's what we were doing on the Bifrost Bridge.'

'Simultaneously, Lord James, there was a massive battle in space,' she stated.

'Between whom?' I asked. 'And how did it manifest itself? What happened?'

'The battle raged over galaxies and galactic clusters. Stars went supernova, galaxies imploded, nebulae exploded.'

'And you saw this?'

'It was clearly visible to all.'

'So what we were doing was only a sideshow,' I remarked.

'No,' said Aradel. 'That is wrong. It was integral.'

'And who were the participants in this war between the stars?' I was still keen to know who had taken part in this cosmic battle.

'Why, you were, of course!' exclaimed the golden dragon. 'The battle was between yourself and Lucifer. The devil was supported by Baal. It was played out in full glory before the inhabitants of the entire multiverse.'

'How can we have been doing that whilst Lucifer was bound in Hell and we were caught at the bottom of Hell's gravity well?' I asked the dragon.

'It was your avatars. You were there as Saint Michael.... a mighty angel with a fiery sword.'

'And Lucifer?'

'I'm sorry to say that for much of the time he took the shape of a dragon, as did Baal,' Aradel seemed genuinely perturbed by this. 'It gives dragons a bad name.'

Chapter 28

The Messiah paused, looked around and listened.

'We have pilgrims at the gate,' he told Simon Peter.

'Really?' asked the apostle with the keys to heaven. 'How did they get past the obstructing hordes?'

'Teleported on a dragon,' replied the kindly, bearded figure of glory.

'Come on, don't josh with me!' rebuked Peter.

The Messiah laughed. 'They really teleported on a dragon. A golden dragon from the southern mountains of Faerie.'

'Gosh!' exclaimed Simon Peter. 'That is utterly astonishing. The golden dragons are rare, really rare.'

'That's as maybe,' replied the resurrected Lord. 'The new arrivals are here now so you must run along and check them in.'

'I will, Lord. I will,' said Simon Peter. 'But don't finish the parable without me.'

*

'Are you able to tell me more about my companions?' I asked. 'Where have they gone? How did they get there and what are they doing?'

'Mary, Harry and Ard have gone to the divine Heaven. Freya, Thor and Vole are in Valhalla and Heimdall, as I said, is back in his position on the Rainbow Bridge.'

Despite the very welcome presence of Lady Aradel, without whom I would still be in the brimstone up to my neck and beyond, I felt bereft of the company of my companions in Hell.

'I feel bad that I did not get a chance to say goodbye,' I remarked.

'We can't always say goodbye to our friends,' replied Aradel. 'Things were happening fast and I felt obliged to move them once I had found you all. But you will get a chance to see them some day.'

'So what are Mary, Harry and Ard doing in Heaven?' I asked. 'Mary told me that she had purposely left Heaven for Hell and Ard was looking for his lost family.'

'I think the experience of being plunged into the sulphurous pit changed her mind,' replied the dragon. 'Besides, she has old friends there. Very old friends.'

I pondered Aradel's reply for a few moments then asked further about Ard.

'Ard was the king of the werewolves,' I said. 'He told me that he had not died but was looking for his family.'

'He had died, Jimmy,' said Aradel. 'He was already a shade or ghost like Mary and Harry and did not know it because he had a quest. But Harry and Ard were also demi-gods as you told me.'

'And will he find his family?' I enquired, hoping that it would all have a happy ending.

'I can't tell you that,' replied the golden dragon. 'All I know is that he is in the divine Heaven and I understand that Heaven is a place of happiness.'

*

Simon Peter soon returned with Mary, Ard and Harry. The Messiah looked on them with great pleasure.

'Welcome back to Heaven,' he said. 'Congratulations on the result of your fight. You have overcome great trials and tribulation and have returned. We rejoice.'

Martha looked on and grumbled.

'I don't know what all the fuss is about. Besides their clothes are filthy. Covered in brimstone and smelling quite sulphurous. Pheww!'

'That's easily sorted,' laughed the Messiah and he turned to his rock. 'Peter, do you have new gowns for our returning heroes?'

'Of course,' replied Simon Peter, holding out the fresh clothes. 'I'll dispose of the dirty ones.'

'Don't do that!' exclaimed Martha. 'I'll clean them in the crystal flowing river.'

Habakuk viewed all this with considerable interest and wonderment ...*who are these new folk?*

'You are probably wondering who these new folk are?' suggested the Messiah who, before Habakuk's eyes turned once more into the Buddha. 'First let me introduce you to the Hindu Lord Krishna. He was known on his recent visit to Earth as Harry, or, in his own words 'Arry.'

Harry turned and executed a deep bow to the group of apostles and saints.

'Caw blimey this is a turn up for the book,' he said. 'Don't know about Krishna but I'm definitely 'Arry. 'Ow do you do?'

'Very soon your memories will return,' said the Buddha. 'And next we have Ard, king of the werewolves who doubles as the jackal-headed god Anubis, who is also known as Saint Christopher the dog head.'

'I thought I saw Saint Christopher the dog head earlier,' Habakuk whispered to Saint Paul.

'You did,' replied the small, serious, loving saint. 'There is some confusion over Saint Christopher but don't worry about it. We don't.'

'Ard has worked valiantly for us in Faerie,' said the Lord, now in Messiah form. 'He also lived a full life in the mortal and semi-mortal sphere and he must now go and find his family. He does know the way, the truth and the light.'

Ard looked up in appreciation when he heard his family mentioned.

'They are here!' he announced. 'They are not far away. I shall find them in the forest.'

With a joyous leap Ard turned into his lupine form and

bounded off into the wood. A few moments later Habakuk heard a happy bark from within the trees answered by a chorus of greeting yelps and howls.

'And Mary,' said the Messiah. 'We all know Mary so she doesn't really need any introduction.'

Who is she? thought Habakuk. *She certainly does not look like the Virgin Mary. Is she Mary Queen of Scots? Or perhaps Mary Anoinette?*

'But for Habakuk, who is still puzzled,' said the tall, bearded figure in the open-toed sandals. 'Yes, for Habakuk and any of the rest of you who have a momentary lapse of memory.'

From somewhere there came a loud drum roll and the Messiah continued....... 'I present my one-time consort, friend of the devil but reformed sinner, Mary Magdalene.'

Mary took a deep bow.

Gee whiz, thought Habakuk. *For a moment then I thought she looked just like a witch and now she looks like a voluptuous young woman. Amazing.*

✶

It was now very early on the Monday. The United Nations was still in emergency session and it was one o'clock in the morning in New York. In London it was already six a.m. and the tired Scotts with the Prime Minister and Chief Inspector Devonport were waking from fitful sleep. They had been taking it in turns to keep watch on events around the world with the computers and locally outside via the cameras. Luckily the effort with the sprinklers had slowed the progress of the besiegers. Inside their bunker the team had to keep a watchful eye on the trussed up MI5 men.

'Look, there's Dad!' shouted Sam as he stared at the monitors with the others.

'Where?' asked Joshua. 'I can't see him. You're making it up. You are still dreaming.'

'No, he's out there,' countered Sam hotly. 'I did see him. He's with a lady. They're trying to find a way in to this place but they don't quite know where it is.'

'Sam's right!' exclaimed Sienna. 'There he is. We had better try phoning him on his mobile.

*

Lady Aradel and I had arrived back on Earth in the United Kingdom. Aradel had told me that we had to find my family and various leaders of the country as things were heating up badly in the political arena. She had also updated me on the crises in the Middle East and in various other sites around the world.

I had very assiduously kept my phone with me throughout our quest and this time it had remained intact. The first thing I did on returning to Earth was to check my text messages and e-mails and I found a huge bunch from the family telling me that they were in a bunker under Westminster besieged by hostile forces. Lady Aradel was standing next to me in her female elf form, looking like a young tall woman, about twenty-five years of age. She had explained to me that she could not simply teleport into the bunker because it was a giant cage made of steel and the iron had a bad habit of negating her magical powers

My mobile rang.

'Hi,' I answered the call.

'Where have you been?' asked Sienna.

'To Hell and back,' I answered. 'How do I get to you?'

'We're in our own little underground prison,' Sienna announced. 'I know of three entrances but there are hostile police controlled by the Armageddon Prophets guarding all three.'

She quickly told me the position of the sites of egress to the underground warren.

'We need a diversion or some such trick,' I suggested. 'I shall ring back as soon as Lady Aradel and I have discussed the situation. I'll ring off now as I don't have much battery power.'

'We should use our powers of illusion,' Lady Aradel surmised. 'We simply do not have time to fight all these folk and fighting would cause unnecessary bloodshed.'

'Perhaps we could persuade the police that we are their commanders and tell them to let us through. That might work,' I postulated.

'I don't think it would,' replied Aradel. 'These guys are very determined and they don't expect to take orders except from the new Church.'

'Then perhaps we could create an illusion that suggests the family have opened the door and are escaping. We could then go in via the opposite entrance and pull them out whilst the police are chasing the illusion.'

Aradel nodded her head, looked around her and selected a small piece of paper from the ground. She let it go and a strong wind from the south-westerly direction blew it away at quite a speed of knots.

'I think I know what you are intending to do,' I said with a laugh.

'Do you, Lord James?' replied Aradel with a twinkle in her eye. 'That's because you have seen me do this before.'

She took a small piece of charcoal from her pocket. Where on her person she kept all this when in her dragon form I had no idea but she undoubtedly had the charcoal now.

'I'm going to use a phantom spell once we have got ourselves into the right place,' she explained. 'We shall both dress as police and then I will go in via the Westminster entrance near here, you go in via Buckingham Palace. In exactly half an hour I will set off the spell. The smoke from the charcoal will be under an illusion that it is your family and the Prime Minister. It will shape itself into the individuals and be blown by the wind away from the entrance.'

'Hopefully chased by the police,' I added.

'I'll be right there and make sure of that,' said Aradel. 'Once the hue and cry is well underway I will join you and we will be able to teleport as the family will be out of the metal box.'

'Are you sure the magic will work here in the normal world?' I asked, knowing that Aradel's powers were much greater in the Faerie Realm than in my reality.

'Since the partial merging of worlds and the manifestations at Stonehenge, magic has been a much more potent force in your reality than it was previously,' she replied. 'Otherwise the god Baal would not have been able to perform miracles in the way that he has and this Armageddon would not have even started.'

'OK,' I said. 'I trust you.'

In reality there was little else I could do.

★

'Now back to the parable,' said the Messiah. 'For those of you who were not here it is a simple tale of a farmer who was disappointed with his genetically modified grain. The GM seed did not do as well as he had hoped. So what did the farmer learn from that experience?'

'That the GM seed was overpriced?' suggested one of the listeners, immediately.

'Possibly,' smiled the Messiah. 'But that is not the main thrust of the story.'

'That the scientists who developed the seed suffered from hubris. The sin of pride that cometh before a fall,' said an elderly, serious man.

'Yes, Joseph. That is undoubtedly correct. Thank you,' replied the Messiah. 'But there is more to the story than that.'

'That you can't predict what plague will come next?' asked Simon Peter.

'That is part of the message. That predictions are not always correct and there are many false prophets,' answered the Messiah. 'But there is still more.'

'That even the weeds are useful and diversity is important?' suggested Habakuk, tentatively.

'Yes,' replied the Messiah and the sun shone for Habakuk. 'That is absolutely right. That is the main point of the parable'

*

Obtaining the police uniforms was a little tricky but careful persuasion and a considerable amount of money did the trick. Lady Aradel's husband, the Dragon King Clawfang, had once explained that a huge amount of gold could easily change people's minds. Lady Aradel teleported to her lair in Faerie, returned immediately with gold sovereigns and then teleported into a   police station. She returned with two perfectly fitting outfits.

'I persuaded a cleaner lady to find the clothes for us,' she said. 'I told her I was a police woman and that my boyfriend was one also.'

'What did she say?' I asked.

'She wanted to know how I had lost our uniforms and I told her we were drunk. She understood that.'

'So she let you have the uniforms?'

'No, she didn't want gold. Had no idea what it was. She wanted money.... ten pound notes. So I had to teleport out to a gold buyer, wake him up, sell him the gold at less than half price and get right back to her.'

'Then she was happy?'

'Then she was very happy.'

*

'In conclusion, Mister Chairman,' orated Sidney Fence speaking to the United Nations Council, his powers of speech enhanced by his great god Baal. 'In conclusion, the only way to save the world from catastrophe is to detonate a neutron bomb in Jerusalem. It will destroy the radical forces in the city. All the civilians have fled so they will not be harmed. The buildings will be undamaged and the crisis will be at an end. I call for a vote.'

There was an enormous clamour of almost unanimous approval from the representatives of countries from all round the world. Fence sat down to thunderous applause.

*

Lady Aradel mingled with the crowd of police outside the Westminster entrance to the bunker and I moved quickly to Buckinghan Palace and thence to the tunnel. I had telephoned Sienna to tell her what we were doing and she had described the tunnels in great detail. I sped down the tunnel in my police outfit and nobody even tried to stop me. They were expecting more police reinforcement so they were not surprised when I appeared. At the exact time that Aradel had appointed a cry went up from police who were listening to their short wave radios.

'They've got out from the other exit,' said a sergeant. 'And we are all to go round there to assist in the chase.'

'I'll stay round here, Sarge,' I suggested. 'Just in case they double back.'

'Good idea, Franklin,' said the Sergeant and for a moment I had no idea who Franklin was, then I remembered that I was wearing an identity card. 'Clarkson can stay with you.'

'No need, sir,' I replied. 'I'll be fine on my own.'

'No, Clarkson will stay,' he growled. 'And don't argue.'

The second the other police had gone I smacked Clarkson on the back of his head with the hilt of my sword. I was worried that he might be an innocent party but a quick examination of his filed teeth told me the opposite. Then I was back on the phone to Sienna.

'OK,' I told her. 'The coast is clear. Open the doors.'

There was an agonising wait whilst the blast door slowly opened and the family came out followed by the Prime Minister and a man dressed as a Chief Constable. I recognised him from pictures in the local newspaper as the man in charge of the Avon and Somerset police, Maxwell J. Devonport.

We dressed the Prime Minister in the unconscious policemen's clothes and then pushed the cannibal into the bunker.

'Can you close the door from outside?' I asked Sienna.

'Samuel can,' she replied.

'No trouble,' said Sam. 'Watch this!'

He pressed a small button on a remote control and the blast door slowly descended.

'It will take them some time to get into there,' I conjectured. 'And if the illusion works well the police will be chasing a phantom into North West London.'

*

A small tanned man stood up. 'I protest, Mister Chairman,' said the man. 'I don't know who this daft bogan is but he speaks a load of complete codswallop.'

'Who are you for that matter?' asked Fence.

'I'm the Ambassador to the United Nations for Australia,' replied the tanned man. 'And I've been listening carefully to your arguments. Firstly I don't believe the civilians have left Jerusalem, secondly I don't for a moment accept that the Israelis, the Jordanians, Christians, Muslims, Jews or whoever would agree to bombing the holy city. Lastly I would like to point out that every speaker so far has been from the new-fangled Church of Prophets or whatever you call them. And you all sound as if you have been drinking too much moonshine.'

'Sit down, sit down. You are out of order, ' screamed the Chairman, baring his pointed fangs. 'I suggest that the security forces take this ex-ambassador for Australia out of the council chamber and dispose of him as they see fit. Does anybody else want to protest?'

There was complete silence apart from some fidgety movements amongst non-aligned delegates.

*

Lady Aradel teleported as agreed right into the broadest and straightest part of the tunnel. The Prime Minister was the only person who had not been at Stonehenge and he was completely overawed by the site of the magical, golden creature. Although the others had seen dragons at the ancient monument they had not been up close to them and were also rather taken aback at the size of Aradel. It did take some getting used to.

'Are you sure that this is safe?' asked Darcy Macaroon. 'I don't want to appear a coward but climbing on the back of this monster is a bit alarming.'

'Who are you calling a monster?' asked Aradel in her sweetest voice.

'Oh, I'm so sorry,' said the PM in his best vote winning voice. 'I didn't realise that you were a lady. I do apologise.'

'Apology accepted,' replied Aradel. Now get up there and shut up.'

We all did so and we were off.

Chapter 29

We teleported out of the underground warren and, with one stop to pick up another passenger, we then teleported straight over to the United Nations building in New York. Lady Aradel turned back into her humanoid elf form and we used illusion to gain entry to the building. We were in the Assembly hall just in time to hear the Chairman, acting Secretary General Balbir Chaturvedi, cry for order and then make a pronouncement.

'We shall move to a vote.'

'I object, Mister Chairman,' cried Darcy Macaroon. 'I have not had a chance to speak yet.'

'Who are you?' asked Chaturvedi, his filed teeth showing up as he sneered the words.

'You know who I am,' replied Macaroon. 'I am Darcy Macaroon, Prime Minister of the UK.'

'We have already had one speaker from the UK,' protested Chaturvedi. 'And we understood that you were dead.'

'Well I'm not,' answered Macaroon, pointing at Fence. 'I'm very much alive. I was ill because I was poisoned and that man is the person who tried to kill me.'

A murmur ran round the assembly.

'How can you prove you are Macaroon?' asked Chaturvedi. 'You might be an impostor.'

'I can prove it with fingerprints, retinal scans, DNA. The lot,' replied Macaroon. 'But you all know who I am so I demand to speak.'

'Then make it very short,' agreed the acting Secretary General. 'It is unlikely to alter the result of a vote so keep it brief.'

'Firstly the UK is completely against a nuclear bomb or any sort of bomb being detonated anywhere in the Middle East, let alone Jerusalem,' said the PM of the UK. 'Secondly we veto a crusade. It must not happen.'

'You're out of order,' screamed Fence. 'You can't use your veto here. It can only be used at the Security Council and I've already agreed it here. Anyway I've done a calculation and we are going to win the vote by a clear margin so you can shut up. The neutron bomb will be detonated and we will wage our crusade.'

'Well spoken,' said Chaturvedi. 'I think you should sit down, Mr. Macaroon. The vote will proceed.'

'Not so soon, chairman,' said Macaroon, refusing to yield. 'First a point of information before the vote.'

'Alright, but make it short,' said the Chairman.

'Is it correct that the head of state of a country takes precedence over any other member of his or her government, including delegates, ministers and ambassadors?' asked Macaroon.

'Yes, of course he does,' replied the acting Secretary General.

'And that in voting in this assembly if the head of state wishes to vote the votes of other members from that country are null and void?'

'Yes of course. It's only one vote per country and by right that vote belongs to the head of state. Now you've had your questions so I move to a vote.'

'Not so quickly,' interjected Macaroon. 'I wish to introduce to the assembly the head of state of sixteen countries and the leader of the fifty-four countries in the Commonwealth of Nations. Ladies and Gentlemen, I present the Queen.'

A little, grey haired, slightly tubby lady with an enormously serious expression stood up. The lady was instantly recognisable to everybody in the room. She opened her mouth and spoke in the plummy way that people the world over had come to love or hate, copy or ridicule.

'Ladies and gentlemen, we are not amused. We are not amused at all!'

✶

'Now we can interpret all of the message in the parable,' said the Messiah. 'People, in their foolish pride, place too much value on fallible prophets and that even the worst sinners, or weeds, may have a place in paradise.'

Habakuk suddenly understood what the Messiah was saying.

'So let them all into Heaven?' he queried.

'Of course,' replied the Messiah. 'Just open the gates and let them in.'

'But their names are not in the book!' exclaimed Simon Peter, indignantly, ruffling through the pages.

'Simon, my rock,' said the Messiah. 'Of course they are. You left two books behind by the outer gate.'

'Did I?' asked Simon Peter, amazed. 'Did I really?'

'Yes, you did,' answered the Messiah.

'That's OK then,' the saint was all smiles again. 'As long as they are in the book.'

The Messiah winked at Habakuk and the priest suddenly remembered that he had seen more books when he sat on top of the gate looking down at Simon Peter. *Yes, St. Peter definitely had several ledgers not just the one.*

'Will it harm the tone of the place if we let just anybody in?' asked Martha.

'Not at all Martha,' replied the Messiah. 'They all change for the better the moment they enter the place and I will expand Heaven to suit the influx. It's not a problem.'

Martha smiled. As long as the proprieties were kept up she would be happy. Again the Messiah winked at Habakuk.

✶

The Queen had finished speaking and the proposal to neutron

bomb Jerusalem and start a religious crusade had been defeated by a small majority led by the example of her royal personage and the fact that she herself could vote for so many states. There was some consternation amongst the representatives of the countries who were Armageddon prophets and wished to vote in favour of the war. Chief amongst them was the right wing President of Canada who loudly claimed that his country would immediately become a republic.

'I don't think so, old boy,' exclaimed Macaroon in reply. 'Not when your voting public realise you are a cannibal.'

There was an instant uproar and Fence climbed on top of the Chairman's podium.

'You won't stop us Macaroon,' screamed the depraved and murderous deputy Prime Minister. 'I represent the all powerful Lord of Lords. He will simply wipe you all out. Great is Dagon! Great is Baal!'

The other Armageddon Prophets started to take up the chant and then it changed.

'We are Gog and Magog and we are the chosen of God.'
'We are Gog and Magog and we are the chosen of God.'
'We are Gog and Magog and we are the chosen of God.'
'We are Gog and Magog and we are the chosen of God.'

The small tubby figure stood up again and such was the power of her fame that the chant died down. They wanted to hear what she said.

'Mister Fence,' she replied to the Deputy Prime Minister. 'Firstly you are wrong that you represent the Lord of Lords. I think you will agree that by precedent and barring the presence of the Pope that one does that in one's role as leader of the Church of England, established in the sixteenth century, unlike your own church that was established only in the last year or so. And secondly you are fired from your position as my Deputy First Minister and therefore have no further right to address this chamber.'

She sat down again to stunned silence. It was now up to their god, Dagon, to respond. The chamber shook and lightning crashed over the building. I knew that Dagon had not been defeated and that he was not chained in Hell with Lucifer. What was going to happen?

*

'Simon Peter how is the roll call going?' asked the Messiah.

'Very well,' said the rock. 'They're all in the book as you said. I have had to recruit Habakuk and Harry to help me on the gates. But they don't mind, they say they are enjoying themselves.'

'Any problems?'

'No, not really,' replied the rugged saint, the rock on whom the church had been built. 'Just a few looking a little confused. The ones who have been in a zombie state for some time.'

'Anybody refusing to enter?'

'Not as yet, boss. They all want to come into Heaven.'

'Good. All is good.'

*

The UN Assembly Room shook as we stood up high at the back. Fence still stood on the podium and he shook his fist at the Queen.

'Precedent means nothing, now,' he cried out. 'What is important is power. These delegates obey our god and will follow my example.'

But as he shouted this he peered round the chamber and realised that his fellow prophets were disappearing. He looked closely and understood that the zombied delegates were dying for a second time. This time they were going with big smiles on their face.

'Stop,' he shouted in a bewildered manner. 'What is going on.'

'The zombies are going to heaven,' replied Lady Aradel.

'Who are you?' cried Fence. 'Why are you here.'

'Lady Aradel,' she replied. 'I am the permitted observer from Faerie.'

'Queen of the bloody elves,' laughed Fence. 'My god will arrive soon and then we'll see if an elf has the right to speak. Not just here but anywhere.'

He laughed in a horrible manner that reminded me of Lucifer, that figure of evil, that giant worm, bound in Hell.

As I contemplated the laugh a chill came across the large hall and something started to coalesce next to Fence. It was a disparate image that flickered resembling for a moment the Statue of Liberty, then the scales of justice and for a second a figure much like Vole and Freya combined. Words came crashing through, sung in enticing close harmony: justice, peace, love, in God we trust.

It's surely not Vole and the Devourer of Souls? I wondered fearfully. *Have I been deceived by my friend?*

But the brightly lit, growing monster did not fix on the Vole shape but became a sheaf of corn, the woolsack, a sack of grain and then the American bald eagle. In God We Trust. In God We Trust.

'I am Dagon, Lord of Lords, God of Gods, God of the Covenant,' cried the eagle-like neon monster. 'All the world bows down before me. Without me there is no justice, no peace, no harmony. All shall obey me.'

Then I suddenly realised who this was. This was Money, with a capital M. Dagon, otherwise known as Baal, had become the embodiment of money. Of course he was the god of the covenant .... legal agreements always involved money.

'You might be Money but you cannot be Dagon,' I cried. 'You represent yourself falsely. Dagon is the name of an ancient fertility god from the Middle East more than four thousand years ago. An ancient god of agriculture and fishing.

'Speck,' said the god. 'You have the gall to address me! But I shall deign to reply. Yes, I am the god of the farmer and the fisheries.

Have you ever met a farmer who did not want to make a profit?'

'You are the god of nothing more than mere money. The dollar, the pound, the yen, the euro..... all currencies combined,' I screamed. 'And money has only been around since about five hundred BC so you cannot also be Dagon or Baal.'

'You are confusing money with coins,' thundered Dagon. 'Yes, coins were invented when you indicate by Croesus and his father in Lydia. Both worshipped me. But at the dawn of recorded time humans used barter, then shells, rings, cattle, anything as money. They all worshipped me.'

'But the empire of Croesus fell,' I countered. 'You are a false god.'

'Money makes the world go round,' cried Dagon. 'You have heard that hymn to me!'

Hymn? I thought. *That's just a song from a musical. A bit of doggerel, not a hymn.*

'My power is immense and all will feel my sway!' screamed the bloated lord of commerce, swelling into a huge creature, part beast and part human. 'You will be the first to die at my hands in this chamber.'

A giant claw reached in my direction and plucked me from my position at the very back of the room.

*

'Boss!' shouted Simon Peter to the Messiah as the be-sandalled figure strode away from him, back into the main part of Heaven. 'I've just got a call from Heimdall on the Bifrost Bridge.'

'So you have,' replied the Messiah. 'Did he just say that it is not all over yet?'

'He did, boss,' replied Saint Peter, just a little crestfallen.

'And that Dagon is about to wreak havoc in the United Nations?'

'Yes, lord,' said the rock.

'Thank you,' replied the Lord. 'Now I know that.'

How does He do it? wondered Saint Peter silently.

Have a guess, replied the Messiah directly into Saint Peter's questioning mind.

*

I drew the elfin sword that I always carried with me and swung at the clawed hand. The god dropped me with a loud grunt of pain.

'You dare to defy me?' cried the monster, the god of money, mammon, Baal, Dagon.

'The love of money is the root of all evil!' I retorted.

'Money, money, money. It's a rich man's world!' replied the god, swiping at me with stinking, razor-sharp claws. 'Everybody worships me, you fool, and worship gives me strength. Without me you can have nothing.'

'You are wrong,' I answered the god with another powerful swipe of my sword. 'The best things in life are free.'

'Try getting a free lunch, speck,' cried the monstrosity of mammon. 'Try buying a chocolate sundae with nothing but air. Try getting accommodation without money. I am all-powerful!'

The monster grew bigger. Where was it getting its extra power from? Then I realised that the whole debate was being televised and the world was listening to our argument. Unlike my fight with Lucifer this was one I was not winning. Suddenly at my side I had reinforcement. Lady Aradel was there as the giant golden dragon but, large as she was, she was dwarfed by the size of the mammon monster.

I looked at myself.

I too had grown and as I grew the memories of past battles came back to me. I was Saint Michael, Mary was right. I could remember my first fight with the fallen angel, Lucifer, before the dawning of time when order had been created from chaos and how I had wounded that devil in a fair fight and bound him in Hell. I could remember fighting evil principalities and powers and how they had fallen to my flaming sword.

But this time the fight was not equal. The monster was gaining in power all the time. I feared deeply that we would be defeated.

*

'Money in itself is not evil,' said the Messiah to a group of disciples and apostles. 'It is the misplaced love of money that is the evil thing and that misplaced love needs to be redirected.'

'But how can that be done, Lord?' asked Saint Paul.

'Can't you just gobble it up, mate?' asked Harry.

'Thank you Krishna,' said the Buddha. 'That is what I shall do.'

'What?' queried Saint Paul. 'Eat up all the money in the world.'

'No, Paul,' replied the one who could walk on water and change it into wine. 'That would create a credit crisis worse than the sub-prime mortgage debacle, the Wall Street Crash and the South Sea Bubble combined.'

'Then what do you mean Lord?' asked Habakuk.

'As the big fish swallowed Jonah, so I shall swallow Dagon. We shall become one again,' announced the Messiah. 'I shall absorb the god Dagon or Baal into my gestalt.'

'But the analogy isn't perfect,' said a serious, older looking man. 'Jonah was spat up again unharmed. I don't suppose you intend doing that to Dagon.'

'Thank you Joseph,' said the ancient of days. 'I was aware of the shortcomings of my analogy but thank you all the same.'

Joseph beamed with happiness at the approval of the Lord. Everyone was happy in Heaven.

*

I felt I could fight no more and my ally, the golden dragon Aradel, had slumped down exhausted next to me. Though I was now the most powerful archangel bar none, I was about to be defeated. I had never known a battle like it. This monster could twist and turn and whenever I thought I had beaten it I found it had cost me dearly in the process. This cost just inflated the monster in front of me. This was the arms race made metaphysical, the military-industrial complex turned supernatural and the banking industry deified. This was the commander of the captains of commercial industry, the lord of the lottery, the master of the mortgage all rolled into one huge, inflated monstrosity that the world kept on worshipping. Money! They all worshipped money!

'Die, you foolish angel,' cried the god Dagon, metaphysical mammon monster. 'Die because of your own righteousness. Selfishness will always beat the selfless as riches always beat poverty!'

His claws had grown to a huge size, each with the razor-sharp edge of the grim reaper's scythe. One came ripping down towards me, I had no defense..... and the monster vanished. It left behind just a single piece of thin plastic about three inches by two which I picked up and examined. It was a credit card past its expiry date!

*

The beautiful light of heaven flickered and the glory that surrounded the Messiah faded momentarily. Then heaven's light took on a slightly gaudier and harsher feel for another picosecond before returning to its usual benign state. The Messiah stretched his arms upwards and outwards, embracing all of creation, and then relaxing with a smile.

'It is done,' he stated. 'We are one. Anybody for a game of poker?'

'I'll take you on at Bagatelle rather than poker,' suggested Simon Peter.

'Best of three,' said the Messiah. 'And I'll put a fiver on it at odds of ten to one that I'll win.'

'You're on,' said Simon Peter. He loved it when the Lord was feeling playful.

The New York Police Department sent their homicide team into the United Nations to investigate the collection of dead bodies but they all appeared to have died from natural causes. There were plenty of other unexplained deaths to investigate in the New York area and the surviving delegates were soon permitted to leave the premises.

The Queen was invited to ride back to the UK on the golden dragon but very politely refused.

'It was a most interesting experience for one but not something that one would really like to repeat. One shall take a trip in an aeroplane,' the Queen very politely told Lady Aradel.

We left the Queen in the capable care of the British Ambassadors to the USA and to the United Nations, both of whom we found tied up in an ante room. The rest of us stopped for a meal in the United Nations canteen and then Lady Aradel teleported Macaroon, Devonport, myself and my family back to London and we all went to one of the many bars in the Houses of Parliament for a debriefing chat.

'As the official police presence throughout all of this, I insist on it,' is what Maxwell Devonport had said. 'Although I was there I want all of your thoughts and impressions of the events of the last few days. As an eye witness I found it all very confusing and I shall have to make an official statement.'

'Can the children come into the bar?' asked Sienna. 'Or are there restrictions?'

'They serve food so its OK,' said the PM, who had himself suggested the venue. 'We'll all go in on my pass.'

Nobody stopped us as we entered the building ... in fact the policemen on duty outside saluted all of us. As we passed a television we could see that it was tuned to an independent twenty-four hour news channel.

"After the astounding scenes in the United Nations building in New York we now have equalling amazing events in the world of finance. Adolphus, Fourth Baron de Ragestein and former Vice President of the United States, arguably the world's richest man, has liquidated all of his assets and given the funds raised to

charities for the poor. Pedro Lupino, rumoured to be one of the five richest men in the world, has done something very similar. His money will go to the chronically sick and crippled. He himself has become a care assistant in a nursing home.

The five top earning investment bankers in the City of London have collectively given their bonuses, with a rumoured total in excess of a billion pounds sterling, to charities that assist the developing world.

"All over the world similar events are unfolding. Dictators have returned their ill gotten gains to their people, bankers have owned up to fraud and the chief executives of the massive   supermarket chains have slashed their prices whilst increasing the amount they pay to their suppliers, improving the wages of the workers and paying more in dividends to their shareholders. We will hear our economic editor's views on these developments but first a message from our sponsor."

"This program has been brought to you by MegaLoan International. Firstly we would like to apologise for the way that we have misled you in the past. We have not always been honest in the way that we have conducted our business and we are sorry about this. Our executives have taken too much money for the little work they do, harming the economy, paying too little to their workers and giving you as little as possible. This has changed. We are rewarding our workers on the basis of their true worth based on real output.

"In addition we are distributing compensation directly to anybody who has previously taken a loan with us or done business with us in any way. We know how much we have cheated you and we are repaying several fold. There is no need to apply for the payment. It is already in your bank."

'This is presumably all the effect of our little battle in the UN,' conjectured Darcy Macaroon. 'How long do you think the effect